Praise for *Dancing with Elvis*

"Voice and characterization are superb, with many scenes that beg to be read aloud. . . . A fine first novel and an author to watch."
— *Kirkus Reviews*

"We're about a half-century on from some significant changes in America, and we've been consequently seeing quite a few books that retrospectively examine the fight against segregation, the entrenchment of small-town ways, and the secrets within communities and within families. Few of them, however, have approached the passion, readable particularity, and sheer vitality of *Dancing with Elvis*. . . . With its quirky individuality and passionate humanity, this is an unforgettable picture of this time, place, and girl."
— *Bulletin of the Center for Children's Books*
Big Picture, starred review

"At once charming, sharp-edged and tragic, the book captures the essence of eccentrics, manipulators, victims and criminals co-existing in pre-civil-rights-era Texas."
— *Publishers Weekly*

"Stephenson has packed this novel with enough action to keep readers from putting it down. . . . A good coming-of-age story."
— *School Library Journal*

"Totally delightful, engaging, and worthwhile."
— *San Antonio Express-News*

"Stephenson sets this ambitious first novel, which is marked by an accidental killing, against complicated questions of black-white relationships during the early days of school integration. . . . The situations Stephenson creates, and the ways her characters wiggle in and out of them, are enticingly fresh. . . . This debut won't easily be forgotten."
— *Booklist*

"Frankilee is a delight — a feisty, impulsive and salty-tongued girl . . ."
— *VOYA*

Dancing with
ELVIS

Dancing with

ELVIS

Lynda Stephenson

Eerdmans Books for Young Readers
Grand Rapids, Michigan • Cambridge, U.K.

Text © 2005 Lynda Stephenson
Published in 2005 by Eerdmans Books for Young Readers,
an imprint of Wm. B. Eerdmans Publishing Co.

Wm. B. Eerdmans Publishing Co.
2140 Oak Industrial Dr. N.E., Grand Rapids, Michigan 49505
P.O. Box 163, Cambridge CB3 9PU U.K.

www.eerdmans.com/youngreaders

06 07 08 09 10 11   8 7 6 5 4 3 2

Library of Congress Cataloging-in-Publication Data

Stephenson, Lynda.
Dancing with Elvis / written by Lynda Stephenson.
p. cm.

Summary: In Clover, Texas, in the late 1950s, high-schooler Frankilee deals with a devious and
manipulative, not to mention prettier and more talented, foster sister, a boyfriend she does not
want, and a community divided over school integration.

ISBN-10:0-8028-5293-9 / ISBN-13: 978-0-8028-5293-9 (hardcover: alk. paper)
ISBN-10: 0-8028-5300-5 / ISBN-13: 978-0-8028-5300-4 (paperback: alk. paper)

[1. Family life — Texas--Fiction. 2. Race relations — Fiction. 3. High schools — Fiction. 4.
Schools — Fiction. 5. Swindlers and swindling — Fiction. 6. Foster home care—Fiction. 7.
Texas — History — 1951—Fiction.] I. Title.
PZ7.S83658Dan 2005
[Fic]--dc22
2004020442

To Gene, Amy, Neil, Sophia, Pauline, and Tom;
to the memory of my parents;

and with gratitude to my critique group,
the Writers of the Purple Page
— *L.S.*

Clover, Texas, 1956

Chapter 1

EVERY NIGHT AFTER I say my prayers, it gives me great pleasure to think about murdering Angel Musseldorf. Hell, I know she's a battered kid, and she's had an unheavenly host of problems, but I've had about all I can take. Then I get to thinking — what about jail time? I don't mean to be wishy-washy, but maybe I wouldn't kill Angel *dead*. Still, I'd like to get rid of her in some kind, Christian way.

I blame it all on Mother. And she blames me. Daddy blames us both and says we've been in cahoots, plotting against him and the rest of the world for too long. Wanita, our housekeeper, says we've put too many crickets in a box and now that some of them are climbing out we've got more than we can handle and it serves us right.

Here's the situation. My mother is a do-gooder. Her motto is "Faith without works is dead." That's why she encourages me to kidnap Angelica Musseldorf one Saturday in September, the morning after our first high school football game. Mother has the distinction of teaching the Mary and Martha Sunday school class at our church

— First Presbyterian — and she always knows the right thing to do. She's beautiful and smart. I want to be just like her.

On that Saturday morning, Mother comes into my room. She sits beside me on my bed and reaches for my shoulder.

"Wake up," she says, gently shaking me. "Angelica is on the telephone, and she wants to talk with you."

I ignore Mother for as long as I can, but she keeps it up. "You promised I could sleep 'til noon." I roll over to look at my clock on the nightstand. It's a few minutes past eight.

"I know, but this is an emergency, Frankilee."

I pull myself up on my elbow and look at her.

"You know what we've talked about. Angelica needs our help," she says.

"Right now?"

"She wants to live with us. At least for a while."

I sit straight up in the middle of the bed. Soft yellow light filters through pale organdy curtains at my north windows, giving my room a delicious glow. The room is filled with dark furniture. One twin bed is rumpled with me in it. The spare bed is piled high with clothes I've worn to school earlier in the week. Above it hangs my autographed portrait of Jesus Christ, which I ordered from the radio station in Del Rio, Texas. Above my bed, slightly lower than Jesus, is my favorite poster of Elvis Presley, held to the wall with thumbtacks. I myself hung these pictures to tell the world I put Elvis on almost as high a level as Jesus.

"Go downstairs and talk to Angelica. She's on the phone," Mother repeats.

I do, and sure enough, Angelica Musseldorf wants to run away from home. I tell her, "Mother and I will be there in a jiff." Then I run back up to my room, where Mother stands looking into my closet.

"Get dressed," she orders, and I pull out a pair of summer shorts. She moves away from my closet. "Don't wear shorts. Wear a skirt today or maybe a pair of jeans. We've got to have dignity for this occasion."

"Angelica's mother isn't home right now, so she can escape. Let's hurry!" I say. As Mother hands me a pair of bobby socks and my loafers, I search for underwear in the highboy.

I'm fourteen. I know how to drive, and every afternoon during this lazy summer of 1956 my parents have let me practice by taking their Chrysler down Cemetery Road. I figure Mother will let me drive the car for the kidnapping, since Angelica lives only three blocks beyond that.

"You shouldn't take the car," she says, "because the neighbors might remember seeing it. We don't want anybody to be able to say we made Angelica run away."

"You want me to go get her by myself? Without you? I can't do that!"

"Of course you can. Easy as pie."

As I pull on my jeans and button them, my hands begin trembling. Then I reach for a long-sleeved white

3

shirt, an old one of Daddy's.

"Wear a nice blouse that fits." Mother hands me my favorite plaid shirt. "Look presentable. This will be a long day."

I can hardly button the blouse.

Mother begins thinking aloud, "You definitely shouldn't take our car. And you without a driver's license!"

"Go call the taxi," I say. She goes downstairs to use the telephone, while I go into the bathroom.

"Lela Belle Walker is on her way," Mother says, coming back. "When she gets here, just run outside and jump into the cab."

"Do you think we can get away from the Musseldorfs' house?"

"Don't tell Lela Belle exactly what you're doing, though, because we don't want this story out all over town."

"What *should* I tell Lela Belle?"

Mother ignores my questions. "Now, be sure to get all of Angelica's things. I think we're in this for a while — at least until her relatives come for her." Mother smiles at me.

"I think I should have Angelica leave a note for her folks, saying she's with us."

"Yes," my mother agrees. "We must be entirely open about this."

Five minutes later, Lela Belle pulls up in front of our house behind the wheel of a spiffy black Chevrolet with a running board. Perched on top of the automobile is a yellow sign that reads "Taxi," and on the passenger's side she has painted "Clover Texas Cab Company" in a gold leaf scroll. Lela Belle, a small, stringy-haired woman, wears a spotted pink blouse, a purple tweed skirt, and black-framed cat-eye glasses. She gets out of the car and opens the back door for me.

"Where to, Miss Frankilee?" she asks, all business-like.

I climb into the back seat and tell her to head for Musseldorfs' house and then realize I don't know the address. "Just drive down First Street. I'll tell you where to stop."

It's a beautiful, crisp fall morning — perfect weather for football, and super weather for a rescue. As we cross Cemetery Road and turn onto First, we drive down one of the prettiest streets in town. Lawns are still green, and the trees and shrubs haven't lost their leaves yet. Tall old elms line both sides of First Street, dipping over us as we pass through, mysteriously leaning away from the yards. A few children play up and down the sidewalks, some zooming along on their tricycles. A blond boy rides a blue bike with training wheels, and as we pass he yells, "Hey, cabbie! Hey, cabbie!"

I realize if I don't start breathing deeply, I'll faint, which could be a calamity. So I sit in the middle of the backseat and inhale slowly, count to five, and exhale. I do this five times. At the end of this exercise, I figure I've got enough air in my upper body to sing "The Star

5

Spangled Banner." Or fight Mrs. Musseldorf.

At the end of a cul-de-sac, the house stands next to vacant lots on either side. Secluded and surrounded by brush and trees, it doesn't fit in with the rest of the neighborhood. "There, the gray house with the black shutters." The one-story house has a dipping front porch, a broken concrete sidewalk, and a lawn that hasn't been cut for weeks. "Turn into the driveway."

Angelica waits for us on the front porch. Dressed in a blue gathered skirt, stretchy cinch belt and long-sleeved white blouse, she appears calm and pretty. She's tied a blue silk scarf around her neck and pulled her blond hair up in a high ponytail. She has Mamie Eisenhower bangs, and on her they look right. Wearing socks and loafers, she looks like she's headed for school.

When I jump out of the cab and run up the cronkey-jawed steps, she announces, "My things are ready. They're all inside." Anxiously, she smiles at me.

Lela Belle keeps her face blank. We carry Angelica's things from her closet and bedroom, put them on the lawn, and then pack them into the cab. If Lela Belle knows she's an accessory to a crime, she doesn't seem to care.

Angelica owns gobs of stuff: clothes on hangers, in suitcases, in paper sacks. She has twenty pairs of ugly shoes, a ragged bulletin board, a green hairdryer, a huge bag of hair rollers, a record player, two faded quilts, a large box of Kotex, and an empty birdcage.

I'm already scared witless, imagining what'll happen

if Mrs. Musseldorf returns before we get the hell out of her driveway. What will I say? "Gee, Mrs. Musseldorf, I'm just helping Angelica run away from home. We'll be gone in a few minutes. Then you and Mr. Musseldorf can have the place to yourselves."

What a spineless approach. No, I've got to be braver than that. "Mrs. Musseldorf, everyone in town knows you beat Angelica whenever you feel like it — and for no good reason! My mother and I won't let you hurt her anymore."

Oh, God! Then Mrs. Musseldorf will probably hit me. Maybe, instead, I'll pretend that no pain and suffering are involved in this runaway situation: "Hot diggedy dog, Mrs. Musseldorf! Angelica has just won a contest, and she'll be living with us now."

An expert at packing her automobile, Lela Belle Walker fits everything in except the birdcage.

"Damned thing can't go," she announces.

I look down the street. "For God's sake, hurry!"

"Oh, but I must take Terrell's cage!" Angelica wails.

"Where *is* Terrell?" I vaguely remember a yellow and green parakeet.

"Mother killed him!" Angelica cries. "Wrung his neck! His empty cage is proof of her meanness."

"Choose between the birdcage and the Kotex," says Lela Belle, taking the Kotex back out of the car. "We can't take both. Which you think you're going to need more?" She climbs into the taxi and turns the key.

I toss the Kotex to the floorboard in the front, and

7

then Angelica and I climb on top of the clothes in the back. Shoving the taxi in reverse, Lela Belle zooms out of the Musseldorfs' driveway and bounces us back down the tree-lined street to my house. Looking back, I see the birdcage forlornly leaning to one side on the lawn. The well-manicured neighborhood is as still as a photograph. Where the hell are Angelica's neighbors? Not a *bon voyage* from anybody.

Suddenly I remember Mother's and my agreement. "Angelica, did you leave a note for your parents?"

"Oh, yes," she says, grinning. "I left them a doozy."

Chapter 2

MOTHER SMOKES A Lucky Strike while she stands waiting for us on the front porch. She wears a tan skirt and a yellow blouse, which makes her curly blond hair look bright, and as always, hose and smart high heels. When Lela Belle turns in our driveway, Mother crushes her cigarette beneath her toe and kicks the butt into the flowerbed. Then she rushes down the steps to welcome Angelica. Opening the car door, she pulls the girl out, gives her a quick hug, and says, "Okay, let's get organized." That's my mother's favorite thing to say.

Mother pats me on the back and says, "Good job, honeybunch!" Then she's back to business. "Take Angelica's things upstairs to the guest bedroom." This is on the same side of the hallway as my room and separated from mine by a small bathroom, which until today I've always had to myself.

Lela Belle unpacks, hoists, and carries. We're the three stooges — Lela Belle, Angelica, and I — unloading the car, tromping through the house and up the stairs, as Mother tells us where to place everything. We're relieved to let her take control, because we believe she's always right. We're sure she'll protect us from Mrs. Musseldorf. After all, she *is* a Sunday school teacher.

When we've finished unloading the car, Mother follows Lela Belle to her taxicab and hands her several bills. What's a fair wage for roping in a taxi driver? Later, I'll ask Mother what Lela Belle charges for rescue work.

Besides the fact that Mrs. Musseldorf periodically beats up both her husband and her daughter, the ladies in the church disapprove of her for other reasons. Mostly they criticize her church attire. "Tacky housedresses," they say, as they arrange floral bouquets for sick folks in the Clover County Hospital, or while they serve ham and potato salad at bereavement dinners.

It's true that Mrs. Musseldorf doesn't look like any other lady in the congregation. When my mother's friends go to church, they wear nylons, high heels, hats, and white gloves. They carefully match their handbags with their shoes, and more often than not they wear pearls.

But Mrs. Musseldorf is built like a short stocky man with breasts. Under her cotton dresses in church, we see her muscular arms and shoulders. Her gray hair twists into tight curls. She never wears a hat and gloves, and she never has a manicure. She wears short white socks with low-heeled black pumps, and she carries a thick black Bible instead of a purse. Every Sunday morning she sits in the front row, directly under the nose of our preacher, the Reverend Farnsworth.

When dressing for any occasion, the West Texas church ladies suck up air and pack themselves into steel-zippered girdles. From beneath their breasts to the middle of their thighs, nothing moves. Sometimes with amazement I watch my mother dress, and I wonder when I'll have enough curves to encase my lower body into one of those cylinders. Shithouse mouse, the way those women suffer.

But no girdle for Mrs. Musseldorf! Her hips are twin hams below her thick waist. And her stomach is a ball of fat. All this flesh bounces and ripples under her clothes.

"Tacky housedresses," the ladies repeat. "What else can you expect from a Yankee woman who runs a tire store?"

In the spring of 1956, just a couple of weeks before school let out for the summer, the Musseldorfs moved to Clover. They bought a tire store and service station out on Route 66, having come from someplace foreign, like South Dakota. Immediately after settling here, Mrs. Musseldorf and Angelica started attending our church, and they're as regular church members as we are.

One habit of Mrs. Musseldorf's fills the church ladies with alarm. That's the way she acts when the preacher starts yelling about evil. Nearly every Sunday, dressed in a black floor-length robe, the Reverend Farnsworth announces that the whole world is going to the bow-wows. He doesn't begin his sermon with this statement, but he gradually leads up to it, as a sort of climax. Bobbing

11

his head and flapping his flabby neck like a turkey, he sounds like a crack-voiced old bird-dog: "bow-wow-wow-wow-wow!"

We don't know what causes him to get so pitifully stuck on that word. It's riotous, but my dad and I are probably the only people in the congregation who think so.

Members of the choir, who sit in the loft behind the minister, report that Mrs. Musseldorf likes this part of the sermon most of all. Her face lights up, and she smiles. And then we all hear her thumping. She thumps on her big black Bible with the heel of her right hand in time with Reverend Farnsworth's bow-wows. The choir members call this "The Litany," and they hate it. Sometimes the minister gets totally carried away, and so does Mrs. Musseldorf. In fact, one Sunday I counted seventeen bow-wows. On and on he went, with Mrs. Musseldorf thumping, and when he finished, "Wow, wow, wow!" she called out, "Oh, yes, yes, Amen!"

A few days later, Mother announced to Daddy and me that the church ladies were scandalized by the thumping and the barking in the church-house. So Mrs. Musseldorf is regarded as a frustrated nutcase with no fashion awareness.

Still, Mother doesn't criticize Mrs. Musseldorf's appearance or her thumping ways. She focuses on the woman as a child-beater.

Soon after the Musseldorfs moved to town, I realized something was wrong. For weeks while I talked on the telephone with friends or primped for chance encounters with boys, I knew something had to be done to help poor Angelica Musseldorf. I brought her home a few times during the summer, and my mother befriended her.

Now Mother and I are cohorts in crime, but we forgot to include my dad as we made our plans. And today, when he walks home for lunch from the bank, he's surprised to learn that he's suddenly responsible for another child.

I hear Mother explaining the situation to him as she makes him a sandwich. Angelica is putting her things away upstairs. For some reason, which probably has to do with her son William's football games, our housekeeper, Wanita, is not here, so Mother and Daddy talk openly in the kitchen.

"I don't know what to say, Abby. I wish you'd talked with me about this before jumping in." Daddy sounds calm but irritated.

"Oh, Jack, I know. But there wasn't time. I had to do something. Angelica called this morning and said her mother beat her last night!"

"You could have called me, for God's sake!"

"I know. I know. But I didn't."

The longer he thinks about it, the more my dad gets steamed. "How long will this arrangement last?"

"What do you mean?" Sometimes my mother is the queen of dumb, and I really admire her for it.

"Do you intend for this to be permanent?" he asks in his cold banker's voice.

13

"Oh, heavens, no. I plan to keep Angelica for several days — or maybe weeks — just long enough for her relatives to come down from Michigan to get her."

"I thought her people were from Iowa."

"Well, wherever," Mother answers. "We'll get that information from Angelica as soon as things settle down."

"My God, you're optimistic," Daddy says.

"Don't worry," Mother tells him. "I'll write out a schedule for the girls to follow. We can make Angelica happy, and she needs us desperately. Surely she'll feel loved and accepted here. And safe. Please, Jack, don't be hard to get along with."

"One more thing. Why did you send Frankilee after Angelica? Putting a fourteen-year-old in that position could have serious consequences."

"Frankilee's a mature young lady."

"She's a *kid*, Abby!"

"Oh, I know. But it turned out all right." Besides her ability to pretend stupidity, Mother is also the queen of vagueness.

After lunch, as Daddy heads out the door and back to town, he says, "Your plan may not work out as smoothly as you think. Call me if you need me. I'm taking the car, so I can get here in a flash."

"Like Flash Gordon!" Mother laughs as she walks to the door toward him. "Hey, wait a minute."

"Two shakes of a lamb's tail," he smiles. He bends to kiss her and then pats her on the rump.

Although the bank is closed on Saturday afternoons,

it's the only one in Clover, and Daddy works every day of the week except Sunday. Today, instead of walking back to the bank, he backs our new white, green-finned Chrysler out of the driveway, and he slowly heads two blocks north to The First National Bank Building, on the nearest corner of the town square. Watching him drive away, I imagine him stopping at each intersection and looking both ways before proceeding. The most boring driver in Texas.

Angelica is pretty, and everyone likes her, but she really doesn't have any close friends, mostly because her mother has frightened all of us girls. The entire summer long Mrs. Musseldorf has refused to let Angelica spend her days in idleness with the rest of us. What's worse, when we've gone to her house to spend the night, Mrs. Musseldorf has made us go to bed at 9:00. Grimly, she marches into Angelica's room — no knocking — and she announces, "It's nine o'clock, girls. I expect you in bed with the lights out in five minutes." Son of a beehive — I call that abusive.

Soon after they moved to town, Angelica invited me to spend the night. Everything in her home is either tan or gray, with the exception of her bedspread, which is covered in blue flowers. But the rest of the house is drab — no pictures on the walls, no knick-knacks or books, no magazines, no television.

Angelica's mother made us go to bed early and get up early. "Jesus got up at the crack of dawn. And I want

15

Angelica to live a good Christian life." She stared at my nylon baby doll pajamas. Even though it was summertime, Angelica wore a long-sleeved cotton nightgown.

"How do you know Jesus was an early bird?" I asked.

"It says so in the Bible. How else could he organize his rascally disciples? Got them up and whipped them in line. And don't call him an *early bird*. That's sacrilegious."

"That's the first I've heard of Jesus getting up early," I said.

"'Early to bed, early to rise, makes a man healthy, wealthy, and wise.' Ever heard of that?"

"Is that in the Bible?"

"It most certainly is. The Lord and Master said it himself! Read your scripture, sister!"

What a rotten hostess! She got me so upset I could hardly sleep.

While eating breakfast the next morning, I made the comment that I just *loved* the new aqua Thunderbird convertible in the Ford showroom window on the town square. Mrs. Musseldorf grabbed me — right where my neck and shoulder join — and she squeezed so hard tears welled in my eyes. She looked me in the face and said, "You don't love *things*. You love *people*."

I tried to dip away. "I *do* love people."

"Who do you love?" she asked, holding me.

"Elvis! I love Elvis with all my heart!"

Then she pinched me harder, and she spat, "Elvis

Presley is trash, you little fool! He's not worth a tinker's damn."

From then on, I couldn't bear to look Mrs. Musseldorf in the eye, and she told Angelica I was shifty and dishonest, because I wouldn't.

So I hated Mrs. Musseldorf. In my judgment, anybody who didn't appreciate Elvis had no business having a family. But the main reason I couldn't look at Mrs. Musseldorf was that by then I'd seen Angelica's scars. She'd shown them to me after breakfast that morning, after her mother left for work. Her father had come home from the tire store and service station and was resting in their cheerless living room.

Angelica's arms and back were cross-hatched with lumpy markings — from being thrown and held down on a hot furnace, she said. "My mother doesn't mean to hurt me. She just has a problem with her temper. Doesn't your mother ever hurt you?"

When I got home that afternoon, I told Mother.

"Oh, Frankilee, we must help that poor girl." Mother was close to crying.

"I know. But how?"

"Bring Angelica home with you every time you can. We'll figure out something."

From then on, Mother and I've conspired to wrest Angelica Musseldorf away from her mother. It's been one hell of a project.

Chapter 3

ANGELICA AND I are organizing her new room when Mother comes to the door. She lightly raps and asks me to step out to the hall. "If we have any trouble here this afternoon, I want you to call your father. I can protect Angelica for a while, but I may need your daddy to convince Mrs. Musseldorf that we intend to protect her daughter."

Shortly after that, the doorbell rings. I hear Mother say, "Yes, you may speak to Angelica, but she's not going home with you." Then she calls Angelica to come downstairs. I immediately run down to the den and telephone Daddy.

"Come home!" I yell into the receiver. "Mrs. Musseldorf is here!"

Hearing screaming, I run into the living room. Mrs. Musseldorf has thrown Angelica to the floor and is kicking her. Swinging her arms, she keeps my mother away from Angelica. I can't move, but simply watch the two women struggle as if in slow motion.

Angelica has rolled herself into a ball, and she

screams, "Stop, Mother, please stop!"

"Goddamn," her mother yells, kicking her again. "What do you expect? Get up, you little bitch!"

Mother's voice shakes. "Please, Mrs. Musseldorf, please calm down." She moves toward them, holding out her hands to protect herself.

But the furious woman punches the air. Then she hits my mother. Mother staggers backward, and I rush in. A sharp pain slices my face. I lose my balance and crash into a lamp table, knocking the lamp to the floor.

Lucy, our orange and white striped cat, has been napping in the living room. Now I see a streak of fur and hear an angry yowl. Dazed, I land with my back against the sofa. I see Lucy's tail beside me, sticking out from under the sofa skirt, and I watch it twitch violently. My ears ring, and my face throbs with heat.

And now Daddy is here. Quickly, he catches Mrs. Musseldorf's wrists. "Now, Mrs. Musseldorf," he says. "Is this the Christian way to behave?"

Mrs. Musseldorf catches her breath and stops her attack. A West Texas farm boy during the Depression, my tall, strong Daddy has hands of iron. He doesn't lessen his hold. "I repeat, Mrs. Musseldorf, is this any way for a Christian to behave?"

"I suppose it isn't," she says.

"If I let you go, can you behave in a Christian fashion? Look at me, Mrs. Musseldorf!"

"I suppose I can."

"Can what?"

"Can behave."

"Look me in the eye and say it!" My God, what a wonderful man.

"I can behave in a Christian fashion," she says, looking at him. Her face is close to his, and she acts a little swoony. For a minute I'm afraid she might plant a kiss on his mouth. Then the weirdness passes.

By now Angelica has crawled away, and Mother is regaining her composure.

"Now what do you want here?" Daddy asks, as he releases Mrs. Musseldorf's wrists.

"I want Angelica's things. All of them. Everything."

"What about Angelica?"

"I don't want her. I made or bought everything she has, and I want it all back."

"But they belong to her," Daddy says. "What would *you* do with them?"

"Sell them or give them away. But she can't have them."

"Do you want her toothbrush also?" Mother asks.

"No, she can keep that."

"Oh, but I think that you should take her toothbrush," Mother snaps.

"Don't you see how ridiculous this all sounds?" Daddy asks.

His presence has given Mother courage. "You may not have Angelica's belongings. What she brought into this house belongs to her, not to you," Mother says.

"That settles it," Daddy says. "I see no reason for

this conversation to continue."

"There's one last thing, Mrs. Musseldorf," Mother says. "If you'll be uncomfortable if I continue teaching the Mary and Martha class, I'll resign."

"No need to do that," says Mrs. Musseldorf. "You're a good teacher. I'll probably keep coming to the class. Don't resign." She seems less defeated, as if giving Mother permission to continue teaching the Mary and Martha class has given her dignity. To me, her reaction makes no sense, but then, neither does Mother's offer. Mother and Daddy glance at each other, and I wonder if this whole day is a hallucination, perhaps brought on by the Russians.

Angelica and I go upstairs together. We put cold wet washcloths on our faces, and we cry, as we hold each other's hands. From a window in Angelica's room, we look down at the driveway through the still-green leaves of the elm tree in our front yard. We watch Angelica's mother climb into her car and drive away. Then Mother comes. Her face is gray, and her hands tremble as she offers us each a glass of water and an aspirin. She holds my face in her hands and says, "Oh, Frankilee. I never dreamed you might get hurt."

After Mother goes back down to talk with Daddy, Angelica puts her arms around me. "Now we're sisters," she says.

Somehow, I don't like the sound of that.

An hour later, Angelica's dad arrives. Like his

daughter, he's small, with delicate hands and fine facial features. The two of them stand in our living room, clinging and sobbing.

"My wife's been out of control for years," he tells my parents. "And whenever I've tried to protect Angelica, Bridget has just beat her all the more."

He wipes his nose and eyes with his hands, then wipes his hands on his overalls. Mother has him sit down on the sofa, while she fetches a box of Kleenex from the bathroom. Angelica sits next to him.

I sit on the bottom step of the stairs in the hall and watch. With all my might, I wish my parents would ask him about the rumors that Mrs. Musseldorf abuses him as well. Holy shit, let's find out the whole truth about this terrible woman, once and for all.

Although Mother and Daddy are too polite to ask, Mr. Musseldorf finally offers the information I'm itching to hear. "You know, not long ago my wife was arrested for beating up a truck driver out on Route 66. Her temper is fierce." So if she attacked a complete stranger, surely she's capable of socking her own husband.

And then my dad brings up another subject.

"Mr. Musseldorf," he says, "let's talk about where Angelica will live."

"Call me Alfred," replies Mr. Musseldorf. He puts his arm around Angelica, and she snuggles close.

"Well, Alfred," Daddy says, "let's talk about where Angelica will live. She can't stay here forever."

Alfred lets go of Angelica, reaches for a Kleenex, and

blows his nose loudly. "I thought you wanted Angelica to stay with you," he says, rubbing his eyes.

"Oh, Mr. Musseldorf — Alfred," Mother says. "We want Angelica to stay with us for as long as she needs to stay. But surely you have people — relatives — that you'd prefer to have her live with. As a permanent thing, I mean."

Alfred Musseldorf sits with his head down.

"Girls," Mother looks at Angelica and me. "Maybe you should go upstairs."

I have no intention of moving, and Angelica makes no effort to leave her daddy's side.

Then Mother says, "Maybe Angelica could stay with us until Christmas and then move to North Dakota — or wherever your people are."

"I have no people, Mrs. Baxter."

"What about Bridget? Doesn't she have family?" asks my dad.

"We have no one."

Daddy leans back in his chair, stunned. Oops! Maybe Mother and I should have researched Angelica's family before we decided to wrest her away from her mother. Oh shit.

Then Mother says something really dumb. "Aren't there ways to get help from the state of Texas in this kind of situation?"

My father gives her a withering glare. "Surely you're not talking about *welfare*," he says.

"No, of course not," she crosses her arms.

By now both Angelica and her father huddle together and blow their noses into wads of Kleenex. Below them, between their two sets of feet, I see Lucy's striped tail.

"I'm sorry to be so much trouble," Angelica cries. "Nobody loves me. I wish I were dead."

Then my do-goody mother says the dumbest thing of all. "Of course, we'll be glad for Angelica to stay with us for as long as it takes you to get things straightened out."

"Of course we will," echoes my dad.

"I'll figure out something," says Alfred Musseldorf. "In the meantime, please keep a record of your expenses. I'll reimburse you for everything." He pulls out a shabby billfold and offers my dad a twenty-dollar bill.

Daddy holds up his hand. "We can talk about money later."

Alfred Musseldorf gently rocks his daughter. She holds onto him and cries. I wonder how they can stand it. How could I bear to leave *my* father?

Then Mr. Musseldorf stands, barely missing the cat's tail.

"You're welcome to come visit Angelica any time," Mother tells him, as she walks him to the front door.

"Thank you, Mrs. Baxter," he says. "You're a wonderful person. You have a swell home and a great family."

Angelica walks with him, arm in arm, to his car. From the living room window, I watch her open the door to the front seat and help him inside. She talks to him for a few moments, and then she bends over and kisses his cheek. Then together — she on the outside, he on the inside — they close his door. Alfred Musseldorf starts his car, she waves, and he drives away.

By now, most of her ponytail has come undone. Held by a rubber band, a twig of hair sticks up tall, and the rest falls in wisps down her neck and around her face. I watch her walk back toward our house, and I feel so sorry for her I start crying all over again.

After dinner, the four of us go upstairs to the guest room, and we christen it Angelica's bedroom. Then we girls get our stuff ready for church the next morning. We press our dresses and wash our hair. Still later, as a newly formed family of four, we sit in the peace of the darkened den, lighted only by the blue halo of our black-and-white television. While watching *The Hit Parade*, Angelica and I eat vanilla ice cream drizzled with Hershey chocolate, topped with a maraschino cherry.

"How much is that doggie in the window," sings Gisele MacKenzie, "the one with the waggly tail?"

As is their custom, Mother curls up on the couch with Lucy on her lap, and Daddy sits in his favorite leather chair, peeling an apple. As he has done a hundred other Saturday nights, he taps his foot to the music.

Chapter 4

RIGHT FROM THE beginning, Mother and Daddy try to treat Angelica as if she were my sister, which is something I hadn't bargained for.

You see, for years my missionary mother has been looking for somebody to save. Succor and aid, as well as improvement of others, runs in her blood.

After the Civil War, when Great Grandmother Hadley and her family moved from their burned-out property in Mississippi to a cattle ranch in West Texas, she was one of the first organizers of the Women's Christian Temperance Union. Great Grandmother Hadley delivered calves and babies, and in her spare time she preached against saloons and drinking. Unlike Carrie Nation, Great Grandmother Hadley never destroyed a bar, and she didn't carry an ax, but she passed down her missionary zeal to my grandmother, who in turn preached the doctrine to her six daughters. Although they'd never admit it, Mother and her five sisters try to outdo each other with good works. So far, nobody else has taken in a child on a permanent basis. So when Angelica comes to live with us, Mother's thrilled to a pink string.

What's more, she wants to protect Angelica from ugly gossip. "If you talk about this openly to your friends," she tells me, early on Sunday morning, "it will just make things worse for Angelica."

"I don't see how you can expect me not to tell anyone," I answer. "This news is just too exciting! My God, Mother! I have to tell Shelly, at least. She's my best friend!"

"Tell Shelly and the others that Angelica has come to live with us temporarily, but don't go into any detail. People will drive you crazy with questions if you let them," she says. "And don't say *My God* that way. You're taking the Lord's name in vain."

"Daddy says *My God* like that. I heard him say it yesterday."

"Daddy is Daddy, and you are you."

Angelica stumbles into the kitchen, crying because she doesn't like the dress she's planned to wear to church. Mother suggests that I lend her one of mine, so I take Angelica upstairs to my closet. She chooses an outfit, and I let her wear it, even though the skirt is so long it almost drags the ground, and the seams hang off her shoulders. Holy crap, she looks tacky. Sharing is one of those Christian virtues I'm not so hot at. Angelica's been in our house less than twenty-four hours, and already she's embarrassing me.

Everything is okay in Sunday school, but, sure enough, in church old Preacher Farnsworth yells out at the end of his sermon that the congregation "is all going to the bow wows." He looks straight at my family. This time, Mrs. Musseldorf doesn't thump. Later, as Daddy drives home, I sit up in the front seat with him, and Mother sits in the back, holding the weeping girl in her arms.

"The preacher said we're going to hell," Angelica wails.

"He likes to be dramatic," Daddy says. "Pay no attention to him. We're doing all right."

As Mother prepares Sunday dinner, Angelica whines that she doesn't know how to set the table. And later, as I wash the dishes and she dries, she whimpers that washing dishes is *her* specialty. Each time Angelica weeps, Mother practically breaks her neck to assure her that, from now on, her life will be wonderful. She can count on us to make her dreams come true.

"One more thing," Angelica says. "I'd like to change my name. From now on, please call me Angel."

By this time Angel is calling Mother Mom and Daddy Pops, and I'm so tired of it all I go upstairs to my room. By the end of the first day, I'm worn out and nervous, and beginning to lose my missionary spirit. Reading my homework for the following week, I can hear Mother and Angel downstairs talking.

Suddenly, a splash of fur leaps up. Lucy stands on the open pages of my American lit book. She lies down across the pages and begins licking her paws. I pick her up, put her out in the hall, and close the door, but Lucy cries loudly, so I open it. There with Lucy stands our gray striped tomcat, Desi. I let both cats in and sit back down to read. Lucy jumps back up on my book, while Desi snoops under my bed. In a moment, she jumps down, Desi emerges from under the bed, and together they head for the door. Like a song-and-dance duo on *The Ed Sullivan Show*, they reach for the doorknob and scratch at it, yowling.

I have a revelation: Angel is like these whining goofball cats, following me from room to room, meowing, wanting who knows what — food? A backrub? A mouse? Angel's needy, all right. Once again, I feel sorry for her.

The next day at school I have another mission. Only two boys in the junior class are taller than I am — James Colton, the football quarterback and everybody's dreamboat, and Jerry Fred Porter, a pitiful specimen of the male gender. For weeks I've been working on getting James Colton to be my boyfriend, flirting with him between classes at our lockers, because I want him to take me to the Homecoming Dance. He's a gorgeous dude, and I have a royal crush on him.

"If I can't marry Elvis, I'll settle for James Colton," I tell Shelly Cox nearly every night as we talk on the phone. To tell the truth, all my friends know about my plan. But today every time I see or speak to handsome James in the hall, Angel rushes between us. She has her flirtation pattern down to an art.

I remind myself that she's simply a lost cat.

After school, as we walk home, Angel starts to cry. She won't tell me what's wrong, so I hope she's homesick. In my daydream, she says, "I've made a mistake. I miss my own mother terribly. Please take me back to her."

I envision calling the Clover Cab Company and having Lela Belle Walker help me move Angel back to her original home. I imagine Angel's mother renouncing her abusive ways and promising to become the epitome of love and gentleness. In my daydream, Mrs. Musseldorf even becomes an Elvis fan.

My heart beats very damn fast. "Please, Lord," I pray silently. "Let it be true." Ordinarily I bother God during the daylight hours only when I need something monumental, and putting Angel back with her mother qualifies as a justifiable reason for disturbing the Lord.

By the time we get home, Angel's wailing. Mother has been waiting for us, but her smile quickly becomes a frown. She takes Angel by the shoulders, "What's wrong? What's happened to you?"

As if she's rehearsed the scene for a year, Angel cries, "Frankilee and her friends were mean to me! But don't get mad at her! She probably doesn't realize she's so cruel. I can't help it if I have ugly clothes!"

Shocked, I watch as if I were in an audience.

Mother glares at me. "What's the matter with you? Go to your room immediately!"

As I climb the stairs, I smell cookies baking in the oven, and know they're for Angel. I try to remember the last time that Mother baked cookies for me. So this is the way it's going to be.

I stay in my room and work on my homework, while Mother makes plans to revamp Angel's wardrobe. I can hear them talking in the kitchen, and, gradually, the little shit's wails become giggles. When they finally come upstairs, Mother brings me a glass of milk and a saucer with two chocolate chip cookies.

"Thought you might like a snack," she says. She bends down and kisses my forehead. I refuse to look up.

The conspirators go into Angel's room and begin pulling dresses out of the closet, while I carry my snack into the bathroom between our bedrooms. Leaving both doors open, I stand over the toilet and throw the cookies into it. I pour the milk into the saucer for Lucy. Sitting on the bathroom floor, I finger-comb her fur as she laps up the milk. I want Mother to see I have no intention of accepting such cheap appeasement. Although I can still tell myself that Angel is just a scrawny, pathetic cat, I now envision her with a bad case of worms.

Watching them together, I'm afraid Angel is what my beautiful mother has wanted all along. Blonde, small, graceful, and pretty, Angel has a curvy figure and a luscious complexion. She looks as if she just emerged from a classical painting. She's like Debbie Reynolds or Doris Day, a girl any sensible mother would love — so why doesn't her old bitch of a mother love her?

On top of that, Angel and Mother look a lot alike. I take after my dad. Tall, awkward, too straight and curveless for description. And it doesn't help that I'm younger than the other kids in my class.

For some reason, when my first grade teacher discovered I could already read, she bumped me up to the second grade — without conferring with my parents. When they found out, they didn't object, because they didn't want me to be bored or burdensome in school.

In the seventh grade, when all the other girls got boobs and periods, I didn't, and when I complained, Mother reminded me that I was younger than the rest of them.

"Then put me back a grade!" I begged. Mother laughed, as though I'd said something hilarious. Doesn't she know I'd gladly give up my reading ability for tits?

Mother was wrong when she predicted I'd grow a bosom in a year or two, because I didn't develop breasts the next year, or the next. Now, my junior year in high school, I wonder if I'll *ever* have boobs — or hips — or a waist. My body is the perfect human matchstick with a head on top of a long, scrawny neck. I look like a damned pencil.

My oily skin and straight brown hair are pathetic. How I long for dramatic looks! How I yearn for beauty! I want to be a Spanish gypsy, like Carmen, and dance on men's hearts. If I could be gorgeously sexy like Marilyn Monroe or have impressive cleavage like Jane Russell, I'd never ask for another thing. But I am plain, bordering on ugly. A beanpole, a scarecrow, a female Ichabod Crane.

During the first week that Angel's with us, I hole up in my room with the cats, read my books, concentrate on homework, and say *Oh shit!* every other minute, while Mother and Angel work on jazzing up her wardrobe.

On Saturday, James Colton telephones. I've been expecting his call. James clears his throat and then asks for Angel. After I hand her the phone, the little sneak says, "Oh, James! I'd love to go to the Homecoming Dance with you!"

"Well, son of a bitch!" I say to Wanita, who stands beside me with her arm around my shoulders. "I wonder how much more I can take from that little shit-face before I have to declare war."

"Watch your mouth, young lady," Wanita answers. "You ain't acting like quality."

Meanwhile, the kids at school accept Angel's circumstances, and they make few comments about our new arrangement. Thanks to my mother's call to the principal, Mr. Johnson, the teachers accept our sisterhood. By the end of the week, everyone in Clover knows all they'll ever know about Angel Musseldorf coming to live with the Baxter family. True to her word, Mother tells people very little about the actual rescue.

"This new arrangement pisses me off," I tell Wanita.

"Don't talk potty-mouth," she says.

"It's my new style," I tell her.

"Dumb style!" she answers.

Chapter 5

WANITA CARVER WORKS for us, and next to Shelly Cox, she's my best friend. She's tall, thin, and as dark as midnight velvet. She's been with our family forever. Silently entering through the back door to the kitchen, she comes to our house four days a week. On Mondays, Wednesdays, and Fridays she stays for the entire day, and on Saturdays she stays until noon.

I love the way Wanita talks, and I enjoy sitting in the kitchen discussing my ideas with her. She says what she thinks, regardless of how outrageous her opinions might be. When she's disgusted, she sings an emphatic "Uhhh-uhhmm," like a blues singer belting out a torch song.

Wanita's husband is Battles Carver, the biggest, strongest, blackest man in the Texas Panhandle. They own a farm on the outskirts of Clover, and every summer Battles brings vegetables to our table — turnips, corn, black-eyed peas, green beans, new potatoes, tomatoes, squash and especially okra. Battles believes okra is the key ingredient for a happy life.

Battles also raises and trains hunting dogs — huge,

rambunctious, spotted pointers, the best hunters in the state. Several times each year my dad and his friends hire Battles to go on hunting and fishing trips with them. "He's the best hunter and fisherman I ever saw," Daddy says. "And he can cook like the devil's own business."

Battles is so strong he's legendary. Sometimes, when the white men are bored, or want to trick a newcomer, they lay bets on what Battles can or can't lift. Daddy swears Battles lifted a railroad car one time when a Rock Island Line train hit a herd of cattle.

The Saturday after Angel comes to live with us, I hear Battles and Wanita fussing in the kitchen. He's brought a load of vegetables, and he's joking her in a deep bass voice that resonates throughout the house.

"What you want to say that for?" Wanita scolds.

"I just say you is cooking them turnips to death. You likes them that way, but nobody else does. White folks for sure don't want their vegetables cooked to death."

"You leave the cooking to me. I ain't heard no complaints lately."

"No, and you won't. 'Cause them white folks is scared of you," he says.

"I sick of listening to your silliness. Who you think you is? Amos and Andy?"

"Well, maybe. I should be on the radio. Or the television. I be so handsome all them Yankee nigger women fall all over theirselves for me."

"Uhhhh-huuhmm!" Wanita sings out. The discussion is closed.

35

Wanita and Battles have two sons, William and Rootie. Handsome, tall William is my age, and everyone says
he'll eventually be as big as his dad. He keeps his head
down, carries his cap in his hands, and acts polite. Unlike Battles, he never jokes. Sometimes William comes
with his mother to do chores at our house, and sometimes little Rootie, six years younger, comes too. Rootie
has inherited his father's sly but funny personality. Slen-
der and sure-footed, he's already a track star.

Twice a year my mother hires William to help wash
the windows. She and I clean the windows inside the
house, while William and his mother clean them outside.
The reckless William shows off by perching on a totter-
ing ladder, arms outstretched.

Once when we were all cleaning windows, I heard
Wanita scream, "What you doing, boy! Ain't you got no
sense? You going to fall and splatter yourself all over the
driveway. Get you a rope and tie that ladder up to the
side of the house!"

William acted disgusted but said nothing. Slowly he
descended the ladder and walked around to the backyard. He found a rope in the tool shed behind the house,
then patiently climbed back up the ladder and tied himself to it.

"What you doing, boy!" Wanita screamed. "You
done tied *yourself* to that ladder, so when it falls, you
fall too!"

William didn't look up, but just kept on working. I tried to imagine how he must feel, with his mother screaming at him in front of us. Through the window, I caught his eye and grinned. "I don't like washing these crappy windows any more than you do!" I yelled.

For the rest of the day he ignored everything his mother said. Crap-a-lap-a-zap, William is a cool dude.

Later, when Battles came by to pick them up, Wanita must have told on William, because Battles took him by the shoulders and began examining his head.

"What are you doing, Daddy?"

"Is there a hole in your head?" asked Battles, "Where the brains leaked out?"

I love that expression and want to use it myself sometime. In fact, I've spent a fair amount of time rehearsing it. Battles is full of great clichés and clever sayings. Now, looking into the mirror, I practice, "Angel Musseldorf, is there a hole in your head where the brains leaked out?"

In no way does William have a leaky brain. He's quite intelligent, a fact which everyone in town ignores. What the townspeople love about William is his athletic ability. He can outrun, out-tackle, out-pass, and out-maneuver any of the white boys on the Clover High School football team. The trouble is, he's never allowed to play with them. And in basketball, he can outplay everybody — white or Negro. It galls Daddy to the bone that William can only play ball in the rickety old Negro high school gym or at the white kids' high school football stadium of Clover, Texas, on Thursday nights, when the Negro teams are allowed in. Daddy goes down to the flats to watch William play whenever he can.

People in Clover know the Supreme Court has ordered integration, and they talk about the 1954 *Brown v. Board of Education of Topeka* case all the time. "We won't do it until we have to," they say.

Daddy says the white people are resentful and think they've done enough for the colored people by letting them live in the bottoms, or the flats. On the west side of town, across the railroad tracks, the bottoms' roads aren't paved, and most of the wooden houses have no plumbing. No lawns, no offices, no stores, and no service stations.

"White folks think the colored people are lucky to live in Clover," Daddy says, shaking his head. "Just because we've never had sundown laws. These fine white Christians brag about how generous they are. Almost makes you want to leave the church."

"What are sundown laws?" I ask.

"Ordinances that forbid Negroes to be within city limits after sundown," he answers. I've never heard of anything so ridiculous.

Once I heard my mother's friends playing bridge and talking about the race issue. "Well, we take good care of our darkies, yes, we do, so why does the Supreme Court want to mess things up for us?"

This made my mother so angry she went to the

kitchen to smoke a cigarette. I was standing there with Wanita, who was ironing and pretending she hadn't heard. While Mother angrily puffed on her cigarette, I whispered, "Mother, why don't you tell those old biddies how wrong they are?"

"Oh, Frankilee," she answered. "You don't know a thing about small town business. Besides, I don't know how to talk about this without going berserk!"

But when she went back to her bridge game, I heard her say, "Let's change the subject now. Wanita is in the kitchen, and your discussion is most upsetting."

They looked up at her, but no one spoke.

In 1956 on the other side of town, the colored people are even more nervous about integration than we are. True, their school is in need of repair, and they never have enough schoolbooks and supplies, but Wanita says that they feel *safe* the way things are.

"Why we want to integrate with you all?" Wanita asked my mother after the bridge players had gone home. "We got a good marching band and great football and basketball teams. And our principal, Dr. Matthis, the smartest man in town. You got a principal puts doctor in front of his name?"

"That's all the more reason we should integrate," Mother said. "Dr. Matthis is the best educated administrator in the county. We could all benefit from his expertise."

"Uuuuhhhh — uuuh! I don't want my boys to go to

school with no white boys! White boys is mean."

But as William develops into a super-athlete, and as we watch Rootie win every foot race in sight, some of the white folks wonder if integration might not be a good idea after all.

For some reason, Wanita wasn't at our house on the Saturday morning Angel came to live with us, so when she comes early on Monday, she's surprised.

Daddy has already gone to the bank, and Mother, Angel, and I are finishing our breakfast. Wanita walks into the kitchen, and she sets her purse down, as Mother explains to her that Angel is now a part of our family.

"Uhhhh-huuuhmmmm," Wanita puts her hands on her hips and looks at Mother squarely.

Then Angel says, "I left a pile of dirty clothes on the floor in my bedroom. You can wash them after you've made my bed."

Mother turns to Angel. "We don't give orders to Wanita," she says. "You mustn't tell her what to do."

Angel's eyes open wide. "What's the use of having a maid if you can't tell her what to do?" she asks. What a stupid idiot.

"Wanita is our friend," Mother says. "We don't boss our friends around. Come upstairs with me, Angel. I'll help you get your room in order before school. Then every morning from now on, you'll do it yourself." She takes Angel by the hand as if she were a small child, and they leave the room. I stay in the kitchen.

40

Wanita stacks breakfast dishes in the sink. "I leaves you people alone for one weekend — two days — and you gets yourselves in trouble."

I clear the table. "You don't understand. Angel needs us."

"Uhhh-huuuhmm!"

"She doesn't have anyone else. We have no choice." I sound just like my mother.

"Frankilee, there something about that girl that just do not ring true." Wanita turns on the hot water. When she looks my way, her forehead wrinkles and her eyes turn cloudy. "The wolf at the door. That's all I has to say on the subject."

Chapter 6

ANGEL HAS LIVED with us for a month, and her father hasn't come by to see her even once. I'm sorry about that, knowing I'd just die if Daddy ignored me under similar circumstances.

One day I mention it to Mother, and she says, "Mr. Musseldorf sure had me fooled. The way he carried on — I thought he loved Angel."

"She acts like she hasn't even noticed he hasn't come to see her," I say. "That's strange."

"You know she must be hurting inside," Mother says. "I can't believe he hasn't come by."

"Maybe Mrs. Musseldorf threatened him."

"You mean threatened to hurt him if he comes over here?"

"It could happen," I say.

"Well, then, he's a damned coward," Mother answers.

But I forget about Mr. Musseldorf, because now we're getting ready for the Homecoming Dance. One

Saturday Mother takes Angel and me to Amarillo to look for formals. Angel's excited about her date with the hunky delicious James Colton, and I'm resigned to going with Jerry Fred Porter. Whenever I think about how the little bitch flirted so outrageously to get a date with James, I could hang my head and cry. Or kill her.

In Amarillo Mother takes us to three dress stores and lets us choose the gowns we want. At least that's what she pretends to do. I want a strapless dress and try a couple of them on, but the saleslady says they don't fit right, and Mother adds that maybe I should wait until my chest develops before I try to go strapless. The whole scene is embarrassing. We look in all three stores for a dress for me, and Mother learns that every pretty dress is strapless. So she complains loudly to the salesladies, because there isn't a variety of styles.

Then suddenly I don't care anymore, and I let Mother choose. The dress I'm going to wear turns out to be ice blue taffeta and lace and strapless.

"Let's emphasize your gorgeous back," gushes my mother, the dolt, the royal piss-me-off.

She shows the alteration lady how to take a panel from the skirt and make a wide strap that wraps around my neck like a halter. Plus, she has the pointy boob fabric taken in, so I look as flat as I do in my underwear.

Angel doesn't get the dress she wants because of her scars. Although the ones on her arms and back aren't as deep and hideous as I once thought, they're still a distraction, especially on a girl as lovely as Angel, going to the ball with the most fantastic hunk in quarterback history. Mother buys her a soft pink tulle strapless gown with a shawl, and she tells the alteration lady to shorten the shawl and attach it to the dress, thereby giving it a Queen Elizabeth back and collar, which camouflages the scars.

So my pretty back is exposed to the world, but my boobless front is covered up, and Angel's big bosoms and tiny waist are emphasized and her scarred-up back is hidden. In Hollywood, my mother could win an Academy Award for costume design.

On the way home, Angel snivels about her scars and how she's ruined for life and she'll be surprised if any man will ever marry her. Before you can say *Jackie Robinson*, Mother agrees to find a doctor and see about getting rid of those scars. I would have thought Mother would confer with Daddy before making this decision, but I must admit the idea is a good one. Nobody wants to walk through life covering up that much skin.

The next week we go to the Homecoming Dance. Jerry Fred isn't an exciting date, and he can't dance worth a shit, but he drives his folks' red and white Pontiac convertible, and he brings me an orchid corsage. Angel lusts after the car and the flower, and I reckon from now on she'll lust after Jerry Fred too, whenever we have to scare up dates for a party.

All in all, considering the fact that I don't get to wear a dress I like and I don't get to go with the dreamy James Colton, I have a pretty good time.

And Angel has a ball. She dances every dance, flirts outrageously, and twists her rear end around like a cat in heat. She puts on such a show it's embarrassing. Then I realize she's probably never been to a school dance before and has gone wild.

Angel doesn't come home by curfew. At first Mother and Daddy are steamed, but after a while they get worried. They're about to call James' parents when she comes dragging in, an hour late. They make me go to bed while they stay up talking to her, but they don't punish her. I can't get used to the injustice of the whole thing. My friend Shelly says I'm a whiner, but I'm not. I'm just mad.

A few days after the dance, Daddy comes home early and tells Mother to come with him into their bedroom. I wonder what's up and tiptoe across the downstairs hall to listen. Daddy closes the door, so I can't hear a damned thing. Later, as she's cooking supper, I ask Mother what Daddy said.

She stirs a pot of green beans. "I'd rather not say."

"Mother, we're partners in crime! You have to tell me!"

She picks up a potholder and walks toward the oven. "I don't have to tell you anything. You need to mind your own business."

"Does it have anything to do with Angel?"

She looks into the oven, checking her roast. "Maybe."

"What about Angel? Tell me, tell me, please."

She closes the door to the range and glances up at me. "Frankilee, hush! I don't want her to hear you."

"So it does have to do with Angel!" I lower my voice. "You can tell me. I won't tell."

"It's bad news," she whispers. "But we're not talking about it until after supper. I don't want to spoil anybody's meal."

"For God's sake, Mother — !"

"Frankilee, hush! You'll know in good time. Now set the table and help me finish up here." Mother is about to make gravy for the mashed potatoes. She totally tunes me out. "Being a good cook is a difficult chore," she says. "You know I can't talk and think at the same time."

Mother and Daddy are quiet during dinner, and they let Angel rattle on about her new clothes and her classes. Finally, after we clear the table, Daddy says, "Angel, I'm afraid I have some disturbing news."

Suddenly I know what the news is. Why hadn't I guessed it until now?

"What is it, Pops?" Angel asks. She's smiling, and I decide the dumb twit doesn't know the meaning of the word *disturbing*. Then I feel guilty and a little sick to my stomach.

"No one has seen or heard from your dad for several days," Daddy announces. "Today the sheriff came by the bank. I was sure you hadn't seen him, and I told the sheriff so. I don't know how long your dad's been missing."

The room is deadly quiet. I look at Mother, who

46

grips the edge of the table, then Daddy, who sits with his hands folded together, then Angel, who stares ahead and clenches her fists.

Daddy continues, "Angel, do you have any idea where your dad might be?"

"No, sir," she says as she wads up her napkin and twists it.

"Was I correct in telling the sheriff you haven't seen him?"

"Yes, sir."

Daddy takes his unused teaspoon and spins it on the table. "Would you like to call your mother or go over to your folks' house tonight?"

"I really don't want to see my mother," Angel replies. "I'm afraid she's hurt Daddy."

"Are you sure he's really gone? Not on a trip somewhere?" I ask.

"Where would he go? Besides, my daddy doesn't take trips." Angel twists her napkin.

"Disappeared without a trace," says Daddy. "That's what Sheriff Billy Joe Baines told me."

Tears stream from Angel's eyes. "When Mother gets drunk, she threatens to kill my dad. She used to threaten me, too."

"Why, Angel," Mother says, "I didn't know your mother has a drinking problem!" I swear to God I can't believe my mother makes such stupid remarks. Already she's been around Angel too long.

"Oh, yes, ma'am. She drinks something awful."

I'm glad Mother waited to tell us this terrible news after our dessert — Wanita's apple pie, with apples from Battles' orchard. I actually feel valves in my esophagus close as I imagine Mrs. Musseldorf attacking her thin, fragile husband. We sit at the table, quiet as sick mice.

"He's crippled, too, you know," Angel begins to sob. "You may not have noticed, but one leg is shorter than the other because when he was a little boy, he had polio."

Mother, Daddy, and I sit in our misery.

Throwing her napkin down, Angel looks at us and begins to giggle. She pushes her chair away from the table, and doubles over with laughter. Then she straightens, rears her head backwards, and laughs maniacally. "He *was* crippled. That's what I mean! He *was* crippled!" Finally, she crumples to the floor and sobs.

"My Lord," Daddy says.

Mother leaves her chair and gathers Angel in her arms. She holds her close and rocks her. I've never seen such a graceful movement.

"What do we do now?" Mother asks.

"Listen, Angel, I need to find out more information," Daddy says. "I probably shouldn't have told you about this, because nobody seems to know any facts." As he rises from the table, he awkwardly pats the top of Angel's head. He walks into the adjoining room, his den, and there he begins making telephone calls. I wonder if he'll talk with Mrs. Musseldorf.

In the meantime, Mother comforts the weeping girl.

"Calm down now, Angel." Mother turns to me. "Honey, while your dad and I take care of this, would you mind cleaning up the kitchen?"

For the rest of the evening, I deeply regret my own shittiness. I wash the dishes, scrub the pots and pans, and scold myself for my selfishness and resentful attitude. It's high time for a prayer.

"Please, Lord," I whisper. "Help Sheriff Baines find Mr. Musseldorf. And let him be alive. Do this, Lord, and I'll never have mean thoughts about Angel again." And I resolve to stop using vulgar words in exasperation with Angel. But I'm careful not to promise God that I'll *totally* give up cussing, just in case I should weaken sometime in the future.

While I put away the dishes, I can hear Mother and Angel talking upstairs. Mother runs bath water and encourages Angel to relax in a warm bath and then go to bed and get some sleep. Sometimes I wonder if Mother overrates the power of bubble bath. She probably has the notion that the North Koreans and the Russians would be our friends if we'd all just take a bath together.

Daddy comes into the kitchen. "I called Bridget Musseldorf," he tells me. "She would hardly speak to me. But she says she has no idea where her husband is. I asked her if she wants to see Angel, and she says no. What a mess."

He goes back into his den and switches on his television set.

I remember Daddy saying to Mother, "My God,

49

you're an optimist," the day we helped Angel run away from home. Is there an optimistic way to look at this situation? Suddenly it occurs to me that perhaps Mr. Musseldorf hasn't been murdered and hasn't disappeared through an act of violence but he's simply taken Angel's cue and run away from home *himself*. If that were the case, wouldn't he establish himself somewhere out of town and then send for Angel? Wouldn't Angel be far happier living with her own father than trying to get the attention of *mine*? This possibility is almost too much to hope for!

I switch my praying tactics. "Oh, Lord, please make it be true that Mr. Musseldorf has simply snuck off somewhere and is getting himself a job and will send for Angel pronto."

In the night I have a god-awful nightmare: Angel's father is scratching on my upstairs window screen, begging me to let him in. When I raise the window to help him wiggle through, Mrs. Musseldorf stands there with a kitchen knife. She slices off both my arms. I wake up, screaming bloody whorehouse murder.

There's one prayer I hate:

Now I lay me down to sleep,
I pray the Lord my soul to keep.
If I should die before I wake,
I pray the Lord my soul to take.

If I should die before I wake! Although I stopped saying that prayer years ago, its scariness is still enough to
keep me up all night.

So now, during my junior year in high school, I negotiate with God. After praying the Lord's Prayer each
night before going to bed, I say, "Listen, you keep me
alive all night, and I'll put up with Angel tomorrow."

Every morning when I awake I thank the Lord and
add, "Now I'll carry out my part of the bargain." And
I'm really trying.

In the days that follow the announcement of Mr.
Musseldorf's disappearance, the town and, consequently,
our school, churn with gossip, rumors, imaginary sight-
ings, and speculation. But after a couple of weeks, the
sensational stories die down and finally, after about a
month, everything returns to normal. Every day I volunteer to walk by the post office on my way home from
school, hopeful of being the first to find the letter from
her father-in-hiding. I'm confident that, in this all-
important missive, he'll beg Angel to join him in another
town, another state or another country. So sure am I of
my theory that I plan to trudge to the post office even in
the middle of fierce snowstorms for the entire winter, or
until hell freezes Hitler.

But Mr. Musseldorf doesn't write. Finally, I ask Daddy
what he thinks has become of him.

"I think he flew the coop," Daddy answers. "And I
don't think we'll ever see or hear from him again."

"So you don't believe Mrs. Musseldorf murdered him?"

"Nah!" he says. "But some people do have that theory."

"My friend Shelly thinks that Mr. Musseldorf lies chopped up and buried somewhere."

"I seriously doubt it," says Daddy, "but I do know this — Sheriff Billy Joe Baines has woefully mishandled the case."

One Monday night, Jerry Fred Porter calls. Like me, he's still unattractive, and like me, he has lots of friends anyway. People think we're witty, charming, tons of fun and excellent dancers. I don't understand it, since we're both such miserable bohunks.

"Do you want to go to the show with me on Saturday night?" he asks.

I'd like to say no, but I don't. "I'd love to. What's on?"

"I dunno. But I'll pick you up at 7:30."

"I want you to do me a favor," I tell him.

"What is it?"

"I want you to help me find Alfred Musseldorf."

He's quiet for a minute. "How am I supposed to do that?"

"I don't know, but we'll think of something. Since your dad's a lawyer, you ought to know how to snoop."

"He's an *attorney*, not a *detective*!"

"Still, he might be able to help us — but don't mention this to him just yet. Pick me up after my music lesson tomorrow, and we'll talk about it." Jerry Fred is so damned easy to boss.

Chapter 7

MABEL KATHERINE HIGHTOWER is my music teacher. She lives several blocks from our house, and across town from the colored flats, in the only true mansion in Clover, Texas.

Mother's friends talk about Miss Mabel's house all the time. It's a gigantic Tudor brick home standing high on the only hill around. Surrounded by intricate landscaping and trees, her estate is so fine and fancy the whole town has been agog over it for decades. Everybody takes pride in this local landmark, and we drive out-of-town guests by it, bragging about the wealth of the Hightowers. When we were in junior high school, my friend Shelly dubbed it the "House of Seven Gables," even though neither of us knew exactly what a gable was.

I love to climb the rounded concrete steps to Miss Mabel Hightower's house. I adore winding around the trees and gardens, and finally, at the top, arriving at the front door. There on the large front porch, which is bordered by black wrought iron railings, I'm always careful to remove my shoes before I go inside.

My music teacher usually leaves the front door un-locked, and on piano lesson days I go early and slip in-side as quietly as possible. A dark green marble foyer leads into the living area. There, in the living room, across from a wall of paned windows, draped with red and gold oriental fringed scarves, stands the ebony con-cert grand piano. As you enter the room, it faces from the corner, with its lid propped up and its ivory keys shining. Many children in Clover have tried to learn to play this piano at some time or another.

To the right of the front door is the library. Dark and cozy, with wooden shelves from floor to ceiling, this room is filled with old books. Smelling like dust and rich leather, the library is where I sit in a dark red chair, waiting for my lesson.

I'm a lousy musician — I hate playing and detest practicing. But I dearly love Miss Hightower's house, so I half-ass do the work so she won't kick me out.

Sometimes, when Miss Mabel is busy with a student and won't notice, I explore other rooms on the first floor. The Persian rugs, oil paintings, fragile figurines, and gold-trimmed furniture make me drool, and I under-stand why the ladies in Clover go berserk whenever they hear the name Hightower.

We kids call Miss Mabel "the Monkey Woman," and with good reason. She's small and wiry and has a great gob of dark, dyed hair piled on top of her head. Her shriveled face has a hundred thousand wrinkles, and she's got huge brown eyes. And when she was young, she "did it" with a traveling man who owned a monkey.

Everyone in Clover knows about Miss Mabel Hightower's lover of long ago. It's no secret that he was a Yankee named Harry Yates, who came to town to work one summer during the Depression. The old-timers say he was a romantic playboy who traveled with his pet monkey, a nasty rascal named Mousetrap.

Miss Hightower met the Yankee at a party and fell deeply in love. He was after one thing only, and it was no trouble for him to seduce her. Since she was quickly becoming an old maid, she might have felt he was her last chance. She probably considered him her only ticket out of town. So they had sexual intercourse — at least once. And when it was over, she'd fallen in love with the entire world. Unfortunately, she didn't realize Mousetrap had witnessed their steamy passion. Sitting on his perch, he was consumed by jealousy.

Getting out of bed, stark naked, Miss Mabel waltzed over to Mousetrap and reached out to pat his head. But the monkey went into a rage and attacked her. He bit down on her right forefinger so badly her lover had to practically beat the little varmint to death to make him let go. Then Lover Boy took Miss Mabel to the Clover Hospital, wearing only a silk robe. Imagine her embarrassment!

There, in the middle of the night, drunk old Dr. Grouse decided the finger couldn't be saved. So he amputated it. Then while Miss Mabel Hightower was in the hospital recovering from the surgery, Harry Yates and Mousetrap skipped town.

The citizens of Clover added this incident to their list of grievances against people from the North. Rallying around the humiliated Miss Hightower, they forgave her for being intimate with a person of foreign extraction.

A few years after Miss Hightower lost her finger, both of her parents died, leaving their estate to her, their only child. As years passed, she became eccentric and then downright paranoid, so afraid of poverty that she started teaching piano lessons. Like many other parents in Clover, Mother and Daddy are making me learn to play.

I hate and love Miss Mabel at the same time. She's a true victim of not one but three horrible men — her daddy, who never let her go anywhere; her lover, who practically ripped her pants off; and her doctor, who snipped off her finger.

In real life Miss Mabel is a terrible bore. Rhythm, scales, and theory — that's all she ever talks about. My God, those lessons are dull.

Some Tuesday afternoons I show up at her house a half hour early, so I can explore and also play with Pope Pius, Miss Hightower's white Persian cat. Miss Hightower likes to joke that she sleeps with the Pope. This may be the only amusing thing she's ever said in her life.

But the music lessons are causing me a lot of agony. Thanks to Miss Mabel having only nine fingers, I can't get my fingering right. When I complain to my parents, they remind me that she has to compensate by having her middle finger work double-time, and that finger moves at an amazing speed. In fact, her entire right hand runs over the keyboard like a scared animal. Or like something under a microscope in biology class.

I watch my teacher zip through scales and exercises and then try to follow her example, but my right index finger gets in the way. So I become frustrated, and Miss Hightower gets angry.

"What are you doing?" She whacks my hand with her pencil. "Use that finger! Are you ridiculing me?"

I'm Miss Mabel Hightower's least favorite student.

After moving in with us, Angel lets it be known right away that she wants to learn to play the piano. She languishes around our upright, sitting on the bench, touching the keys, and laying her head above the keyboard next to the damned sheet music, like some forlorn movie star. She picks up my John Thompson music book, calls me over and asks me to identify the notes. Then she presses the same keys down again and again with a pulsating rhythm. Lord have mercy, what drama.

Soon Angel's taking lessons from Miss Hightower. And now she spends hours every day at the upright, far exceeding the maximum time required. When I head toward the instrument — which isn't often — she flops down on the seat and begins her scales first.

Angel has made it so difficult for me to practice I'm

not getting my work done, and today my pieces are in pitiful shape. Consequently, I receive more scolding from Miss Hightower than ever.

"You're a terrible disappointment," Miss Mabel says. "Your playing is a mutilation. You must practice more, or you'll never become a musician."

I want to say, "Listen, you witch, I'm doing the best I can. *You* try living with Angel Musseldorf. I never get a chance to *practice*." But I keep my mouth shut and try again.

"No, no, no, no, no!" She puts her hands over her ears. At that moment Pope Pius leaves his warm fluffy bed beside the piano and huffs out of the room.

"See! See! Your playing today is so bad even the Pope refuses to give you audience." And she cackles.

"Well, call me a nun and serve me fish sticks on Friday," I say to her, standing and reaching for my music. "I think Pope Pius is a loyal pal. He refuses to witness my humiliation."

I am so mad I'm practically in tears, and suddenly Miss Mabel changes her mood. Smiling brightly, she takes my music, stacks it neatly, and hands it to me.

"See you later, alligator." She tries so hard to be hip.

"After a while, crocodile." What else can I say to a woman with a screw loose?

Angel's lesson comes after mine, and she's so talented and well-prepared Miss Hightower goes into a rapture.

Sometimes, in my sock feet I sneak away from the

piano room and continue exploring. They never notice me, and I usually have thirty minutes of good snooping before either of them comes up for air. Usually this is the most fun I have all week.

But today I have another mission, and I immediately leave Miss Hightower's house. I am especially pissed, since I know Angel heard Miss Mabel scolding me. Gads, I hope she doesn't tell Mother.

Jerry Fred waits for me outside in his old blue jalopy. I climb in, and we head for the Dairy Queen. I tell him I'm going to wring Angel's and Miss Mabel's necks, and as he shifts gears he laughs. On the radio Bill Haley sings, "Rock Around the Clock," and I sink into the softness of the squishy seat, close my eyes, and breathe.

"What about it, Jerry Fred," I say, as we drink our lime and cherry Cokes. "Will you help me find Mr. Musseldorf?"

"What if we can't? What if he's dead?"

"My dad thinks he's just skipped town. He doesn't believe the murder rumor at all."

"Well, what if you do find him? Then what?"

"I'll send Angel packing. She needs to be with her dad."

"Will you be nice to me if I help? Really nice?" he asks.

"If you mean will I sit around smooching with you, the answer is probably not." I look at him. "Well, maybe once." He can't help being tall and skinny and revoltingly ugly, any more than I can help being the way I am.

Then I make up my mind for good.

"I'll kiss you a lot, Jerry Fred, if you'll help me get Angel out of my hair."

"For your love, I would do anything."

"It's a deal?" I extend my right hand.

"It's a deal." He shakes my hand. He pulls me over and kisses me on the lips. Phooey and gooey.

But how to do it is the big question.

That night, as I sit down at the piano to practice, it hits me that I can solve the mystery of Angel's missing father by casing out Mrs. Musseldorf's house. It'll be tricky, but Jerry Fred will help. I leave the piano to call him.

"Finished so soon? That was fast," Mother says.

"You should have heard Miss Mabel gritching at Frankilee today," Angel says. "I'd be embarrassed if she fussed at me that way! But she loves *me*. She says I'm her most talented student." I could scratch Angel's eyes out and give her an enema.

When I get Jerry Fred, I say, "Let's plan a little investigation tomorrow night. In the meantime, let's pay a call on Sheriff Baines tomorrow."

After school we head for the sheriff's office in the basement of the courthouse. We walk into the dreary place and find the sheriff smoking and reading a *Field and Stream* magazine, his wide feet up on his desk. Clearly he's irritated at being interrupted. I explain that we're doing research on missing persons for our English class.

"There are lots of stories in American literature about people who disappear without a trace," I say. "I'll bring a real gruesome one for you to read sometime. It's called 'A Rose for Emily.'"

The sheriff grunts.

"Anyhow, it occurred to us that we have a classic case of human disappearance right here in Clover, Texas. The case of Alfred Musseldorf."

Another grunt.

Jerry Fred says, "We'd sure appreciate it if you'd tell us the facts of the case. You'd help us make a really good grade."

"You two writing this paper together? I never heard of that."

"Oh, yes," I answer. It's called 'investigative team essay writing.'"

"Can you tell us what you know about Mr. Musseldorf's disappearance?" Jerry Fred asks. We're both poised with pencils and notebooks, ready to write down every word.

Sheriff Baines puts his feet down, leans back in his chair and scratches his belly. "I can't tell you anything. We don't know it was a disappearance. The old boy probably just took off."

"But why? With a wife and child here in Clover?"

"Have you seen his wife?" the sheriff laughs. "And I understand his child is living with you, Frankilee. Why wouldn't a man take off?"

"If that's true, where is he?" I ask.

"Nobody knows."

"Are you sure Mr. Musseldorf is alive?" I ask.

"Of course! This sort of thing happens all the time."

"Men just walking off and leaving their family, home, and business? I don't think so," Jerry Fred says.

"Are you calling me a liar?" asks the sheriff, glaring at Jerry Fred.

"We wonder who reported Mr. Musseldorf missing in the first place. How did the investigation get started?" I ask.

"Someone called in to say he's missing. I don't know who it was. Probably an employee at the tire store."

"What does Mrs. Musseldorf say?" I ask.

"Why do you kids need all this?"

"Oh, you're doing great, sheriff," I say. "Just tell us what Mr. Musseldorf's wife told you about her husband's disappearance. Does she have any idea where he is?"

Suddenly the sheriff stands up. "I've told you all I know. I don't see how you can get an English paper out of it. Now you two kids skedaddle."

"One more thing," I say. "Have you closed the investigation?"

"You kids watch too much television!" he answers, as he shows us to the door.

Driving home, I ask Jerry Fred, "Do *you* think Mr. Musseldorf is alive?"

"I don't know. But if he's alive and determined not

to be found, we haven't got a chance."

"What do you mean?"

"Even if you found him, you'd never get him to take Angel."

"You don't know that. Let's see what we can find out tonight. Pick me up at seven. Wear dark clothes and bring a flashlight."

When Jerry Fred picks me up, we immediately drive out to the Musseldorfs' tire store and service station. Jerry Fred stops to get gas, and as he talks with the attendant, I walk into the building. Dressed in men's overalls, Mrs. Musseldorf argues with a man out in the garage. She hasn't noticed us. Quickly, I look through papers on the counter and the desk, but everything I see pertains to the station. I have only a minute to decide that I'll find no clues here, and I get in the car as Jerry Fred pays for the gas.

Next, we head back into town, down First Street to Musseldorfs' house. Jerry Fred parks on the street, down near the dead-end, and we walk quietly. Although there is a streetlight, most of the area is dark, with no lights coming from inside the house. When we walk up the sidewalk, Jerry Fred stumbles over the uneven, broken concrete, and he falls.

"For heaven's sake, be careful," I whisper, as he gets back to his feet.

First, we try the front door, which is locked. All the other doors and windows are locked also. Shades are pulled down, and we can't see anything inside.

"Come on, Jerry Fred! We've got to figure out a way to get in!"

He jiggles every window and tries every door again. "We need a locksmith," he says, and I realize how much he's counting on the kisses I've promised.

"We can break a window to get in," I say.

"And the sheriff will know damned well who did it," he answers. We continue walking around the house, pushing and yanking at the windows.

"Mr. Musseldorf might be tied up. If we can hear any noise from inside, let's break in, come hell or high water."

This time, when we go to each window, I softly call, "Mr. Musseldorf, if you're inside, make a noise!" But we hear nothing.

"We gotta give this up, Frankilee. It's ridiculous," Jerry Fred finally says.

So that's the way the cookie crumbles.

When we arrive back at my house, I thank Jerry Fred for his help. I'm disappointed to extreme unction, but true to my word, I sit and kiss him for nearly ten minutes.

"What were you and your string-bean boyfriend doing out there in the dark?" Angel asks, as I climb the stairs. "I'm going to tell Mom and Pops I saw you two smooching!"

"Leave me alone, Angel," I reply.

The next week I'm back at the music teacher's house. My lesson is tolerable, and when Miss Mabel dismisses me, instead of going out the front door, I turn to the left, and head down the hall toward the staircase. I want to go someplace where I can forget about Angel.

I tiptoe up the staircase as close as possible to the inner wall, and I reach the second floor without making a sound. The upstairs bedrooms are beautiful. Heavy walnut furniture, marble topped washstands, mirrored dressing tables, canopied beds, and fainting couches galore. Rich velvet draperies, hand crocheted bed linens and oriental rugs. I glide from room to room, carrying an antique fan from one of the dressing tables and whisper, "Why, Rhett, I can't give you an answer right *now*. Don't worry me so. I'll have to think about *that* tomorrow."

In Miss Mabel's room, I notice the door to a closet has been left open, and I can't resist the temptation to look inside. There in the gloom, hanging from a satin hanger, is a crimson feather boa — very different from the drab and sloppy clothes Miss Mabel usually wears. I weave my fingers through the old feathers and wonder if she might have worn it the night of her tragic monkey bite.

As I turn to leave the closet, I notice an old trunk back in the corner. Its lid is up, and on top of a pile of clothes there's something that looks like a basket. And sitting inside is a monkey — wearing a dress. The truth about Miss Mabel hits me. She has killed and stuffed

Mousetrap!

But when I turn on the closet light and crouch next to the trunk, I see that I've been mistaken. The basket is made of the carcass of an armadillo — shell, head, feet, and tail, lying upside down, with its innards scooped out, its belly lined with purple silk. And the dead monkey isn't a dead monkey after all.

Instead, it's an old-fashioned rag doll stuffed with cotton. It wears a Ku Klux Klan robe, the head completely covered with a pointed hood. On its chest, over the heart, a plain Christian cross is embroidered in red.

I can hear Angel running through her scales. Miss Mabel taps the piano with her pencil.

Inside the closet, my back to the door, I can't decide which artifact is more fascinating. Who would even *think* of resurrecting road-kill? And why would *anyone* preserve a symbol of such evil as the KKK?

The door creaks, and I realize the music downstairs has stopped. I feel a presence behind me. The hair on my neck stands up, big-time. Oh, Lordy, I wish I hadn't come into this closet! I'm surely about to be murdered, but I can't move. Could this be the way my life will end? Slaughtered in the closet of the Monkey Woman?

I hear a light humming mew and feel soft fur on my arm, as Pope Pius sidles up against me. Then he quickly jumps into the trunk and lies down to rest.

The music downstairs starts up again. "Oh, no, you don't," I whisper, as I pick up the cat. "If you even *try* to get me in trouble, I'm going to snatch you bald-headed!"

I'm so weak I can hardly hold him. I drop him to the floor outside the closet. Then, shaking, I creep away.

That evening I ask Daddy to tell me everything he knows about the Hightower family.

"Mabel Katherine experienced a sad love interest when she was young," he says, looking up from the evening paper. "She comes from a family of southern plantation owners in Georgia, but they lost their fortune during the Civil War. They moved to West Texas to start ranching almost a hundred years ago. Then they struck it rich in the oil fields. Miss Mabel is well fixed for the rest of her life."

"Why does she act like she's poor?" I ask.

"She's a little off-center," he answers. "I've tried to convince her she has plenty of money to live on, but she's so frightened about her future she plans to start taking in boarders."

"Don't you think her life has been sad?"

"Oh, yes. Miserable."

Chapter 8

DADDY'S FAVORITE MOVIE is *Citizen Kane*. He says everybody has something in their childhood they want to hold onto — even if it's one happy moment on a sled. Mother's favorite picture show is *Picnic*. She goes gaga over William Holden and Kim Novak in their romantic dance scene. Mother says every woman secretly wants to run off with a handsome guy who knows how to dance sexy.

I agree with them both. Like Old Man Kane, I once had happy childhood moments — before Miss Angel Musseldorf came on the scene. When I'm a hundred years old and dying, my last words will be "Before Angel."

And as far as Mother's statement about running off with a sexy man goes, when Elvis Presley comes to Clover, which I fully expect him to do any day now, I'll run off with him in a *trice*, which I believe means "quicker than quick."

My favorite picture show is *The Greatest Show on Earth*. I love the story, the characters, the circus, the costumes, and the train wreck. But I especially love Cornel Wilde. When he falls from his trapeze, my heart breaks. Even with a paralyzed, purply, shriveled-up hand, he's a handsome hunk of a man. I wonder how it would be to alternate between dating Elvis Presley and Cornel Wilde. Nothing below the neck, of course. Wouldn't I be the luckiest girl in Texas? With Elvis I could bop and swivel, and with Cornel I could lean and sway.

Mother and Daddy love to dance. They belong to a dance club that meets one Saturday night a month at the National Guard Armory — when the soldiers aren't there — and they dance practically all night, like Ginger and Fred. Some afternoons when Daddy comes home from work and Mother is cooking dinner, he puts a record on the phonograph player in the den, turns the volume up loud, and asks her to dance in the kitchen. Harry James is Daddy's favorite orchestra leader, with Glen Miller and Tommy Dorsey coming in second and third.

I like watching Daddy take Mother in his arms — she, pretty and graceful, and he, as handsome and rugged as John Wayne. I sit at the kitchen table and watch them foxtrot or waltz while whatever we're having for dinner warms up in the oven.

But when Mother is frying okra or chicken fried steak, she can't concentrate on dancing, so Daddy asks me to take a whirl. He waltzes across our wide kitchen floor, extends his right hand to me, and asks, "May I have this dance, Miss Cyd Charisse?"

I stand up straight. He bows, and I curtsy. He leads me into the middle of the kitchen and then we fold together. I call him Arthur Murray, because he teaches me steps.

Angel likes to watch Mother and Daddy dance. When the music plays, she can't be still. One day Mother is cooking a complicated meal that has to be timed right. Tommy Dorsey music plays in the den, and Angel begs Daddy to dance with her. He tells her that Mother is his dance partner, and he doesn't enjoy dancing with anyone else.

"What about Frankilee?" Angel asks. "You dance with her, don't you?"

"Well, yes, sometimes I do, but usually my partner is Abby."

Angel has perfected a dejected look, and she tries it on him now.

"Tell you what," he says. "You two girls dance together. Frankilee can teach you a few steps before dinnertime. Or why don't you turn on the television and watch *American Bandstand*?"

"No! I don't want to dance with another girl."

Daddy takes his newspaper into the den, turns down the music, and reads.

So poof! No more ballroom dancing before supper for anybody, anymore.

Mother says that someday someone will love me as much as my dad loves her. But I don't want Jerry Fred

Porter. My greatest fear — besides Mrs. Musseldorf cutting off my arms — is that I'll have to marry Jerry Fred, on account of he's the only guy I can get. The only complimentary thing I can say about him is he's tall. With shorter boys I have to bend my knees, hunch my shoulders and hunker my back. You have no idea how painful it is to shrink yourself four or five inches for an entire evening.

With Jerry Fred I don't have to do any contortions at all. Plus, I can say *shit* and *hell* whenever I damn well please. So maybe he really loves me. Unfortunately, the feeling isn't mutual.

There's another good thing about Jerry Fred. He's smarter than a tree full of owls.

For Halloween I dye Jerry Fred's amber hair black and dress him up as Elvis. He already has a pair of black slacks, and I take one of Daddy's old white shirts and dye it black in the washing machine. It takes about a hundred packages of Rit, but I finally get the shirt right. The whole project is messy, and Wanita has fourteen cats when she sees what I've done. She gets hysterical and makes me bleach the whole damn kitchen and laundry area where I've dripped dye. Honestly, sometimes she just wears me out.

"Wanita, you are radical," I tell her.

"Uuuhhh-huuuuh!" she says. "Don't you mess up my work place no more!"

Then I glue some sparkles and sequins on an old gray

jacket of Daddy's. This time Wanita insists on helping me. She says she wants to teach me to be neat, but it's also because she's clever with her hands and wants to show off. When we get through, Jerry Fred's costume is fine.

So he goes to the high school Halloween party as Elvis, and I dress up as a fan, which isn't original, but it is effective. I wear my best poodle skirt — a black felt circle skirt, decorated with a white fuzzy poodle with flashing red eyes operated by a battery hidden under my can-can petticoats, at least twelve. I put on my red sweater, bobby socks, and saddle shoes, and to my flat booberamas I pin a sign saying, "President, Elvis Presley Fan Club, West Texas Chapter."

When we arrive at school, I hear some smart aleck boy yell, "Oh, no! Here comes Frankenstein!" Referring, of course, to Jerry Fred. It makes me so damn mad I stop by my locker for a piece of paper, and then stomp down to the home economics department for a safety pin, Jerry Fred trotting behind me. I'm seething while I make a sign that says ELVIS in big letters. I pin this sign to his chest, and we proceed to the gym. I'll deck anybody who says anything derogatory to him. After what I've put him through, I've got to stick up for him.

At the party I take dues and sign up new members to Elvis' fan club. Many of the girls in school are already members, but I'm able to get a few more. The boys won't join. Angel won't join, either, saying she wants to save her allowance. That makes me want to spit, since I know where the little pea brain's allowance comes from.

Since it's a school night, the party doesn't last long, so afterwards I talk Jerry Fred into taking me trick-or-treating. We go to some of the neighborhoods that have small children still running amuck. I've coached him to quote Elvis extensively at every house. If a man answers the door, Jerry Fred says, "Don't step on my blue suede shoes," and if the man is rude to us, Jerry Fred says, "You ain't nothing but a hound dog."

If a woman answers, he says, "Hello, baby." And then I go into my spiel and politely ask her to join the Elvis Presley Fan Club. Most of these women whoop and laugh and run to get their purses, even though their husbands are saying, "Don't do it. That's the silliest thing I ever heard of!"

After a woman joins the club, Jerry Fred says, "Thank you very much," and curls his lip in a seductive way. He does everything I've taught him to, and everybody has a big time.

At one of the homes, the lady of the house is having a bridge party. Instantly, I sign up twelve new members, the most remarkable haul of my career.

As he drives me home, Jerry Fred says, "I just don't get it. What's so special about Elvis Presley?"

"I can't explain it," I answer. "But Elvis has sizzle, and we all want some sizzle in our lives."

"Well," he says, as he shifts gears, "that *is* silly."

"It may seem silly to you, but tonight seventeen women and several girls joined the West Texas Chapter of the Elvis Presley Fan Club."

Chapter 9

EVERY THANKSGIVING WE drive to my grandparents' house, which is on a ranch about twenty miles
away. It's the home my mother and her sisters grew up
in — spacious and filled with heavy furniture, each piece
with a story of its own. It's a happy, pointed house with
deep porches, gingerbread trim and tall windows in every room.

Today is the first time for the rest of the family to
meet Angel, and I dread it. I know she'll probably flirt
with my cousin Charlie, and he won't pay any attention
to the rest of us. Charlie, a tall handsome heartthrob, is
the oldest boy cousin, and a freshman in college. If he
weren't my cousin, I'd have a crush on him.

As we drive down the highway, Mother tells Angel
about her family: "My daddy is gruff," she says, "but
he's really a teddy bear. And my mother is a saint."

She doesn't say that her father is a little bit touched,
and in my opinion, it's because he's been a Baptist too
long. But she does warn Angel about his prayers.

"Mother will ask Daddy to give the blessing," she

continues, "and it will be very long. Parts of it won't make a whole lot of sense. And at the end, he'll ask God to forgive any of us who aren't Christians and help us see the light."

"When he does that, Angel, he's talking about *me*," says Daddy.

"Yes," Mother agrees. "My father always prays for Jack, because he thinks he's too liberal."

"It's really because I led Abby astray and caused her to become a Presbyterian."

Then Mother goes on to explain that she and her sisters are named after her father's favorite presidents. "My daddy didn't think he'd have boys, and he was right. So he gave us men's names."

"Why'd your mother let him do it?" Angel asks.

"After a long labor, Mother was too weak to argue, and that's when Daddy and the doctor filled out the birth certificates. We're George Washington, Thomas Jefferson, James Madison, Abraham Lincoln, William Henry Harrison, and Theodore Roosevelt."

Angel giggles.

"Don't laugh. Giving boys' names to girls isn't too unusual in the Texas Panhandle. What is unusual is this presidential thing."

"And what name did he give you?"

"I was baptized Abraham Lincoln, but everyone calls me Abby," Mother says. "In fact, Mother always shortened our names and called us Georgia, Tommie, Jimmie, Abby, Billie, and Teddy."

"The same thing happened to me," I say. "When I was born, Grandpapa came to the hospital and talked Daddy into naming me Franklin Delano Roosevelt Baxter."

"It's true, I'm ashamed to admit," Daddy says.

Mother adds, "When I found out about it, I was mad enough to kill them both. But then I decided I could still call my daughter a name I liked, so it was Frankilee, right from the start."

"Odd," says Angel.

The rest of us agree.

When we arrive at my grandparents' house, Grandpapa comes out to greet us. He's a combination of an American bald eagle, a giant penguin, and Mark Twain. His blue eyes are sharp, and his nose is hooked. His silver-white eyebrows and hair blow in the wind, and he hugs and kisses us women, even Angel. He shakes Daddy's hand cordially. You'd never know he's about to zap Daddy in a prayer.

Grandpapa wears a black suit and vest with a white shirt and string bow tie. And his best black cowboy boots, of course. The rest of us are dressed up, as well. Mother and Daddy in church clothes. I'm in my red and black Elvis fan outfit, and Angel wears a gray poodle skirt and white sweater, which I've given her, since she hankered like hell for them and wouldn't give me any peace.

Inside, we all hug and kiss, sometimes more than

once. Everybody talks at the same time. In the past, our holiday has been very predictable, but because of Angel this year things are different.

First of all, Mother acts like Angel is some sort of trophy. Just because Mother's mother and sisters haven't saved a battered kid lately, that's no reason for Mother to lord it over them. But she does. When she introduces Angel, you'd think the girl was some delicate flower from the South American rain forest. And the way the others *oooh* and *aaaaah* over her, like she's some sort of rare Egyptian gem, is disgusting.

You haven't lived until you've walked into my Grandmommy's kitchen and smelled pumpkin pies, turkey and dressing, sweet potatoes and marshmallows, green rice casserole, all baking. Or until you've tasted her Texas pecan pie, crunchy Waldorf salad, and cranberry sauce. And hot rolls rising! My God! Or, as Preacher Farnsworth would say, "My Geeuuuooooaaaad!" He can turn a monosyllable into a polysyllable any day of the week.

After a while, the women put the food on the buffet and on the table, and we gather in the dining room for Grandpapa's prayer. We crowd together — all thirty-plus of us — and bow our heads. Grandpapa thanks God for everything under the sun. Then he scolds God for problems we're having here on earth. Lack of rain! Integration! The Communists! Then he asks for help with unrelated problems and says a bunch of stuff that makes no sense. Finally, Grandpapa says, "And now, Lord, if there is anybody here who is not a Christian, please forgive him and help him to see the error of his ways. Help the rest of us become a beacon shining out to that person so he may see the light." That's his dig at my dad. Finally he signs off, and we're ready to eat.

During the meal, Angel wedges herself between Charlie and me at the huge kitchen table and finagles her way into our conversation about college. She asks Charlie about fraternity life, and he's off and running, ignoring my questions about his classes.

As always, everybody eats way too much, and afterwards, as the sisters are cleaning up the kitchen, the noise and clatter of the kids gets on the adults' nerves. Since it's a pretty day, Grandpapa tells us we can saddle up his champion stallion, Jeff Davis, and a couple of the other horses and take turns riding. All the kids change clothes — out of their church outfits and into their jeans. They put on their jackets and then head down to the horse pasture. With Charlie in the lead and Angel close behind, they form a regular parade. Angel is practically on top of Charlie, her fingers twined in his belt loops. I won't be surprised if she climbs up on top of him and makes him carry her piggyback. Honestly, when she gets close to a cute guy like Charlie her butt twitches like she's some kind of feisty animal. It's worse than weird.

"Frankilee, aren't you going with the others?" Mother asks.

"No, I have a sore throat. I don't feel like it."

Mother knows I'm lying, but she's not going to cause a scene with her own daughter after proving what a saint she is by mothering Angel. She lets me stay.

All the women are in the kitchen, finishing up, so I get to hear the aunts' opinions and questions about Angel. Mother tells the complete story — fairly accurately, not embellishing too much. When they finish their work, Grandmommy tells her daughters and me to come into the living room and rest, and we all follow her, sit down, and get comfortable. The men have gone out with Grandpapa to see his new barn.

"How long will Angel stay with you?" Aunt Billie asks.

Mother replies she doesn't know.

"Isn't it strange Angel's mother still comes to your Sunday school class? What do you make of that?" asks Aunt Teddy.

Mother doesn't understand that either.

"So the Musseldorf woman is active in your church? Doesn't she feel uncomfortable?" asks Aunt Jimmie.

Mother doesn't know.

"The woman obviously is crazy. Has anybody located the father?" Aunt Georgia wonders.

"Don't know."

"How are y'all going to manage putting two girls through college at the same time? Is Jack pretty well fixed?" asks Aunt Tommie.

Turns out Mother doesn't know a damned thing.

"Well, I'll swan," says Grandma, as she stands up, takes off her apron and sits back down. "Beats anything I ever heard of."

"I'll admit the whole situation is strange, and not exactly what I expected," says Mother, "but Jack and I've gotten ourselves into it, and we're determined to see it through."

"I don't know how smart that is, Missy," says Grandma, folding the apron. "A girl like that can carry off your husband."

"Mother!"

"I mean it. She acts like a Paris whore." Grandmommy irons her skirt with a flat hand and looks at my mother.

"And how would *you* know?" Mother shoots back.

"I may be old, but I ain't stupid, as the saying goes. Didn't you see her make a play for Grandpapa?" Grandmommy looks straight into my mother's eyes. "You're acting like this girl has the same kind of rearing as Frankilee, but she hasn't. She acts ill-bred and boy-crazy to me."

"Oh, Mother, my stars! Angel is just friendly." Mother sits up straight in her chair.

"She was flirting with Grandpapa. And the damned old coot liked it."

"Well, I certainly didn't notice anything like that. Did the rest of you notice Angel flirting with Daddy?" Voice quavering, Mother looks at her sisters.

"Oh, yes," they say, "we saw it, all right." So the sisters aren't buying Angel as a delicate flower.

Sitting on the fringes, I speak up. "I wonder if Angel has a physical problem that causes her to twitch around men."

For a minute, nobody says a word, and the room is quiet. The sisters look at each other and share secret smirks, and then Aunt Georgia says something that really gets my goat, "Well, what do *you* know about this, young lady?"

I shouldn't have popped off. I should have sat quietly in this inner sanctum of women. Being female isn't enough. I'm an interloper who shouldn't be seen or heard, and no one values my opinions anyway. What a royal monkey-butt piss-off.

Then Grandmommy looks at me and smiles. She pats the couch beside her and says, "Come here, Frankilee. I haven't had a chance to talk with you yet." She ignores her daughters and scoots over to make a place for me. As I sit down, she puts her arm around me and asks me about school. I tell her about working on the annual staff, editing the high school newspaper, and recruiting members for the Elvis Presley fan club.

"What do you think of Elvis, Grandmommy?" I ask. "Most adults don't like him much." The other women are talking among themselves.

"I think Elvis Presley is a sweet boy," she says.

Aunt Georgia has been listening and is obviously surprised at her mother's answer. Stupid old Aunt Georgia's eyes are round and vacant.

I adore my dear little grandmother. Grandmommy is like Jesus and Wanita: she likes me just the way I am.

"There's something I'd like to mention to you girls,"

Grandmommy says after a while, snuggling closer to me, "and that is, be good to your husbands. Y'all are lucky to have good men who've given you great children. Don't press your luck."

But what she has to say next is even more shocking. Grandmommy announces to her daughters she's expecting them to start having Thanksgiving at *their* houses.

"Your father and I won't be with you much longer. I want you to experience the joy of entertaining while we're here on this earth. And I want to make sure you can do it right." She gives me one last squeeze. "Frankilee, honey, please help me up." When I do, she tells the others, "Come with me to the kitchen."

On her huge wooden table, Grandmommy makes six piles of serving pieces and linens. Then she hands out handwritten recipes. Their mouths hanging open, her daughters stand and watch.

"I have boxes in the hall closet. I want you to take every bit of this stuff."

Aunt Billie says, "This is sad."

"I've given up cooking for crowds. From now on, I'm eating at your houses, while I wait for heaven or the 'home,' whichever comes first."

"Oh, Mother, don't be so dramatic," Aunt Jimmie says.

"I'm passing the torch to you," Grandmommy continues. "One foot in the grave, that's me!"

She takes down a shallow bowl with folded pieces of paper inside and has each of her daughters draw one out. On each, she has written a number. "Who drew number one?" she asks.

Mother raises her hand.

"Good. Abby, we'll come to your house next Thanksgiving."

Mother's sisters silently agree to follow this holiday plan. They're afraid not to, because Grandmommy has a knack for making a person feel hugely rotten if her wishes are ignored. Otherwise, she's as sweet as maple syrup.

Late in the day, when we're ready to leave, we put on our coats and head for the front door, hugging and kissing for the zillionth time. Angel steps over to Grandpapa and smacks him a good one, right on the mouth. Instead of being offended, the old codger is thrilled. He kisses her on the forehead and then starts to dance a slow softshoe. Picking up the rhythm, Angel joins him, and they hold hands and shuffle toward the front porch together. Hopping a little more, Grandpapa starts singing,

You go home and get your scanties,
I'll go home and get my panties,
And away we'll go.
Whooooooooooooo!
Off we're going to shuffle,
Shuffle off to Buffalo.

Everybody laughs, and then we all dance to the driveway toward the parked cars. When Grandpapa and Angel get to our car, he hugs her again and says, "You make them bring you back real soon." He turns to Mother and Daddy, "You've gotta keep this girl. She's a dandy."

Grandmommy has her arm around my waist, and I can feel her thin frame under her blue woolen dress. "There's no fool like an old fool," she announces loudly. And the crowd breaks up with bloated laughter.

On Monday after Thanksgiving, Mother waits for Angel and me in her car after school, which means I can't go to the Dairy Queen with my pals. She drives Angel to her dental appointment and drops her off. Then Mother says, "I need to have a little talk with you." That's never good news.

"Okay," I say. "Talk."

Mother clears her throat. "Have you ever heard the word *nymphomaniac*?"

I'm shocked. Where the hell did *she* hear that word?

"I've heard of it," I keep my eyes on the road.

"The reason I'm asking is I wonder if that might be Angel's problem." Mother speaks slowly. "I have noticed she acts a little crazy around men. I want to know if she's the same way at school. When you said Angel twitches, what did you mean?"

"Oh, I don't know what I meant. She's weird, but I didn't mean she's a nympho!"

Everyone's heard the story of the nymphomaniac who drank a potent sex drug. After she slurped it down, she went mad with desire and had sexual intercourse with the gearshift in the family car! I sure don't want to talk to Mother about *that*.

"So you didn't mean she has wild, uncontrollable urges?" Mother asks.

"No, of course not!" Looking at Mother, I can't believe she's so dumb. "Listen, Angel's cagey. Everything she does is controlled."

"Are you saying her flirtations are calculated?" When Mother talks like Jane Austen, it means she's serious, scared, or mad as the devil.

"Sure. On Thanksgiving Day Angel totally ignored all the men except Grandpapa and Charlie. She picked them out and then gave all her attention to them. She knows what she's doing."

Mother talks to herself as she drives to our house. "She picked out the richest one and the most eligible one. Why didn't *I* see that?"

All the leaves have fallen off the trees, and the entire neighborhood is drab brown and gray. Even the sky is tan, and the dusty wind blows fiercely. The air has turned nippy, so I yank my jacket up around my neck as Mother pulls the car into the garage.

"There's another subject I want to discuss with you," she says. I get the feeling this one won't be so simple to deal with.

"What is it?" I turn to look at her. If she's going to criticize me, she can do it to my face.

"On Thanksgiving, I heard you using foul language."

"Oh, Mother. Not me!"

"Don't be a smart aleck. Yes, you."

"Well, so — ?"

"I don't like it. Your father doesn't, and we want you to stop. You talk like the poor white trash in *Tobacco Road*."

"You can't be serious! Using bad words is my style!"

"I'm telling you to change your style."

"What will you do if I don't?"

Stiff and formal, super steamed. "Your father and I will withhold privileges."

"Mother — have you ever heard of Molly Brown?"

"Of course. She's a hairdresser, isn't she?"

What a dumbbell! "Molly Brown was a very rich lady from Denver — notorious for cussing. I read about her in English class last year."

"That has nothing to do with you."

"She wasn't popular in Denver," I continue. "The old socialite fuddy-duddies thought she was vulgar and wouldn't invite her to their parties. So she went to France and — now get this — she was the toast of Paris! Everybody thought she was unique and charming."

"You're way off the subject," Mother says.

"And listen to *this*. Molly Brown was a heroine during the sinking of the *Titanic*! Kept her head cool and saved a whole bunch of people! She's called 'The Unsinkable Molly Brown.'"

"What is your point?"

"I don't think you should punish me for my self-expression. I'm imitating Molly Brown. All those other rich bitches twiddled their thumbs while the *Titanic* was sinking, but she tried to do something. I want to be just like her."

"My stars, Frankilee. You exasperate me so!" Mother gets out of the car, slams the door, and walks into the house.

When I come through the back door a minute later, she's waiting for me. "I'm not finished with you."

"Listen, Mother! Y'all are lucky to have me! I don't drink, smoke, get wild with boys, lie, cheat, or steal! The worst thing I do is cuss! What're a few *hells* and *damns* compared to all that other stuff?"

Mother reaches into her purse and gets out a pack of Luckies. She lights a cigarette. "We know we're lucky to have you," she says. "And I'm glad you don't smoke or do any of those other things."

"That's more like it."

"Listen, I'll make a deal with you. You can say *hell* and *damn* occasionally and I won't complain, if you just won't take the Lord's name in vain or say *shit*. Do you think you can manage that?"

"It'll be very hard."

"Well, try," she looks at me with the meanest eyes she can muster. "Oh, and there's another word you absolutely are forbidden to say."

"Oh, really? What is it?" I take off my jacket.

"The word that begins with an *f*," she says. "I don't want to ever hear you say it."

"I don't know what word you're talking about." I take my jacket to the hall closet.

"I'm talking about the four-letter word that's written all over public restroom walls!" She's really pissed off and follows me into the hall.

"Sorry, don't know that word at all, but I'll watch out for it." I'm *not* going to talk to my mother about *F-U-C-K*! Holy Moly.

So now I've got her on my back. Just like the Thought Police in *1984*. One by one, my civil liberties are being taken away. And I blame Angel.

Chapter 10

BESIDES STARTING PIANO lessons and getting her teeth fixed, Angel convinces my parents she needs help with her scars. Just after Thanksgiving, Mother and Daddy take her to a burn treatment center in Amarillo. I spend the night with my friend Shelly so I won't have to go with them. The burn specialists send Angel to a dermatologist, who sends her to a plastic surgeon, who says the scars are mostly superficial.

When Angel gets home from Amarillo the next day, she's exuberant.

"The doctors can totally erase these scars," she tells me, prancing through my bedroom. "By the time I go to college, I'll be able to wear strapless, backless dresses! I'll be beautiful! The belle of the ball!"

Hearing her chortle, I'm doubly glad I didn't go with them.

"Well, I'll be a cat-eyed fart face," I say. "That's wonderful, Angel."

So a series of skin planing and grafts begins in Amarillo. Gradually, Angel's getting beautified. Meanwhile, my hair's still stringy, my skin's oily, and my feet are long, high-arched, and narrow. Like two fish, they flop and squirm in uncomfortable shoes. And my breasts still don't grow. I take to wadding bobby socks into C-size bra cups. Mother acts like she doesn't notice, but Wanita says, "Hey, you, girl! Come here! Get that stuff out the front of your blouse!" So I'm back to my flat-fronted self.

I look like a boy in a dress, and I can't stand myself. I'll never get a husband — or even a cute boyfriend. And if Elvis comes to town before I fill out, I'll leave a tragic note of my desperation and then jump off the water tower.

I gotta keep up my ravishing personality, or else I'm a goner.

One evening Mother and Daddy ask Angel and me what we want for Christmas.

"Oh, absolutely nothing," Angel answers quickly. "You've done so much for me I couldn't possibly ask for anything more." Good grief.

"Well, we want to put something for you under the tree," Mother says. "Please, just give us a few suggestions, and we'll choose a couple of things." Gads, what a sucker.

"Well, if you insist," Angel answers, "I want a puppy." It serves Mother right.

"Angel, we can't have a dog. We already have two

cats."

"It's all right, I understand. It's just that I've never had a pet in my whole life, and I've always wanted a dog."

"I'm sorry, but we can't manage a dog. Think of something else." Mother pauses, then turns to me. "What about you, Frankilee? Have you thought about what you'd like Santa to bring you?" Mother plays this Santa game to the hilt, as if Angel and I are cases of arrested development. Good grief and shoot the preacher.

"I want a typewriter. And a camera. If I'm going to be an investigative reporter, I'll need both."

"When did you decide to become a reporter?" Daddy asks.

"Just now."

"That's quite an ambition," Daddy says.

"It is. I plan to write articles for *National Geographic* and take pictures of ferocious animals and totally naked Africans."

"Well, that *is* an ambition."

"With their boobs sagging and their genitals hanging down."

"The animals or the Africans?" he asks. It's hard to rattle my old man.

Sure enough, on Christmas morning I find an Olympia portable typewriter under the tree, along with a new Minolta camera. And Angel finds a wiggling puppy. Black and white, shorthaired, long tailed, an adorable little swash of energy. Angel cries when she first holds it, and for a moment I'm sorry for acting like such a shit, but the remorse soon passes, and I'm back to normal.

"What will you name him, Angel?" Mother asks, laughing at the way the puppy shreds the wrapping paper with his needle-knife teeth.

"Oh, I know exactly what I'll name him." She sits on the floor with her puppy. Wearing soft pink flannel pajamas with matching robe and slippers, she's as beautiful as a Christmas card. We watch her expectantly, and when she's sure she has our attention, she grins. "I'm going to name him Elvis." Angel gives me her I-gotcha-where-I-wantcha sonofabitchin whorehouse smile. And my heart sinks lower than it's supposed to be.

I'm in a lowdown funk when Grandmommy and Grandpapa drop by. Every Christmas they spend the entire day driving from one West Texas town to the next, bringing gifts to us grandchildren. They have packages for both Angel and me. In hers is a yellow woolen sweater — the perfect color, the perfect fit. In mine is a red cashmere hat, scarf, and gloves set.

When I try mine on, Grandmommy says, "I hope this set will match the red sweater you wear with your Elvis fan outfit." Then she adds, "Listen, Frankilee, you should always wear red. You're gorgeous in that color."

Mother serves mugs of spiced apple cider, and she passes around trays of homemade candy — fudge, divinity, and caramels. I inhale the allspice and cinnamon and watch Elvis playing on the floor, biting and pulling on Angel's socks. I hope he drives her crazy. Soon Grandpapa is ready to leave.

"We've got miles to go before we sleep," he says.

"Is that biblical?" I ask, hoping to stump him.

"No, it's Robert Frost," he answers with a wicked grin. The old geezer is sharper than I thought.

Suddenly, Grandmommy grabs me and says, "For goodness sakes, I almost forgot something. Frankilee, please bring me my purse."

After I've fetched her handbag, she reaches deep inside and pulls out a package of folded white tissue paper. "Here," she says. "I want you to have these, honey."

I unfold the paper. I'm shocked to find a strand of perfect pearls — which Grandpapa gave her to celebrate their thirtieth wedding anniversary almost twenty years ago! I look at Mother and realize she's as surprised as I am.

And Grandpapa's shocked, also. For once, he's speechless.

Grandmommy has me sit on the carpet in front of her, while she fixes the clasp at the back of my neck. "Go look in the mirror, sweetheart. They're perfect for you."

She's right. The pearls make me look good. They even help ease the pain of Angel naming her canine after my lover man.

"Let's go." Grandmommy starts putting on her coat and pulling on her gloves. We walk them to the door and then out to the front porch. "No, don't come outside," she says. "It's too cold!"

When I hug my wonderful grandmother goodbye, she laughs. "Now, don't forget what I told you, Frankilee. Wear red every time you can." I put my arms around her and hug her light birdbones. It's like hugging air. Then she and Grandpapa are gone.

One cold gray January morning I come downstairs to the kitchen and find Daddy making coffee. I pour myself a bowl of cereal and grab juice and milk from the refrigerator. Setting it all on the counter, I pick up a banana. Angel is still upstairs playing musical clothes in my closet, matching my stuff with hers, but I'm in too much of a hurry to care.

Daddy plugs in the coffee pot, and as it begins to perk, I hear him sniffing. I look over at him, and realize he's crying. "Your Grandmommy died last night," he says. "It was her heart."

I stand in front of my father. My world has come to an end.

Grandmommy's funeral is on the coldest day of winter thus far. The West Texas skies are a deep blue gray, and when we walk from the house to the car, the wind blows through our clothes, fiercely. Luckily, we have no snow or rain. When we arrive at my grandparents' house, everyone focuses on the weather. Over and over again my relatives say, "Oh, thank goodness we have no snow." I agree. Grandmommy wouldn't want to be buried in the snow.

The family gathers in the living room of the old ranch house, and we wait for the funeral director to come lead our string of automobiles to the Baptist Church in town. Grandpapa will ride in the undertaker's limousine, and the rest of us will follow. He has chosen two of his daughters — Georgia and Teddy — to ride with him. My mother and the rest of my aunts will ride with their families. That is the monumental plan for burying my grandmother.

Waiting for instructions, I decide to go to the bathroom one last time, so I head in that direction. The door's open, and I hear someone scurrying around inside.

"Anybody in here? Can I come in?"

"Sure, you might as well." It's Charlie's voice. I go into the bathroom and immediately smell a powerful fragrance. Broken glass is on the floor.

"What in the world?"

"I was putting on aftershave and dropped it," he says. "I've spilled it all over me!"

"Charlie, this isn't aftershave." I pick up the shard that contains the label. "This is Grandmommy's perfume."

"Damn!" he croaks.

"Oh, Charlie, you smell stronger than shit!"

"Thanks a lot." He's almost crying.

"Here, let me help you wash some of this stuff off. Then I'll pick up the glass. You might cut yourself."

I take a wet washcloth to Charlie's face and neck as

he rolls up his sleeves and washes his hands and arms. But it does no good. His clothes are saturated.

"Hey, kids," calls my mother. "It's time to go!"

"Don't worry, Charlie," I say. "When we get out in the wind, this stuff will dry. You won't smell anymore."

But I'm wrong. Charlie reeks to high heaven, and nobody wants to sit by him at the funeral, not even Angel.

During the service, the preacher is so morose and the music so dirgey I can't stand it. Everybody's crying, which makes me mad. Why should *they* cry when *I* loved Grandmommy, and she loved *me* best? I should be the blubbering baby. I'm so damned angry I'm not going to shed one tear.

I shift in my seat and get a whiff of Charlie's perfume. Remembering him in such a panic in the bathroom, I begin to giggle. Gorgeous hunk of a fraternity man, Charlie, soaked in his grandmother's perfume! It's too rich.

Before I know it, I'm laughing out loud. The other kids look at me, and they crack up, too. We try to stop, but a terrible scourge has us under its power. Grandmommy's grandkids are overcome by uncontrollable laughter. Even Charlie.

Our parents look at us, horrified, and then finally they pretend they don't notice our snorts and cackles.

"What made y'all laugh at the funeral?" Mother asks, as we drive in the procession to the cemetery. "Y'all carried on like a pack of hyenas."

"I'm sorry, Mother. We couldn't help it."

Following the cars in front of us, Daddy drives down Main Street. It's so cold, and the wind is so blustery there's no one on the streets to watch us drive by. One lone policeman — Sheriff Baines — stands at attention in the middle of the street, holding his hat over his heart.

"It was a dreadful service," Mother says. "I didn't like the music, and I can't stand that grim old preacher. Your grandmother would have hated it, too. The only thing she would have liked was you kids laughing. I hope she knows that today her grandchildren celebrated her life that way."

"She knows," Daddy says, driving through the cemetery gate down the zigzagging dirt road toward the open grave. "Grandmommy could always find humor in everything, and she's tickled to pieces."

At the funeral I didn't cry. But by the time we reach the gravesite, I'm sick with sorrow and weeping.

Chapter 11

IT'S THE SUMMER after my junior year. I'm a fifteen-year-old beanpole. Nearly every day I put on a bathing suit, and Daddy takes me to the Clover city swimming pool, where I meet my friends. Daddy has bought a second car, and he lets me drive whenever we go anywhere. He's usually very quiet, and sometimes we go from our house to the pool without speaking. He's probably wondering when we'll get my mother back.

One morning he says, "I swear I believe your mother's gone off the deep end."

"What do you mean?"

"She's too involved with Angel."

"Sometimes I wish we hadn't rescued her."

"How would you feel if you hadn't tried to help Angel? You wouldn't like yourself much."

"True. But I didn't know it would turn out this way."

"You mean that she would live with us? None of us knew that."

99

"I'm not a very good person, Daddy. I don't like Angel."

"I know. But you're still a good person. We're all doing the best we can."

I spend most of my free time at the pool for another reason as well. Recovering from the skin treatments, Angel's forbidden to be in the sun, so the pool is my great escape. I'm becoming a strong swimmer and as tan as a cowboy boot. Toward the middle of June, Todd Mason, the manager, asks me to take lifeguard training so I can help out as a substitute lifeguard in August, filling in for the football players who usually hold down the job. So when football practice starts, my career will begin. Just call me Esther Williams.

With my short, sun-bleached hair and bosomless body, I look more like a boy than ever. Would anyone notice if I went swimming in my shorts with nothing on top? Every day I stand in front of the upstairs full-length mirror in my underwear. Shoot a monkey, and I don't mean Miss Mabel's. Are my tits ever going to grow at all?

Without Grandmommy my grandfather is lonely, so we go to see him often, and he drops by to visit us occasionally. One hot day toward the end of June, he comes to visit. Still wearing my bathing suit, I answer the door.

Today Grandpapa's on the prowl. Shortly after sitting down in the kitchen with Mother and me and stirring his tumbler of iced tea, he asks to see Angel. Says he wants to give her something. Mother tells me to go upstairs and ask her to come down. Wanita is in the kitchen also, serving our tea and baking a peach cobbler, which smells fantastic. We're waiting for it to come out of the oven.

Upstairs, Angel is lying on her stomach, with her head hanging over the edge of her bed, reading a *Seventeen* magazine that's spread open on the floor. She looks pitiful, in a pair of pink baby doll pajamas with bandages taped to her back and shoulders.

"Grandpapa wants to see you. I'll find a robe," I say.

"No, I can't stand anything on my back," she says. Slowly, she sits up and groans as she moves from the bed. We go downstairs.

Angel slops into the kitchen in flip-flops and then turns on the charm like Miss Astor when she greets her gentleman caller, my Grandpapa. He stands and bows, and she struts and prisses. Mother and I watch them dance a pussyfooty two-step around each other. Finally, Mother asks them both to sit, and Grandpapa pulls up a chair for Angel so she sits down next to him — her hand on his knee.

Mother says, "Frankilee, please go get Angel a robe."

"Nope, don't need one. Hurts too much," she answers.

"Angel," Grandpapa says, "I'm so sorry about your operation. Honey, I hope you'll feel better real soon." He reaches into his cream-colored suit coat pocket, and he pulls out a small blue box. "Here, sweetheart," he says. "I want you to have this little present. Maybe it'll make you feel better."

My mother knows what's in the box. Oh, this is rich and also terrible, and I look around, hoping to make eye contact with Wanita, but she's made herself scarce. Poof, disappeared!

Like a five-year-old, Angel opens the box and squeals. Inside, between thin squares of cotton, are Grandmommy's sapphire and diamond earrings, which Grandpapa bought ages ago in New York City. I hear my mother sucking in air. She looks as if she's been stuck in a deep-freeze for about ten years.

"Do you like them, sugar?" Grandpapa asks.

"Oh, my God!" Angel shrieks. "Ohmigod, ohmigod, ohmigod!" She jumps up and down and grabs him around the neck. Pretty soon she'll be crawling all over him. And she has practically no clothes on.

Grandpapa's surprised and pleased he's made Angel so happy. He tries to hug her and starts to pat her on the back but then feels her bandages, so he laughs a little guffaw. He acts like a schoolboy giving his first girlfriend a valentine. I never saw such a foolish old coot in my life. His face is so red I'm afraid he'll fall over from a stroke, and it might be better if he would, because he's about to feel the wrath of my otherwise peace-loving mother come down like gangbusters on his head.

"She can't have them, Daddy," Mother says.

He looks at her as if she's lost her mind. "The hell you say," he growls. "They're mine to give, and I'm giving them to Angel."

"No!" Mother says. "They belonged to Mother. They are *not* yours to give away. Angel, give them back."

Angel clearly doesn't know what to do. She desperately wants the earrings, but she doesn't dare disobey my mother.

"I'm only doing what's fair, Abby," Grandpapa says. "At Christmas your mother gave her pearls to Frankilee, and I'm just trying to even the score."

"Frankilee is *my* only child, my mother's *granddaughter*," answers Mother. "Don't give me this bullshit about evening the score."

When Mother says *bullshit*, Angel sticks out her arm and hands Grandpapa the blue box. Her bottom lip trembles, but she says nothing as he takes it.

"Angel appreciates the gesture, but she can't accept your gift," Mother says.

Suddenly Grandpapa stands up. After he puts the box back into his pocket, he takes one last deep swig of his tea and sets the glass down on the table with a bang. I wonder if it's ice or glass I hear cracking.

"Go upstairs, Angel," Mother says. We watch Angel walk out of the kitchen in those thin shortie pajamas, and then Mother turns to me. "You, too, Frankilee." Damn! She expects me to miss the most exciting thing that's ever happened in our kitchen. I can't stand it.

Slowly, I drag myself to the door of the kitchen and

103

turn the corner. I see that Angel has already climbed the stairs. I walk across the downstairs hall to the stairway and quietly sit on the second step, my spot for eavesdropping. I hear Angel close the door to her room.

"Daddy, I don't want to embarrass you. But you must realize how inappropriate it is to give jewelry to a teenaged girl. If you wanted to give the earrings to someone, why not one of your granddaughters?"

"Don't you dare question me, girl," he says.

"I'm questioning your judgment."

"I'm leaving," he says.

"No, don't leave yet. I want you to realize what you're doing."

"I realize my daughter is getting old and cranky and as selfish as hell!"

"You can think whatever you want about me," my mother's voice gets louder.

"Old, cranky, selfish!"

"Don't be ridiculous!" She pauses, and I assume she's smoking. "For you to give a family treasure to a girl who's not in the family is crazy."

"So I'm crazy, is that it? Listen, I'll give whatever I want to whomever I choose!"

"You act like you're courting Angel."

"What do you mean treating me this way?" he thunders. "Who do you think you are, young lady?"

"I know *who* I am! I'm the only person in this room who has an ounce of sense!"

"I'm leaving!" he shouts.

I zip up those stairs lickety-split before they catch me. I crouch at the top of the steps, behind the banister.

"And one more thing," I hear him say, as he stomps to the front door. "You smoke too much! You're going to wreck your health!"

"What do you care!" she yells, following him.

"I don't care! Just thought I'd mention it!" He opens the door.

"I'm fully capable of handling my life and my health!" They're standing at the front door now, toe to toe.

"You're too old and cranky to handle anything!" Grandpapa walks out and slams the door.

Mother opens the door. "At least I know who I am!" she yells. Then she slams the front door twice as hard, and the house shakes.

So my mother stood up to her old dad. Later, up in my room, I think about that. I never imagined my mother could be so fierce. I want to help her, and wish I could figure out how. I need to make Grandpapa seem so unappealing Angel won't ever flirt with him again.

A few days later, Angel has another appointment with the surgeon in Amarillo. Only a routine check-up and removal of the bandages. By now I've come up with a plan.

I beg Mother and Daddy to let Angel and me ride the bus to Amarillo and spend the day horsing around after the appointment. By now, Mother's so sick of driving back and forth to the doctor she agrees.

In high heels and sundresses, Angel's back covered by a bolero, we catch an early Greyhound. On the way, I bring up the subject.

"Angel, I'm sure glad you get along with Grand-papa."

"Oh, I love Grandpapa! He's so lovable, and he's been great to me! I wish Mom could understand what good friends we are. I was very hurt when she wouldn't let me keep the earrings."

"Of course you were. But you know how worried Mother is."

"What's she worried about?"

"Grandpapa's finances are in awful shape. He has no business sense. Mother and Daddy say he's about to lose everything!"

"How could that happen?" Angel sounds alarmed.

"I don't know, but I think he owes everybody in the Texas Panhandle."

"What does he owe money for?" she asks.

"He's been borrowing for years. And he loses it with bad investments. Grandmommy used to control him, but things are real bad now."

"How do you know this?" she asks.

"I hear Mother and Daddy talking. Don't you dare tell them I told you."

When we arrive at the bus station in Amarillo, we take a taxi to the medical complex. After a short wait, Angel sees the doctor, who pronounces her A-OK. Now we have the rest of the day to do as we please. We catch another cab to the downtown shops, and then we eat lunch in the cafeteria. I know exactly what I'm going to say next.

"Angel, don't be too shocked if Grandpapa has to move in with us. My folks are talking like he's liable to lose the ranch — and his house. If that happens, he'll live with his daughters. Everybody will take a turn."

"He can't live at our house!" Angel says, wide-eyed, as she leans across the table.

"Of course he can."

"Where will he sleep?"

"He'll take your room — and you can move in with me. It'll be cramped, but we'll manage."

"Why can't he take that storeroom in the upstairs hall?"

"Oh, Mother would never put him there! But she might let *you* have the storeroom for your room. It could probably be fixed up all right."

"My Lord, Frankilee, that room's tiny."

After shopping all afternoon, we head to the station for the last bus home. As people mill about, and buses whush in and out of the loading area, we sit in the busy waiting room, eating sandwiches and drinking Cokes. I have one more surprise to spring on Angel.

"If Grandpapa does have to move in with us, it's going to be hard on everybody. Especially Wanita."

"What do you mean?" she asks.

"I'm not supposed to tell," I say.

107

"Tell me what?"

"Nothing."

"Frankilee, tell me! Why will it be hard on Wanita?"

"Promise not to tell?"

"I promise."

"Well, Grandpapa has a slight physical problem."

"What?"

"Sometimes he wets the bed. Sometimes he does worse."

"A grown man? You must be joking."

"I'm not. It's an old bowel injury, maybe from one of the wars — or maybe from riding horseback too much, I'm not sure," I answer. "After he soils his bed, he wakes up and yells out, and whoever is sleeping nearest to him has to help him change his bed. It's a mess. Just wore Grandmommy out."

"Good Lord, Frankilee! Has he seen a doctor?"

"Of course. Lots of them." I take her hand. "Now listen, Angel, you've promised not to tell anybody about this."

"I'm shocked!" she says. "Grandpapa seems so healthy and so *viral*." What an idiot, she can't even pronounce the word *virile*.

I have one final bit of information for Angel. "The reason it'll be hard on Wanita is all the extra laundry she'll do. I'm sure we'll have to help. Especially on the days she doesn't come to our house. Think about all the extra sheets and towels — very smelly — as well as the

108

wet trousers and underwear."

"What do you mean?"

"Haven't you noticed how Grandpapa pees on himself?"

"No!"

"Oh, he does." I whisper. "It's a mess."

"I've never seen him pee!" Angel shrieks. But in the crowded bus station, nobody pays any attention.

"Yes, Angel. Grandpapa pees on himself all the time. If he doesn't do it around you, it's because he's wearing a diaper."

I've had my revenge. It's time to board the bus home.

We find our seats toward the back of the bus. Immediately after we pull away from the station, Angel starts up a conversation with two servicemen headed toward Wichita Falls.

We haven't traveled five miles before Angel suggests that one of the boys and I shift places, so we can all get to know each other better. That's fine with me, and I awkwardly climb over her and change places with the outgoing, handsome one. After a few minutes, I realize that my army boy is a dullard, as dumb as a hammer. I can easily carry on a conversation with him and eavesdrop on Angel and her guy friend at the same time.

They become quite chummy. Angel tells the soldier about our purpose for visiting the doctor in Amarillo. Looking into his eyes, she smiles at him and then slowly she takes off her bolero and shows him her scars. Asking him to hold her jacket, she slowly stretches and twists. With a little bump and grind, she pulls up her hair, bends over his lap, and asks him to examine the red spots on her neck. I hear stripper music in my head. Then she goes into her "Oh, woe is me" routine, and Handsome Army Boy puts his arm around her and pulls her close. They cuddle together for the rest of the trip. Well, hell, if Angel can't get Grandpapa she'll just make out with some horny soldier she meets on the bus!

"Boy, your sister is really something," breathes my serviceman, watching them. I realize that he's as disappointed with me as I am with him, but for different reasons. Well, fill my bra with radiator fluid. Once more this girl had pissed me off to extreme unction.

I listen to the conversation of the sex-crazed neckers.

"How did you say you got those scars?" Handsome asks.

"I was burned in a car accident. The car caught fire, and I was trapped inside," Angel answers. "My mother and daddy were killed in the accident. I was only three years old."

"Is this girl over here — Frankilee — your sister?"

"No, I lived with my aunt for a while, but then Frankilee's family adopted me."

Watching Angel and listening to her story, I want to cry. Why, oh why, has the Baxter family been saddled with this manipulative, lying slut? And why, oh why, did I think I could ever out-maneuver her? The whole damn situation makes me so mad I could have a royal fish-eyed seizure.

Later, after we're back home, I knock on Angel's bedroom door. Then I smash into her room without waiting for a response.

"Why did you tell that guy a lie? Why did you tell him you got burned in a fire and your parents were killed in a car accident?"

"I didn't realize you were listening to our conversation." She shakes her head in disgust. "You didn't expect me to tell him the *truth*, did you?"

She's standing under the ceiling light in her room. For the first time, I notice that her pink and white room isn't at all attractive, and wonder why she's never asked to redecorate it. Maybe she figures she'll just be here until she can get somebody like Grandpapa or Soldier Boy to take her in.

Looking at her, with the light shining on her gorgeous head of golden hair — so luscious and curly, I have the strongest impulse to reach over and grab that thick mane. I wonder how it would feel to pull it, to make Angel tiptoe as I drag her along. Talk about a dance! Why, holding onto her hair I could jump up on her bed and bounce like a crazy girl, never letting go, snatching Angel Musseldorf bald-headed.

I can hardly control myself. If I don't leave her room immediately, I'm liable to pull out every hair on her head. I go to my room and think about my lies as opposed to Angel's. Which of us is worse?

Sometimes I worry that when I die and go to Heaven, God's going to be in one of his Old Testament bad moods. He may not let me in. I'm hoping that dear Jesus and his mother will jolly God along and he'll admit me on probation.

I may be a bad person, but I do love God. I'm crazy about Jesus, and I have great admiration for the Virgin Mary. And the Holy Ghost! Mercy. The Holy Ghost is *so cool*.

The most exciting event to happen in our town this summer — which is far more significant than Angel and her scarred skin — occurs in August, when the new football coach moves to town. He's single, so the town talkers are atwitter. Everyone agrees that he'll have his hands full with the load our high school principal, Mr. Johnson, has given him. Rumor has it he'll teach senior English, as well as coach the football, basketball, and track teams.

"If we could just win a few games this year, I'd be satisfied," Daddy remarks when he announces the arrival of the new coach. "These high school boys are plenty capable; they just need a decent coach. I wish they could just win a few games, just three or four, to get the taste of victory under their belts. We can't stand another losing season!"

"Why is winning so important?" I ask.

"Why play a game if you don't intend to win it?"

I have no answer for that, but I agree that Clover

High School has a pathetic record in sports. Personally, I think our school fight song is partly to blame. Who could ever muster up guts and courage with a non-heroic fight song like "I'm Looking Over a Four-Leaf Clover"? Somehow the song doesn't inspire a body to get mean and fight. But it's the tune our band does best, and so they play it after everything that happens during a game: after the opening prayer, after a first down, after the possibility of a first down, after a touchdown or a field goal, during half-time, after the other team's half-time show, after a win or a loss. When they're not playing that song, they feebly try to toot out our alma mater, "When Irish Eyes are Smiling," which is so pitiful everybody begs them to quit playing and get some rest.

The new coach is twenty-one, lean and lanky, and not at all what we expected. He has sorrowful dark eyes and a hank of straight brown hair over his forehead. He doesn't stand up straight, and when he walks he shuffles like an old man. He doesn't even look particularly athletic. We wonder how he got a degree in PE, and then we learn that he recently graduated from college with a bachelor's degree in English. This news sends most of the town into a rage.

"Oh, hell," they say. "He's a shrimp. He won't know the first thing about coaching."

"Damn! Another losing season!"

But we girls think the new coach is adorable. During his first few days before afternoon practice, he often comes to the pool for a swim. We hush whatever we're saying, sit on our towels by the side of the pool, and watch him. He wears a skimpy green bathing suit. Thin and pale, he teeters on the diving board. Then he leans forward and dives a beautiful arc into the water. Magnificent.

"My dad says he looks like a twelve-year-old, but I think he's cute," says Shelly Cox. We both agree that on a scale of from one to ten, he scores a nine.

"Guess where he lives!" somebody says, just a few days after the new coach's arrival.

"Tell us!"

"In Miss Mabel Hightower's garage apartment!"

This delicious news brings shrieks and cries.

"Do you mean he's going to live with the Monkey Woman?"

"Well, not *with* her, but *near* her."

More shrieks and cries.

"My dad calls him the original ninety-eight pound weakling," Shelly adds.

I can see now that Coach Calvin Morris will have major difficulties with the likes of us. Already he's a celebrity, a heartthrob, the brunt of monkey jokes, and a major disappointment to the middle-aged drugstore jockstrap guys. And he's just moved in.

Chapter 12

ANGEL HAS LIVED with us for almost one full year. Big mistake, as far as I'm concerned. Sometimes when friends remark about how generous my folks are to take care of her as if she were their own daughter, *I* want to regurgitate. Just urp. I'm tempted to ask, "But what about me? Does anybody ever think to ask how I feel about this whole shootin' match?"

Angel is upstairs, throwing a ring-tailed fit about her school clothes. Nothing in her closet suits her; nothing that she brought with her is acceptable anymore. Every time I turn around, the little pissant has stolen one of my garments or talked Mother into buying her a new one. Good grief. She's a demanding little bitch, and Mother's a weakling.

Sometimes I tell her, "Consider the lilies of the field. They don't worry about their clothes, and neither should you!"

"You know, I enjoyed being an only child," I tell Wanita the day before school starts.

"Yes, well, I 'spect you did," Wanita answers.

"Nobody asked me how I felt about starting this four-person family," I add.

"That ain't true. *You* thought the whole thing up your own self. Now it's happened, and it ain't going to suit you, but you just as well be a good sport about it."

"I'm sick of being a good sport. Wanita, I'm not a good person. I don't like to share."

"Honey, I know what's the matter with you. You think your mama done fell in love with another child. But that ain't it. Your mama see Angel as a big project to work on. She still love you and you know it."

Well, butter my buns and call me a biscuit. Is that all the sympathy I'm going to get from Wanita?

School starts in September after Labor Day. Angel and I are both in Coach Morris's first hour English literature class. She sits in the front row, and I sit halfway back. On the first day of class, she fidgets and squirms so much anybody would think she has burrs in her underwear.

Holy Helsinki, if she ruins this class for me, I will stab her in the heart.

After a while she settles down, because the nervous little coach has interesting things to say. First, he explains his expectations of us — very reasonable, as far as I'm concerned. Next, he tells us what we can expect of him. No teacher has ever been so forthright with us before.

Then he has us thumb through our textbooks, and he shows us the works we'll discuss. He demonstrates how to skim, how to read, how to memorize, and how to seriously study.

He says we'll read literature as it relates to theme, and to demonstrate his point he has us turn to a section of love poetry in the book. Our ears perk up.

I want him to notice me. I raise my hand and clear my throat. "What is *your* favorite type of literature, Coach Morris?"

"I like stories of adventure," he smiles. "And what is yours?"

Oops! I hardly know what a literary theme is.

Then he says, "Many girls your age like stories of unrequited love. In fact, that's probably the most popular theme of all."

I say, "Unrequited love. That's a good one. Would you spell that, please?"

He spells it, and he explains it. He gives examples, and by the time he's finished his definition of unrequited love, we're all a little crazy with desire for him.

No teacher has ever done *that* to us before.

When we return home from school, Angel and I sit in the kitchen, having milk and cookies, as we tell Mother and Wanita about our classes. Angel starts talking about the theme of unrequited love.

"Give us an illustration," says Mother.

"The story of *Romeo and Juliet* is perfect," I say. "Or even 'A Rose for Emily.' *The Scarlet Letter, The Sun*

Also Rises . . . It's being in love with someone you can't have."

"What about in real life?" asks Mother, teasing us.

"Well," says Angel. "Suppose that Wanita's boy, William, and I fell in love. Say that we wanted to get married, but you, Mom, sent me away to boarding school because you didn't want me to marry a Negro. His love for me would be unrequited, and my love for him would be unrequited. In other words, we'd still have passion for each other, but we couldn't get married or have S-E-X or anything because you and also society wouldn't let us. We'd be like Romeo and Juliet, in love but forbidden to love."

No one says a word. I can't bear to look at Wanita.

Before Mother can change the subject, Angel continues. "It's not that I personally have anything against Negroes, but a lot of people do. I think it would be fine to marry a Negro, just as long as we didn't *intermarry*. We could be married and be perfectly happy, but if we *intermarried* and brought children into the world, why that would be awful! They wouldn't be Negro and they wouldn't be white; they wouldn't know *what* they were. They wouldn't have any friends. So marriage without intermarriage is just fine, I think. But most people don't agree and don't want any mixed marriages at all." The everlastingly stupid Angel looks at Wanita and realizes she's offended her. "Don't get me wrong," she says. "If I were to marry William, I'd *want* to intermarry with him. Because I think that S-E-X is normal, and I'd want to

118

make him happy. Even if it did cause grief in the long run, with children and all."

"Uuuuuhhhh-hhhhuuuuuhhhhmmmm!!!" belts out Wanita, her voice sliding up and down the scale.

"What?" asks Angel. "What did I say?" I almost feel sorry for her, but I hate her so much I won't let myself soften. You can let stupidity go only so far.

Mother says something, but it comes out as a squeak. Then Wanita interrupts. "I's leaving now." She looks directly at Mother. Her eyes are on fire. "You get this young lady straightened out, or I will!" She grabs her purse and charges out the back door.

Later, when Battles comes to pick up Wanita, we realize she's *walked* all the way home, from our house to hers, out in the country. Mother looks sick, and her lips quiver as she finishes preparing the dinner Wanita started. "I must talk with you after supper," she tells Angel.

We eat in almost total silence, and Daddy says, "Well, you girls must have had a busy day. Too tired to talk."

After our meal Mother and Angel disappear to Angel's room, while I rinse off the dishes and load our brand new dishwasher. I hope with all my heart that Mother will wring Angel's neck. But when I go upstairs, I hear no screaming or crying coming from Angel's room. So she's going to get away with being a shameless shit-heel.

Later, as I'm climbing into bed, Mother raps on my door. I already have Lucy and Desi situated in the covers, and I won't get up and open the door, on the chance that one or both of them will escape. Mother comes in.

"I want to be perfectly clear about something," she says. "You know that Angel hurt Wanita's feelings today, when she talked about falling in love with William. You do understand what an inappropriate thing that was for her to say, don't you?"

"Yes, I guess so."

"A Negro mother must be especially careful with her children. Those two boys — William and Rootie — are smart and good looking, but they may face some danger in their lives. Sometimes white women cause trouble for Negro men, just as sometimes white men cause problems for Negro women. Do you understand?"

She's so vague I don't really know what the hell she's talking about. But I'm fairly certain it has something to do with sexual intercourse. Anyway, I don't want to hear any more, so I nod my head.

"I won't allow Angel to speak in such a familiar way about William. Is that clear?"

The woman is getting on my nerves. *I* am not the person who brought up the subject of unrequited love. *I* am not the one who mentioned doing it with William. Still, I'm thrilled to a mountaintop that Angel's in deep shit.

"Does this mean Angel isn't going to live with us anymore?" I ask Mother.

"Oh, I didn't say that! Of course she'll live here. She just has to learn what is and is not proper to talk about."

Mother kisses me good night. Well, scab my knees and put me on roller skates.

I'm turning off my bedside light when Angel scratches at the door. "Are you alone?" she asks. She comes into my room and plops on the foot of my bed. She reaches out for Lucy, who snuggles up next to her, purring loudly, the disloyal little creep. Angel's Elvis is downstairs in the laundry room, locked up for the night.

"I really don't understand why Mom is so upset with me," Angel says. "You'll have to explain what I said that was so wrong. And Wanita! Talk about the wrath of God!"

"Don't you understand why talking about doing it with William upset Wanita?" I ask.

"Doing it, having sexual intercourse, having inter-marriage, whatever you call it. No, I don't understand why Mom got mad at me for talking about having sex with a nigger. It's not as though I'm actually going to *do* it!"

"Don't say that word! Mother will slap you from here to Christmas if she ever hears you!"

"What word?"

"The *n* word, you idiot! Mother and Daddy won't put up with it for a minute. Use *Negro*. Where have you been, Angel? We try to treat those people with respect."

"But that's not the way I was brought up! Where I come from, you'd be called a *nigger-lover*!" Angel spits out her words, and drops of saliva hit Lucy's head.

"Listen to me!" I spit back. "You've lived here for

121

a year, but you haven't learned much. Wanita and her family are real live human beings — with cares and worries. That's why both Mother and Wanita are so mad at you. Wanita didn't like for you to use her son as an example — as if she has no feelings!"

"I never heard anybody talk the way you're talking. I don't care if they do have feelings. I wasn't brought up to care."

"Good! Then go back to your mother! Act shitty in her house if you want to!" I jump out of bed, and Lucy and Desi scatter. "Come on, Miss Priss Pot." I start down the hall. "I'll help you pack." I head toward her closet. This is my opportunity to get rid of the bitch! I sling open her closet door.

I feel like Superwoman. I could strap Angel and all of her belongings to my back and fly straight to her mother's house, dropping everything, Angel included, down, headfirst, into her front yard.

"The trouble with you, Frankilee, is you're jealous!" she says, as she follows me to the closet.

"Jealous?"

"Yes, jealous! Because I'm prettier than you! And because I can do everything better than you! And most of all, *because I have breasts!*"

I look at Angel's golden halo shining under her bright bedroom light. I grab her hair with both hands and try with all my might to pull it out.

She screams bloody whorehouse murder.

Then I hear my dad's voice at the bottom of the

stairs. "Girls! What's happening up there? Is everything all right?"

The little hypocrite begins to cry. "I didn't mean it. Please don't tell Mom and Pops about our quarrel."

"Angel, this isn't a *quarrel*! This is a *fight*!" I yank her hair harder. Her soft golden locks curl around my clenched fingers. Bird feathers in my hard grasp.

"I didn't mean it. Come on, Frankilee, let's make up. Please let go!"

"Girls!" comes the voice from below us.

"I hate your guts, you little shit-ass," I say, pulling her head closer to mine.

"Girls!"

"We're fine," I call back. My heart is pounding out of my chest. I wish to hell I didn't have to let go of that fine nest of hair. For some reason I think about poor Samson in the Bible. Hanging onto a huge wad of hair can give you superhuman strength. Slowly, I let go.

"Don't bother me again, Angel. Just don't bother me." I'm shaking.

Leaving Angel's room, I head for my own. What have I gained from all of that fire and fury? As Wanita would say, "Is you any better off than you was, Missy?"

Rubber-kneed, I climb back into bed and try to calm down. What good have I done by letting Angel unhinge me? Why do I let her drive me up the wall?

I try praying the Lord's Prayer, but I can't concentrate. For about the millionth time I wish I could pray a really zesty prayer — like many of my freewill friends do. They can truly pray to the Lord Jesus with such fluid fervor you'd think he was their boyfriend. They know just how to wheedle and cajole Jesus and order him around.

I want to get God's attention once and for all. I want to let him know I don't appreciate having to put up with this girl who's as dumb as a box of Kleenex. I wonder if God even knows who I am or gives diddly-squat about me. If so, he's probably going to send me straight to hell.

Well, I don't care! Screaming like a banshee is infinitely more satisfying than controlling my temper, and Angel *is* a shit-ass. I know Mother and Daddy expect me to be more mature, but I've been kind to that little bitch for one whole year, and that's long enough.

You know what they say about the communists — they move into a place and take over everything. I wonder if Angel could be a part of a communist plot, coming into Clover, Texas. Thinking about it for a minute, I start to giggle. Angel's not even smart enough to *vote*, much less work for a political cause. Remembering her inane speech about *marriage* versus *intermarriage*, I laugh until tears run down my cheeks. Finally, I'm calm.

On the brink of falling asleep, I remember Angel's delicious scream. Although I don't have boobs, I do have long bony fingers just itching to sink into that gorgeous head of hair again. Next time I won't let go.

Chapter 13

I START GOING to the Booker T. Washington High School football games with my dad. I go partly to get away from Angel, partly to support Wanita's family and William, but mostly just to be with Daddy. The games are usually held on Thursday nights in an open field, newly mown and marked, surrounded by hand-me-down wooden bleachers, down in the Negro flats. Prior to this year, the colored team was allowed to play at the Clover High School field, but our new coach put a stop to that, insisting on having our team use the field every night for drills, practices, and scrimmages. Rumor has it that Dr. Matthis himself went to Coach Morris and asked if the colored team could continue using the field, but Coach Morris wouldn't budge.

"I wonder how Coach Morris can be so selfish," I say to my dad.

"You have to understand," he says, "this new coach has the right to insist on everything he can get for his team. He wants to build up a sports program, and maybe he feels he can't do it by sharing space with another team. After all, he's been hired to try to shape up the Clover High School football team. He may make some people angry before he gets it accomplished, but he has to try."

"Since you put it that way, I do understand how Coach Morris feels about sharing space with someone else," I reply.

"I'm sure you do," Daddy answers.

So, late every Thursday afternoon, loaded down with blankets and folding yard-chairs, we head across the railroad tracks down to Booker T. High School, to watch William play. The games are scheduled during daylight, because there are no lights on the new field. Early in the fall, the teams finish their games as the sun goes down. Later, headlights from cars and pickups will light the games. Occasionally, a game will be held during the day on Saturday. The principal, Dr. Matthis, is ingenious in the way he provides for the team.

The people in the flats always act glad to see Daddy and me, and they make us feel welcome. Dr. Matthis, especially, comes over to us to greet my dad, and every week the two men shake hands as if they're long lost fraternity brothers.

William is marvelous. His calm personality, which makes him such a rock, is a great quality for a football player. As quarterback, he hurls the ball with total accuracy. As a tailback, he can carry the ball anywhere. He's slippery and hard to tackle, and if he's hit, he simply won't fall down. And on defense, William out-tackles the other players. He's our fearless William, and Daddy and I brag about him, gloating over his ability to outplay everyone else.

Although William is definitely the best, he isn't the only good player on the team. Daddy says that these boys are coached well, and often he comments on the decisions of the Negro coach, Mr. Jacobs, who teaches strategy, as well as lots of different plays. Also, Daddy says that Coach Jacobs insists on tough conditioning, and as a result the players are rarely injured. But most important, the coach teaches them to expect to win. They're strong, self-confident, happy guys of all sizes, and they love to play the game of football.

Not wanting to sit up in the uncomfortable, rickety bleachers, we always set our chairs up near Battles, Wanita, and Rootie, who likewise sit near the playing field in canvas folding chairs. Sometimes they bring food, since there's no concession stand. When the weather gets cold, we'll huddle under blankets, and Wanita will bring hot water bottles to keep our feet warm. Daddy will bring his thermos full of coffee or hot chocolate to keep us both from freezing to death.

But nobody cares much if the weather turns cold. Attending a football game in the flats in Clover, Texas, is by far the most entertaining thing we do. I wonder how Mother and Angel can stand to miss these games, and I tell my friends that they're foolish to miss so much excitement.

Watching the BTW band is almost as much fun as

127

watching the ballplayers. The kids wear royal blue, silver, and white uniforms — hand-me-downs from another school in another state, we've been told. The BTW High School is tiny, but over fifty kids are in the band, because Dr. Matthis insists that every student be involved in some activity as a way of helping the school. Every student has to play football, march and play an instrument in the band, serve in the pep club, or work as cheerleaders.

Before the games and at halftime, a tall skinny drum major in a royal blue and silver uniform leads the band onto the field. His chest is covered with silver braid and buttons, and a tall white plumed hat is strapped under his chin. Keeping time with a long baton carried high in his right hand, he bends backward in an upside-down U shape until the plumes drag on the ground. Following him, the members of the band strut out on the field, marching like crazy. Rhythmically, the kids twist their bodies in unison, while they keep their lines as straight as pencils. They march to the drums in double-time, and they move so quickly that if you blink, you'll miss something. And no sissy four-leaf-clover song for them! They know how to play fight-songs! From the moment the band enters the field, they play loud, wild music: Go!!! Fight!!! Win!!! Horns, cymbals, and drums! Syncopation deluxe!

They have about a dozen cheerleaders — boys who wear blue jeans and white shirts or sweaters, and girls who wear royal blue felt skirts and white sweaters, saddle shoes and bobby socks. Some of these uniforms are a little worn, but the girls decorate the faded spots with colorful rickrack and ribbons. All the cheerleaders are exuberant and creative:

Orange crush! Lemon fizz!
We's the Eagles! Who you is?

Sometimes they flip over each other's shoulders or make pyramids and climb over each other to the top and jump off. Their fast moves are unpredictable, as are the words of their cheers:

Yea, Chartreuse!
Yea, Fuchsia!
Yea, Booker T.!
We's for you-sha!

There's no way to keep from comparing the kids in the flats to the kids in my school. At Clover High, we have no pep club. Only five girls — of similar size, jumping ability, and hair height — are chosen to wear the green and gold cheerleader uniforms. We call them our Wild Irish Roses. With synchronized steps, crouches, salutes and gestures, the Wild Irish Roses lead us through the ritual:

Two bits!
Four bits!
Six bits!

A dollar!
All for the Leprechauns,
Stand up and holler!

The rest of us kids sit together, bored to death, pessimistically cheering our boys to victory. Sometimes when the score gets hopelessly bad, we give up on the cheering and sneak out to the cars in the parking lot with college boys home for the weekend to enjoy some serious smooching. Sometimes we meet beneath the bleachers for a quick drag on somebody's Winston and a gulp of beer.

As far as I'm concerned, the acrobatic feats and the deafening, boisterous yells of the Negro cheerleaders make the carefully choreographed and big-haired white cheerleaders at my school look like scared babies.

Coming home from William's game one night, I ask my dad, "What would it take to get the white and colored teams to play together? I'd like to win at least one game before I graduate, and I don't think we can without the colored boys' help."

"It'll take integration," he says, "and I don't know when it'll happen."

"The white people aren't being fair, and we're the ones suffering for it," I say.

"That's probably true."

"I want you to tell me something."

"I will if I can."

"We call them *Negroes, nigras, colored people,* and *darkies.*"

"Yes," he says, "we do."

"I want to know what they call us."

"Frankilee, I can't answer that question, because I don't know."

Chapter 14

BESIDES GOING TO both white and colored ballgames and holing myself up in my room studying, I spend my leisure hours either dragging the town square, talking on the telephone, or writing articles for the *Elvis in Clover Newsletter*. For a long time our family has had a telephone down in the den, and for ages I've begged Mother for my own private one. Finally, she agrees and has an extension installed upstairs in the hall, with a long cord attached so that either Angel or I can carry it into our bedrooms, close the door, and conduct conversations. This sorta pisses me off, because I really wanted my own separate line, like my friend Shelly has, but Mother gets on her high horse and tells me if I don't like her offer I can continue to run downstairs each time I get a call. So I have to backtrack fast and act grateful to share a phone with Angel. To tell the truth, this isn't much of a problem, because Angel takes every kind of private lesson under the sun and doesn't have time for gossip and small talk.

Not only is Angel receiving piano lessons from Monkey Woman Mabel, but she's also enrolled in dance lessons — ballet, tap, and jazz. She taps all over the house, making my teeth clink. Starting the first of September, her latest musical project is taking singing lessons from the choir director at the Presbyterian Church. So every day and night, if Angel isn't practicing the piano, she's knocking holes in the floor with those tap shoes, or she's gliding around in ballet shoes, practicing the Five Positions. Or else she's singing her head off in the living room, usually accompanied by Mother at the piano.

Mother and Angel remind me of a picture in Shelly Cox's bedroom. It's a print by Renoir, a picture of two beautiful girls — the older one playing the piano, the younger one standing behind her. Ditsy blonde heads together, reading the music, oblivious to everything else. When I get all I can take of their mutual admiration society, I let Angel's stupid dog Elvis in, because I can count on him to ruin their concentration, he's such a royal asshole mess.

People in Clover think Angel Musseldorf is definitely Broadway bound, and everybody raves about how she's blossomed in the past year. It's irritating beyond belief. Sometimes I sit in my room with Lucy and Desi, listening to the radio or playing records, trying to figure out how I might bait her into doing something stupid enough to warrant another good hair-pulling. So far, I haven't come up with anything. In fact, she's been on her best behavior ever since the night I lost my cool.

Mother says I spend too much time on the telephone, but if I'm going to be a good reporter, I'll have to practice gathering information. I tell her visiting with my friends qualifies as research. One topic we discuss in depth these days is Coach Morris and unrequited love. We can cite examples galore of love gone awry. Our major source of information is *Photoplay* magazine, which gives blow-by-blow accounts of who's rejected whom — when and why. And our favorite people to discuss are Eddie Fisher, the rotten shit-heel; Elizabeth Taylor, the man-eater; and Debbie Reynolds, the victim.

One evening I realize that the greatest, most spectacular example of unrequited love in our town is Miss Mabel Katherine Hightower and her Monkey Man, Harry Yates. When I mention this to my friends, we all suffer a paroxysm of delight. Miss Mabel has experienced a classic literary episode.

I've decided I need an unrequited lover. Not Jerry Fred, because I can't stand him. Don't want him to touch me, hold my hand, or kiss me. Ugha Bugha! I'll give him only one small sloppy kiss in exchange for an entire evening of entertainment. I tell him I like him for his mind.

Elvis Presley is my unrequited love. He's absolutely unavailable, and he won't lurk about, getting on my nerves. He's incredibly handsome, sexy, a real hunk of fantasy love. Someday, when I'm ready, he'll be traveling down Highway 66 with his entourage, and his big white limo will practically explode with a flat tire. He and his band will limp into Clover. There, standing on the town square, dressed in a fine white suit, Elvis will hunker over his guitar, singing "Love Me Tender," and he'll look straight at me. I'll be the gorgeous girl with big boobs and a clear complexion.

I'll take Elvis home, and Wanita will feed him her special chicken-fried steak, melt-in-your-mouth mashed potatoes and gravy, and crunchy fried okra. Mother will pass the hot rolls to Elvis and say, "Butter 'em while they're hot," and he'll want to stay forever. Eventually, Elvis and I'll get married and have sexual intercourse.

I tell Shelly about my fantasy, and she thinks my plan is cool. Then I warn her not to tell Angel, because she'll ruin it for me, if she can.

Since Elvis hangs over my twin bed and Jesus hangs over the other, and Lucy and Desi are usually asleep in the covers, and I've got the phone nearby, I'm never lonely in my room. On the wall over my desk, I've tacked up my Certificate of Service to the National Elvis Presley Fan Club, along with my "Ode to Elvis," which Mother had framed for my fifteenth birthday. It's long and mournful and ends with this stanza:

And then one night Ed Sullivan did some changing,
He took the liberty to do some rearranging!
You lost your swing, you lost your smile,
And when he got through you'd even lost your style —
Oh, Elvis Presley, what have they done to you!!!!

In our telephone conversations, my friends and I

don't limit ourselves to love and movie star small talk. We also talk about school business: specifically, about how the new coach is stirring up the town about integration. Everything we see and hear scares us, and we argue and debate about who's right and wrong and what should be done. Daddy says at our age most of us are just reflecting the viewpoints of our parents, but that's no comfort.

We watch the news on television every night. Plus, I read the newspapers and magazines my dad brings home. What's happening at Central High School in Little Rock, Arkansas, is atrocious. I've seen pictures of a colored girl named Elizabeth Eckford. A girl with a cute hairdo, wearing a pretty cotton dress with a full skirt and lots of petticoats. In one picture, Elizabeth is walking to school, and in the background a bunch of white students with hateful faces are screaming at her. Another picture shows Elizabeth on a bench, waiting for her bus, and white kids surround her, calling her names. More pictures show the Negro kids being kicked and beaten. But the worst is the picture of the Arkansas National Guard blocking the kids' entrance to Little Rock Central High.

I don't know what I'd do if I were a colored girl in that situation. But I do know I'd want William and Rootie and their friends to feel safe and welcome in our school. Those nine colored high school kids in Little Rock are brave, and they deserve for somebody white to reach out a hand to them and then say to the others, "Hey, wait a minute! Where're your manners? Didn't your mother teach you to open the door and say, 'Welcome! Come in this house this very minute!'?" That's what we always say. And even though my mother is mad at Grandpapa right now, if he came to the door tomorrow, she'd fling it open and say, "Come in this house!" She'd hug him and grab his hand, and pull him inside. That's the real way it should be.

Mother and Daddy and I are proud of President Eisenhower for talking to the American people on television and for sending federal troops to escort those nine kids. Some people don't agree, but we like Ike. We like Mamie, too, but she needs a new hairdo.

Rumor has it that Coach Calvin Morris has paid a call on both Dr. Matthis at Booker T. Washington School and Mr. Johnson, our high school principal. In both visits, he brought up integration, and he pushed them into admitting they don't have either the funds or the facilities to accomplish what they should. Then he argued that if the schools were consolidated, all the students could have equipment and supplies we need. Finally, he reminded them they were running a segregated system in defiance of the law.

Coach Morris took his argument to the superintendent and then the school board. They pretended to listen, but they did nothing. Then he wrote a letter to the editor of the weekly city *Clover Leaf News*, but the editor printed only part of the letter, stating that it was too long to quote in its entirety. My friends and I have nightly reports on his efforts. Shelly Cox is a student secretary for Mr. Johnson, and she says Coach Morris is about to drive everyone in that office crazy.

But Coach won't give up. He writes another letter to the *Clover Leaf* and challenges the community to hold a town meeting to discuss integration. This time the editor publishes his letter, and it raises such a hullabaloo the mayor and city council call a town meeting just to quiet things down. They expect no one to come, and they schedule it on the last Tuesday night in September in the high school auditorium. I insist on attending with Mother and Daddy. Wild horses couldn't keep me away, but wild horses couldn't make Angel go.

The place is packed with white people, but no Negroes, not even Dr. Matthis. This really burns me up, but my dad says, "Those people probably figure this is an exercise in futility."

The town is split on the issue, but not evenly. Sarah Daniels' dad stands up and says since integration is inevitable, we should go ahead and integrate, especially since the Negro football team is outstanding. In closing he argues, "It would be wonderful for Clover to have a winning football team!" A few men cry, "Hear, hear!"

Matthew Jordan's mother replies, "Integrating just for the sake of sports is stupid!"

The Smithson twins' father, a C.P.A., argues that from a financial standpoint, it makes sense to combine school budgets and provide all the students with the best education possible.

The Adamson kids' parents both speak, saying that

the school systems should be separate but equal.

Shelly's dad, an attorney, argues that the schools are now separate but certainly not equal and never will be.

Brenda Jones' parents warn that the Negro boys will try to date the white girls.

James Colton's dad says he's afraid the Negro girls might try to date the white boys. Then a lot of people get carried away and talk about that subject for a good twenty minutes.

Our government teacher — shy little old Mr. Clancy — slowly stands to speak. He waits until the auditorium is quiet. His voice is soft and low. "We live in a democracy, and in a democracy everybody should have equal opportunity. Under our system, the Supreme Court is the Law of the Land. Why even debate it? We should obey the Law of the Land!" People are surprised at Mr. Clancy's passion.

Not to be outdone, the Reverend Farnsworth takes the floor. "If we were all living right and praying right, none of this would be happening," he says. "We should ask God for deliverance and forgiveness. Clover, Texas, is like Sodom and Gomorrah! In fact, the whole world is going to the bow-wows!" As usual, he gives no practical advice.

My dad is the last to speak. "I know that these ideas are hard for some people to hear," he says. "But isn't it wonderful that we live in a country where everybody can come together like this and speak their minds?" Some people applaud, and Daddy continues. "And I know that what I have to say will anger a few folks. But I'd like for us all to consider what things would be like if our schools were the very best they could be. If we had the money, the equipment, the teachers, the supplies, what would it be like? What if we *did* have the very best sports program, the very best music and band programs, the best science, the best English and math? Seems to me we'd all be better off. Not only the kids, but our entire town. And don't we have a better chance of improving our schools if we pool our resources and our talents and all try to work together?" The room is quiet.

"Integration will happen. It's a fact. It's here. Why drag our feet about it?" Daddy's expression doesn't change, but he sounds irritated. "Fighting integration is foolish. And if you want an example of stubbornness, and unwillingness to work for the betterment of the community, look at Central High School in Little Rock. How could adults possibly put their kids through such an ordeal? I'm not talking about the Negro adults. I'm talking about white parents and the white citizens who have encouraged their kids to believe that states' rights are superior to federal law. You know, belief in states' rights can translate into white supremacy."

People in the room are becoming restless. I can't tell if they agree with Daddy or if they think he's loony. He pauses briefly and then continues. "There's no such thing as white superiority. You know it, and I know it. If I remember correctly, a man named Hitler believed in white superiority, and we all know he was wrong. Let's face it, folks. There's no good to come from continuing to separate our kids in the Clover schools."

Daddy sits down, and soon the meeting is over. As we leave the auditorium and walk toward our car, someone says, "A veritable hornet's nest, that's what Coach Morris has stirred up!"

And then another voice in the dark: "There are plenty of other banks in our area, and I intend to take *my* business to one of them."

The next morning Wanita is in a terrible mood. She comes to work early, and she asks Mother and Daddy about the town meeting. After their report, I add, "People are really mad at Coach Morris."

Wanita puts on her apron and starts clearing the breakfast dishes from the table. "He don't give a rat's ass about us." She bangs plates and silverware. "He sure don't give a rat's ass about Rootie or William! He just need to leave them be."

"It's going to happen, Wanita," my father says. "Maybe not while William is in high school, but certainly before Rootie graduates. You'd better get ready for it."

It is the first time I've ever seen Wanita cry.

"Why don't you want your kids to go to school with us?" I ask.

"If all the white kids was like you, honey, it would be all right. But like I said before, white boys is mean to colored boys."

"I wouldn't let anyone hurt William or Rootie. You

could trust me to watch over them," I answer.

"Oh, honey," she replies, "You got no idea what I'm talking about."

The white people in Clover have me so upset I take more and more comfort in thinking about Elvis. Daily I become more obsessed with him, and I fantasize every night, to the point of sometimes forgetting to say my prayers.

Thinking about Elvis makes me sleep better. My favorite fantasy before dozing off is of Elvis driving to my house in a shiny pink Cadillac convertible, picking me up for a date. He wears black slacks, a black and white tweed jacket, a white shirt and black tie. He stands at the bottom of our wide staircase, with his legs spread apart and his arms stretched down straight. He keeps his chin down, but his eyes look up at me. As I descend the stairway to him, his sweet mouth curls with that cute little twitch, and he smiles.

"Hey, cool cat," I say.

"Hubba hubba, honey," he answers.

One morning after English class, Coach Morris calls to me, "Frankilee, please stay for a minute," and when I stop at his desk, he asks, "What are you doing fifth hour?" Without waiting for my answer, he says, "Please come to my office in the gym. There's something I want to ask you."

My heart is aflutter. All day I wonder why he's singled me out. Maybe he wants my help in his crusade for integration. Maybe he wants me to assure Wanita that he'll protect William and Rootie from the dark, evil forces of the men's locker room.

I appear at his office at the appointed time.

He asks, "Why aren't you on the girls' basketball team?"

"The truth is, I've never even thought about it. I guess I'm not very good at sports," I answer.

"You swim, don't you?"

"Yes, but — "

"You need to play some basketball," he says. "A tall girl like you would be a perfect center on the court. I need you, and I want you to play."

Just like that. What a damn egotistical whippersnapper!

"Think about it. I need you to start right away," he says.

When I get home that afternoon, I tell Wanita, "You're right. Coach Morris doesn't give a rat's ass about anybody beside himself. All he wants is to *use* people and build up his teams, regardless of what the students want."

"That's right!" she agrees.

But when I tell Daddy of my conversation with the coach, he gets more excited than I've seen him in a long time.

"I don't have time for it, Daddy," I say. "I can't keep up my grades, edit the school newspaper, serve on the annual staff, take piano lessons, chair the Elvis Presley fan club, and play basketball."

"Sure you can!" he says.

The idea of me playing ball makes Mother laugh, and she says, "It would be fun to go to the games and watch you play!" She acts more cheerful than she has since Grandmommy died.

Before the end of the week, Daddy installs a basketball goal at the edge of the backyard terrace, near the trio of elm trees that sway as their leaves begin to fall. And I'm enrolled in girls' basketball, sixth hour, five days a week.

I'm a lousy player. Unsure and clumsy, I can't play with the same fluid movements with which I swim. But I do practice, and every afternoon, if William comes to pick up his mother after his football practice, he gives me a few suggestions and shows me some moves. Sometimes he pitches me the ball and guards me as I try to shoot.

"Run!" he yells. "Pick it up, girl! You as slow as molasses on a cold winter morning." Towering over me, he swoops down and grabs the ball out of my hands, and he tosses it through the hoop, before I can say "Sonofamonkey!"

When William and Rootie come for Wanita, they usually bring their hunting dog, Alice, a red short-haired mongrel. Larger than most of Battles' hounds, Alice is docile and silly, and she follows the boys, nose to the ground, tail wagging. Wanita insists that they take Alice with them for protection, especially if they're going into white neighborhoods, but everybody knows Alice is harmless. Except for a stomach disorder that sometimes makes her objectionable to be around.

My dad has nicknamed William's dog "Flatulent Alice," and says she's an embarrassment to the canine world. Once, when he was preparing for a hunting trip, I heard him tell Battles not to bring her along.

"She's disgusting," he said, and Battles laughed.

Sometimes on the pretty autumn days while William coaches me, Angel comes out to the terrace. Dressed in black dance leotards, her blond hair tied back with a red ribbon, she looks as if she should be on the cover of *Glamour* magazine.

"Hey, William," she calls. "Look at this new dance step I just learned." And she taps along the concrete, or pirouettes into the area where we're playing. She irritates the hell out of me, but I'm proud to see William doesn't pay any attention. Occasionally, I look up and see Wanita watching from the kitchen window, and I'm glad. Surely, sexy, crazy Angel won't try anything outrageous with William as long as Wanita hangs around.

One cold, crisp day we're all outside. Somewhere nearby a neighbor burns a fire, and we smell scrub oak smoke. The three elms in our yard stand like flat, friendly skeletons against a scrim of blue. Cloudless and bright, the sky curves over and around us, making us feel as if we stand on top of the earth. William and Rootie and I play ball, as Flatulent Alice and Elvis the dog follow us — tripping us up, panting, jumping, and barking — and Angel dances on the sidelines.

This will do, as far as I'm concerned. This will do just fine, until the real Elvis comes along.

Chapter 15

WANITA MAKES APRICOT fried pies so delicious you want to slap your grandma. "Absolutely laruppin!" Mother calls them. "So good they melt in your mouth!"

The apricots come from Battles' orchard, and he brings bushels of them to our house each summer. Mother and Wanita make apricot preserves with about half of them, and Mother always gives about a ton of these pint jars to the First Presbyterian Church Bazaar. On each jar, she attaches a fancy label, which reads, "Golden Jar of Heaven from the Kitchen of Abby Baxter and Wanita Carver." These preserves sell like hotcakes.

Then Mother and Wanita cram the rest of the apricots into quart-sized plastic bags, tie them with silver twisties, and put them in the freezer. There they sit, frozen, darkening, until one by one, they're plopped out and defrosted. Then, after simmering in sugar on top of the stove, the apricots are spooned into envelopes of fresh dough and fried in deep grease.

Everybody loves these pies, especially Battles, who brags he can eat ten at one sitting. Sometimes Daddy cranks up a freezer of ice cream while Wanita's frying pies, and later we invite neighbors to come for dessert. To make enough for all these people takes Wanita the better part of an afternoon.

Although it's Thursday, Wanita has agreed to come to our house to teach me to make fried pies for the basketball team bake sale tomorrow. Coach Morris says we need new uniforms, so he's planned several fundraisers. When I get home from school, Wanita, wearing the pink cotton dress that she calls her uniform, starts showing me how to cook the apricots and roll out the dough. It's a messy project, and we have stuff scattered all over the kitchen. Saying she wants to help, Angel stands around watching, getting in our way.

That's what we're doing when Mother's best friend, Martini Laremore, calls us on the telephone screaming, "The desperados are coming to town!"

Mother yells for us to come into the den as she turns on the radio. Rinky Fines, our local radio announcer, gives us the news: "There are two young men, possibly teenagers, driving down Route 66 from Oklahoma, where they held up a filling station in Elk City. Sheriff Billy Joe Baines set up a roadblock just to the north of the Clover city limits. The alleged criminals crashed through the roadblock, shot at the sheriff, and they're coming our way!"

We're beside ourselves with fear and excitement. When the telephone rings, Wanita, Angel, Mother, and I shriek and nearly jump out of our skins. On the other end of the line, Daddy says, "Lock the doors, and don't let anybody in. I'll be home as soon as I can lock up the vault. I'm letting all of our employees go home immediately."

When Mother reports this conversation, Angel screams like a wild thing. Mother looks so disgusted she could spit, and she takes Angel by the shoulder and shakes her. "Angel, if you don't hush, I'm going to slap your face!"

Soon Daddy arrives, with more news. The fugitives ran out of gas and abandoned their car. The sheriff believes they are somewhere on one of the farms outside of town.

"What direction?" asks Wanita.

"Northeast," says Daddy.

Wanita and Battles' farm is located southwest of town, so Wanita is relieved, and she goes back to the stove to fry her pies. Soon Rinky Fines announces on the radio, "The outlaws have run out of gas, and they are now on foot. Authorities believe they may be hiding in one of the shelterbelts north of town. Sheriff Billy Joe Baines is forming a posse, and he's requesting men in the area to join up. These fugitives are armed and dangerous. I repeat: these two men are armed and dangerous. If you see them, call the radio station or the sheriff's office right away!"

Because the outlaws are far away, we feel relatively safe. The telephone rings again. Daddy answers and says, "Yes" twice. Then he hangs up. Mother looks at him expectantly, just as Battles raps on the back door. Wanita lets him in. My dad ignores the rest of us and says to Battles, "Do you have the dogs?"

"Yessir, sure do!" Battles says, as William follows him into the kitchen.

"What the hell you think you doing?" Wanita rushes to Battles. "Where you think you going?" she grabs William's collar. "Where you taking him?" She moves back and forth between them, like a switch.

"Sheriff come by and say he need my dogs to track them outlaws," Battles answers, not looking her in the eye. He turns to Daddy. "I got them loaded up. Don't know how they'll do, though. Never tracked no white boys before!" he laughs.

"You not going!" announces Wanita. "You two think you going out there with a bunch of white men with guns? Is you crazy? And you damn sure not taking William! You both get shot!"

"It ought to be all right, Wanita," Daddy says. "They'll be with the sheriff and me."

"You can take the dogs yourself," Wanita says to Daddy.

"I's going," says Battles. "Mama, I take these men hunting all the time. There's not a white man out there I ain't took someplace, sometime. Don't you think they would of shot me by now if they wanted to?"

"Them outlaws don't know you!"

"It's getting dark," says Battles, laughing. "William and I be the safest men there! I trained them dogs and

I always goes where my dogs goes. William, you can go or stay."

"Goddamn you, Battles Carver," Wanita says.

"Woman!" He looks around at us and then back at her. "If you're born to hang, you'll never drown!" And with that, Battles storms out the back door. William follows him. And then my father, still wearing his business suit and striped tie, brings up the rear, carrying his rifle.

We stand in stunned silence. Then Wanita turns, with a moan, to the stove and her pies.

Angel sees this as an opportunity to hone her theatrical skills. She walks over to Wanita and pats her shoulder. Wanita moves away.

"Poor Wanita," Angel says. Then she looks at Mother and me, wrings her hands, and cries, "Poor William. I'm afraid he'll be shot! Poor dear William will be killed. Oh, what'll we do?"

Wanita looks at Angel, and I know she'd love to kill that sorry girl. Mother and I have our mouths open. Now Angel shrieks, "I can't stand it!" With that, my mother moves as quick as a cat, grabs Angel, and slaps her. Pop! I can't imagine Angel's nose surviving such a hit!

"Go to your room," Mother says to her. "I don't want to see or hear from you again tonight."

It's given me infinite pleasure to see my mother tear into Angel that way. I move to put my arms around Wanita, but she pushes me away, blows her nose, and washes her hands.

In a minute, Mother asks, "Wanita, where's Rootie?"

"With his grandma. Safe," Wanita says with her back to us. Then I wash my hands too and join Wanita at the stove, and we fry the pies.

When the pies are done, draining on white cup towels on the kitchen counter, we clean up the kitchen. Then Wanita sits down at the table, her back as straight as a rod, her arms stretched out over the table, and her hands clasped together. As still as stone.

Mother has found a dust rag. Starting in the living room, she dusts everything she can reach. Carefully moving each object and putting it back in its place. Painstakingly slow.

"Frankilee, please bring me the Hoover," she says. "I might as well sweep this carpet while I'm at it."

"This house ain't dirty," Wanita says.

"I know it," Mother says. "But I have to do *something*!"

The clock ticks in the kitchen. Rinky Fines plays Frank Sinatra records. He sings, "It's Witchcraft." Wanita sits and Mother dusts.

"Does anybody want a sandwich?" I ask.

Mother says, "No, thank you, honey."

"I ain't hungry," says Wanita.

I open the refrigerator door, look inside, then realize I'm not hungry either. So I walk back and forth from window to window and wonder how it feels to have your heart break.

Finally I go into the downstairs bathroom, close the door, and sit on the edge of the tub. "Now listen, God," I whisper. "I know I'm not a good person, but *Wanita and her family are good.* And *Daddy* is good. You've got to make this right. You must protect those men out there tonight." I wait for a moment, and then I choke back tears and add, *"Please, please, please!"*

I can hardly stand the fear and waiting. Finally, I grab the cats' brush, find Lucy, and start in on her fur. Sensing the tension, Desi runs upstairs and hides under my bed, but Lucy lets me work on her. She makes sad, throaty noises.

As I brush, I formulate a plan. One which will keep Wanita and me from going crazy. I let Lucy go, find a sheet of paper and on one side, I write, "Say NO." On the other side, I write, "Say YES." Then I get my camera and put it into my purse. I go into the kitchen and stand across the table from Wanita. Mother is piddling in Daddy's den, straightening his bookcase.

"Wanita," I say, loudly. "Would you like to play cards? I can get some out and we'll play Hell." I hold the paper up for her to read.

"No," she says.

"Wanita, would you like for me to take you home so you can check on Rootie?" I turn the paper over and hold it up.

"Yes," she says. Then she improvises, "I'd like that real well. I need to check on that boy. My mama there, but she probably tired and want to go sleep in her own bed. I be very grateful to you, Frankilee. I ain't doing nobody no good here." I signal her to hush by making

153

the sign of cutting my throat.

I walk into the den and look at Mother, who's standing on a chair with the rag in her hand. "Wanita wants to go home," I say. "I'll take her and stay with her until the men get back."

"I don't know about that."

"Please, Mother, can't you see how she's suffering?"

"Straight to Wanita's and right back," she says.

"Yes, ma'am," I dash into the kitchen and grab my purse and the car keys. "Come on, Wanita. Let's go."

In the car I start the engine. "Okay, let's head for the shelterbelt!" She doesn't argue but settles back.

We head out of town on the northeast highway, and it's after dark when we leave the pavement and turn onto the dirt road. To cheer up Wanita, I tell her the story about how I got my name, which was partly on account of the shelterbelts in West Texas.

When President Franklin Roosevelt was trying to stop the Great Depression and looking for jobs to put people back to work, he came up with the Civil Conservation Corps, which planted long, wide lines of thick shrubs and trees in the Dust Bowl of Texas and Oklahoma.

"This was to keep the soil from blowing away," I tell her, "and I guess it worked, because we don't have dust storms like we used to."

"What that got to do with you?" she asks.

"Grandpapa was so happy with Mr. Roosevelt for the shelterbelt idea, that he got real sad he didn't have another daughter to name. Not long after that, I was born, and he talked my dad into naming me after F. D. R."

"That take the cake," Wanita says.

We bounce along in a line with several other cars driven by people who probably don't have any business being here either. Finally we come to a roadblock and wait in line as most cars are turned away. When we get up to the actual roadblock, I tell the officer, "I've got the wife and mother of two Negro men who're helping with the search. She wants to see them."

He bends down and looks in my window. "Oh, hello, Wanita. I'm afraid Battles is gone. He and the other men have took off with the dogs."

"That's fine," I say. "We can wait. Just show me where we can pull over and park."

He points to a group of other cars, all lined up with their headlights on, facing the shelterbelt. We can see men carrying guns, walking back and forth, milling about lazily, or standing and talking, taking sips from brown paper sacks.

Then we hear gunfire. The men start running around and shouting.

"Hold your fire! Hold your fire!" I think it's the sheriff. "Be careful now, men!"

"Wanita," I say. "Those stupid men don't know what they're doing! They need someone to organize them."

"You stay in this car and keep your mouth shut," she says. In a little while, she adds, "Sheriff Billy Joe Baines don't know shit from shinola."

155

It's a beautiful October night — cool, crisp, and clear. The harvest moon, set against a suede sky, is almost full. A perfect night for a hayride or a romantic drive with Elvis, or possibly Cornel Wilde. Not a night to search for two armed thieves. Wanita and I sit in silence. In a while, the officer comes over to our car to chat; he's been making the rounds. You'd think he was running for office.

"Where's Sheriff Baines?" I ask. "And the rest of the men?"

"Most of the posse is following the dogs," he answers. "And some have gone back to town for burgers and coffee."

"Where's my dad?" I ask, and instantly regret it. Damn! Why do I have to give too much information? I sure don't want Daddy to know I'm out here.

He looks at me closely. "I didn't recognize you, Frankilee. Your dad is with Battles and the dogs."

"What's happened so far?"

"It took a while for the dogs to get the scent, but Battles finally got them to understand. Then they took off howling. That's the last I seen of anybody."

"How long ago was that?" I ask.

"An hour or so," he says. Then he strolls off.

Suddenly, we hear a hullabaloo in the thick brush and all hell breaks loose. A volley of shots, then shouting and barking. Someone screams. Wanita and I jump out of the car. Not bothering to slam our doors, we run toward the light and the noise. When the deputy sees us heading for the shelterbelt he yells, "Hey, y'all get back! You can't go in there!"

And then we see the men, rushing out of the thicket, surrounded by yapping dogs. They're jubilant. Everybody's talking, laughing, yelling. Barking. You'd think they were a bunch of hounds with a fox.

I take my camera out of my purse and start snapping pictures like crazy. Nobody notices the flash.

Battles crashes through the shelterbelt, dragging one of the criminals. "I got him!" And the kid is kicking, fighting, and bawling. Battles holds the boy's head under his arm, like a football, as he drags him along. More men and dogs emerge, and I see the sheriff and another man pushing the other fugitive, who holds his hands up in surrender. Then comes my dad and a few more men. You'd think Battles had just made the winning touchdown, the way all the guys cheer. It's pandemonium, and I get pictures of everything.

Then from behind them, we hear a few scattered shots. Wanita and I look at each other, and she shakes her head.

"Men!" she says.

I turn to walk back to the car, saying, "Lordy, what a relief! Now I gotta get home. If Mother realizes we came out here, she'll ground me for the rest of my life."

Wanita doesn't move. "I ain't leaving until I see William."

The sheriff handcuffs the criminals, who look like high school kids. Then the deputy shoves them toward

157

the only police car in Clover, Texas. I search through the faces for William. There must be at least a hundred men.

Wanita approaches them, all white except her husband. I can't distinguish her words, but about a dozen of them turn and run back into the shelterbelt, yelling, "Flashlights, we need more flashlights!" One of those voices belongs to my dad.

I hear the men call, "William, William!"

Wanita screams, "William! Come out!" Then she follows the men.

No one notices me as I enter the shelterbelt, following a different trail from the others, still worried my dad will see me. I can hear them and see their flashlights nearby while I make my way through the brush. I walk about fifty yards, listening to them and watching their lights. Soon, I'm relieved to hear someone thrashing through the woods, coming toward me. Assuming it's William, I yell, "Hey, hero!"

Relieved he's safe, I lift my camera to take his picture. But when the flash goes off, I see it isn't William. This guy is white. He runs into me and knocks me backward into the brush, plowing right over me and running down the trail. Stunned and hurting, I try to pull myself up. He's knocked the breath out of me, so by the time I'm standing, he's gone. Although I'm dazed, I know something about him is familiar.

And then I hear a moan. Although it's dark, I can see well enough to follow the sound. A voice deep and miserable. Still hearing the others as well, I make my way through the woods and finally reach a figure on the ground. William.

"Help!" I try to scream, but my breath won't come. I crouch beside him. He's lying flat, face down, groaning.

"William, it's Frankilee. Are you hurt bad?" I put my arm over his shoulder, and he shudders. He's so big and heavy I can't roll him over. Again, I try to scream, but my voice comes out of the top of my throat in tiny, use-less wisps. He's cold, so I lean over him, trying to cover him, rubbing his arms to give him warmth.

"Hang on, William. Oh, God, please help us."

I'm no damned good at this. All I can do is cry.

I hear another yell, Battles' deep bass voice, and I look up into the glare of the flashlights.

Four men carry William. Battles holds his son's feet, a white man at each shoulder. My dad leads the way, cradling William's head in his arms. I hear Daddy say, "Easy, now, easy." William's Flatulent Alice follows them, cringing, with her tail between her legs.

Someone has found a blanket, and they spread it on the grass.

Someone else says, "Don't put him on that hard ground."

"We've gotta get the doctor!"

"Put him in a car. We'll take him to town."

"To the hospital!"

All the while Wanita is pushing, picking at them

with her large, black hands. She claws at the men carry-ing William.

I move as close as I can, and try to put my arm around her, but she jerks away.

My daddy and the sheriff's men lay William on the blanket as Battles squats beside his boy. Daddy kneels and gently lowers William's head. From where I stand, William looks fine. He should say something and stop scaring us, for God's sake.

"It's too late," someone says. "He's gone."

Flatulent Alice nudges into the circle, pushing until she rests her nose on William's hand. She licks it.

One of the men yells, "Yah! Get away!" Waving his arms, he lunges at Alice and kicks. "Yah! Now git!"

Whimpering, Alice retreats to the edge of the lighted area. From there, she watches.

When my dad stands up, his white dress shirt is cov-ered with blood.

I don't get it. Only a few minutes ago, these same men were playing cops and robbers, whooping and hollering, calling for drinks to celebrate the capture of two kids.

And now, what is there to celebrate?

I hope I live to be a hundred years old. Or maybe two hundred. Long enough to forget the sight of Wanita, in her pink cotton dress, taking William's head in her arms, and rocking, rocking. She pushes at the men who try to help her.

A sound rises. We hear it building, mounting, and

finally erupting, in a rich contralto. Not a shriek, not a moan, but something in between. Loud and long, Wanita roars, "Whoooa! Whoooa! Whoooa!"

And soon, from her place at the edge of the light, Alice joins sounds with Wanita. A faraway, older than human life, more ancient than history, howl.

It's nearly midnight when I pull into our driveway. Mother is on her hands and knees, scrubbing the kitchen floor. She stands up. "Where on earth have you been? I've been worried sick about you!"

She has made a pot of coffee and put out tall glasses to be filled with milk. She's arranged some of the apricot pies on a tray, and set the table for a midnight snack. The kitchen is a mess.

I don't want to tell her about William, but then, I don't have to. As I open my mouth to explain, we hear Rinky Fines on the radio: "Ladies and Gentlemen, Sheriff Billy Joe Baines has just informed us that the two fugitives are now in custody. Battles Carver and his son William helped the posse track the outlaws down. Thanks to these men, the criminals are in the county jail." Rinky clears her throat. "The sheriff says that William Carver was shot and killed during the search." Rinky's voice breaks. "Now we'll return to *The Music Hour*."

"Whoooa! Whoooa! Whoooa! — " All night long, I hear Wanita.

Chapter 16

I HARDLY CLOSE my eyes all night. When I go downstairs to the kitchen on Friday morning, my dad sits at the table, reading the Amarillo paper. He looks up. "Frankilee, you don't have to go to school today if you don't feel like it."

"I'm already dressed, so I might as well. Besides, Coach Morris is counting on me to bring the pies for the bake sale."

"Well, if you need to come home during the day, it's all right with your mother and me."

"Where's Mother?"

"She's already left for Wanita's. To see if she can help. She might be gone for a while."

"What can she do to help?"

"Probably prepare food." His voice sounds tired and wooden.

"Daddy, does anyone know who shot William?"

"I don't think so. But Sheriff Baines was talking last night about charging those two Oklahoma boys with murder."

"Do you think they did it?"

"I don't know, Frankilee!" Suddenly, he's as cross as hell with me. "We'll have to wait for the coroner's report."

Angel walks into the kitchen, and when Daddy tells her about William, she says, "I knew it! And Mom made me miss the whole thing!"

"Angel, you're beyond redemption," I say.

"What's *that* supposed to mean?"

In our classes, many of us kids don't have our lessons done, claiming that the trauma of last night kept us from doing them. Although Coach Morris tries to keep us on the subject, we can hardly concentrate. Our other teachers allow us to talk about what happened. Desperate outlaws zipping along Route 66, wreaking havoc on Clover's citizens, and killing William Carver. For once, in every class except English lit, I have the floor, and I tell the story of watching the men snare the criminals. I won't talk about what happened to William, though, because I can't. Ordinarily, it would give me infinite pleasure to have firsthand information, while Angel can only tell about it second-hand. But today I'm too numb for gloating.

Still, nearly every time I speak, Angel interrupts and embellishes my story with her dramatic magpie chatter. She's loving it.

Toward the end of the day, during fifth hour I realize that James Colton hasn't come to school today.

After classes, I return home via the post office, once more hoping to be cheered by the long awaited letter from Alfred Musseldorf, asking Angel to come live with him. No such luck. So I drop my film off at the drugstore to be developed and head to our house.

Angel attends her dance lesson, while Mother and I drive out to Wanita's and Battles' farm. We're taking a ham, a sweet potato casserole, black-eyed peas from Battles' garden, and an old fashioned pound cake. When we arrive at the house, Negroes stand in the yard and on the porch. A couple of the men help us carry the food into the house, but no one else says a word to us. Not even the people who always welcomed me to the colored kids' ballgames.

Mother and I are the only white people in a sea of black folks, and they move out of our way, murmuring among themselves. I can't understand what they're saying, but it's clear they don't want us here.

Mother and I take the food to Wanita's kitchen. The counter, the table, and several chairs are filled with dishes, brought by Wanita's friends. Food nobody eats. We make room for our offerings and leave them.

We walk into Wanita's bedroom, tiny and dark. There she is, practically my very best friend, still wearing the pink dress smeared with blood. She lies on her back, staring up, so strange she scares me. I don't think she even knows who I am. Nor how bad she smells.

Mother sits on the bed and takes her hand. "Wanita, it's Abby. And Frankilee." Wanita doesn't look at Mother, nor does she speak, so after a while we go back into the kitchen. Rootie and his grandmother come from the living room, and speak to us politely, as if we were strangers. The grandmother wonders what we've come for.

"Is Battles here?" my mother asks.

"No, he ain't."

"Has a doctor seen Wanita?"

The old woman doesn't speak.

"Listen, I'd like to bring my doctor out here," Mother says, "if Battles will let me. Wanita's in shock, and she needs some medicine."

"Wanita don't need nothing from no white doctor. You let her be."

"Just something to help her rest — "

"Your family done enough to help out mine." She takes Rootie by the arm, and they walk away from us, into Wanita's room.

The folks in the flats blame us for William's death.

"Why wouldn't they?" Mother asks, as we drive home crying. "After all, Wanita works for us. Battles takes your dad and his cronies hunting and fishing all the time. Battles and his dogs were with your dad last night. And then William came along. Those people might even think your dad *made* Battles and William go to the shelterbelt."

"They both went against Wanita's will," I say.

"Yes, and look what happened." Mother struggles to speak. "Not only have we lost William, we've lost the whole family. The dearest people in the world!" She

165

pulls the car over, takes a handkerchief from her hand-bag, covers her face with it and cries. "How they must hate us," she says. "And I don't blame them."

Even though Mother nearly knocked Angel's nose off last night, the girl hasn't let up on her demands. She's standing in the kitchen when we return. "Listen," she says, "I need new taps for my shoes. In fact, I need a whole bunch of things. Can we plan a shopping trip soon?"

For the next few days, Mother, Daddy, and I wrap ourselves in invisible cocoons, each of us hoarding our grief and mulling over the events leading to William's death. I personally feel that God has let me down. After all, I specifically prayed for William's protection. Then I begged God to save his life. I don't ask for much, but when I do, it's pretty darned important, as it was on the night of the manhunt.

If this is as good as God can do, then what's the point? I mean, why do millions of people go to church and pray like crazy? I've learned firsthand that in a real pinch, he's no help at all.

I consider taking the autographed portrait of Jesus Christ down from my bedroom wall. I want to rip it up, throw it in the trash barrel out in the alley, and burn it. As soon as I can find another poster of Elvis Presley, down comes Jesus. The whole situation makes me sick. During the days we wait to bury William, I seethe with rage.

The day of William's funeral is beautiful. A bright, Indian summerish October day meant for football, wiener roasts, and walks home from school. Great weather for biology students to collect leaves, for the golf team to tee off early, for the Future Farmers of America to groom their stock outdoors. But a terrible day for a star athlete's funeral.

Grandpapa drives over from his ranch to go with us to the service. Watching him hug Mother and shake Daddy's hand, I wonder if he'll be the next one to get zapped by God. My throat and chest throb with rawness.

When we arrive at the African Methodist Episcopal church, it's already full. An usher seats us directly behind the pews reserved for the family, which forces some folks to scrunch together. They politely do so, but they don't acknowledge they've ever seen us before. The only other white person I see is Coach Morris; he's treated the same way.

No one makes a sound, not even the small children present. Looking around, I see William's teammates and their families. They sit with downcast eyes. Everyone is dressed up. Unlike Mother, Angel, and I, who wear boring felt pillboxes, the colored women have large, swooping hats decorated with flowers, veils, ribbons, or, in one case, tiny birds. I never saw such a beautiful assortment of colorful hats in my life.

We wait a while before the funeral director leads the family in. When they enter, wailing rises from the congregation. Entirely in black and clutching a white handkerchief, Wanita comes first, supported by her brother and Battles. Then Rootie, then the grandmother, wearing a hat laden with fruit and flowers, then many family members I don't know.

Wanita is a thin shell of herself, and I wonder if she knows where she is.

The preacher starts out by reading Psalm Twenty-Three: "The Lord is my shepherd, I shall not want. He maketh me to lie down in green pastures. . . ."

In white robes and on risers, the choir sings energetic gospel, which leads to a solo by a large woman with a rich alto voice:

Deep river, my home is over Jordan.
Deep river,
Lord, I want to cross over into campground.

Everybody cries.

The preacher, Brother Reynolds, stands. He's wearing a long, black robe. "Brothers and Sisters! For the rest of our lives, we'll remember where we were and what we were doing when we heard the bad news about William Carver. Yessir!" His voice is similar to Wanita's in that it slides up and down and keeps your attention. But it has a gravelly quality, and listening with my eyes shut, I'd swear he was Louis Armstrong.

"Brothers and Sisters! Today we have to deal with

168

that bad news."

Someone in the congregation shouts, "Amen!"

"Yessir, we are dealing with *terrible* news." He draws out the word *terrible* like a musical note. His voice is an instrument, playing words and phrases with such rhythm we're mesmerized.

"That bad news is William Carver, wonderful athlete, good scholar, young man with a brilliant future, is *gone*."

"Amen!"

"The bad news is his mother's heart is breaking! His father is racked with *pain*! And his brother will never be the same." His voice drops.

"Oh, Lord!"

"Amen, brother!"

"The bad news is William's light was snuffed out for no reason!"

"No reason!"

"William was innocent, doing what he always did, helping his daddy with the bird dogs."

"Yessir!"

"Bad news is we're *a-a-all* suffering! And we wonder if this business of Negro men getting shot will ever stop."

"Yes, Lord!"

"Help us, Jesus!"

"The bad news is we're *angry*, and we want to *hurt* somebody!" Brother Reynolds drops his voice to a low, grinding note, as he drops the threat of *hurt somebody* over the congregation.

Voices swell. "Amen!"

Others join in. "That's right!"

Brother Reynolds leaves the pulpit and marches down the center aisle to the back of the church, where he screams, long and hoarse: "We've got bad news, we've got bad news, a son is gone, he's lying in the coffin cold, cold, cold! Lord, Lord, Wanita and Battles Carver have lost their boy!" He comes up for air, with a loud gasping sound as if his throat were sore and bleeding. Then he races up the aisle.

"Oh, Lord!"

"Help us, Jesus!"

"But listen to the *good* news!" he shouts. Stepping up to the pulpit, he grabs his black Bible and waves it in the air. "Here's the good news, right here in the Holy Book!"

"Amen! Amen!"

"The good news is William isn't suffering! In fact, William will *never* suffer, never be hungry! Not thirsty! Not tired! Not poor! He'll never worry! He'll *never be afraid!*" His voice runs up and down the scale, until he loses his breath, and sounds as if he's choking.

Now he speaks softly. "William will never, ever be afraid, because William is with the Lord."

Members of the congregation are holding handkerchiefs, crying, clinging to each other.

Brother Reynolds is soaked through. He takes a large white handkerchief from inside his robe. Mopping his glistening face with the handkerchief in his left hand, he waves the Bible in his right.

By now his voice has begun to set me on edge, like fingernails on a blackboard. We don't belong here. This is Wanita's and Battles' world, not ours. We can't help them, can't possibly understand. We're fools to try.

The preacher stretches his words like taffy. "The good news is this: right now, William, noble, strong, and true, our William Carver, is sitting with the Lord God Almighty right there in Paradise."

A woman stands. "Oh, yessir, Praise God!"

"William is where we *all* want to be someday. That's the good news!"

A Negro athlete shouts, "Amen!"

"The best news of all — Wanita, Rootie, and Battles! The best news of all is that when each of you pass — pass over into campground — William will be there to meet you."

Everyone's crying and shouting now, "Alleluia! Come down, Lord!"

I look at the colorful hats, the white rafters, the tall pointed windows. Anything to keep from falling apart.

"The best news is you'll spend eternity — I said *eternity* — with him. We'll all spend eternity with William, our friend." The preacher mops his face again.

"Thank you, Lord Jesus!"

Preacher Reynolds looks out over his congregation. When he speaks again, his voice is soft. "William Carver was a good boy. If he ever committed a sin, it was so small only God knew about it."

"That's right!"

The preacher continues. "No, he wasn't the kind of young man who tries to rassel with God."

"So true!"

"Not the kind of boy to go against the Lord."

"Amen!"

"Not the sort of child who refuses to love his neighbors."

"Nossir! Praise Jesus!"

"Not a person who wouldn't forgive."

"Right, preacher!"

He lifts his Bible up and raises his voice. "Love and forgiveness! It's here in the Holy Book! Here are our instructions, here's what we're supposed to do."

"Tell it to us, now!"

"Lord Jesus knew pain!" the preacher cries. "And resentment!"

"Yes, Lord!"

"He knew disappointment and betrayal! There's nothing we can face that Lord Jesus hasn't faced before us, a long time ago."

"True!"

"And Lord Jesus asked his Father to forgive his enemies, because he *loved* his enemies! We can't do anything less," the preacher says.

"Amen!"

"You hear what I'm saying?" He scans his congregation again. "You understand now, *we can't do anything*

172

less than forgive those people who persecute us. Forgive those people that don't love us! Forgive our enemies, just as the Lord Jesus Christ did on the cross!"

"Alleluia! Amen!"

I'll swear I don't see how any of this applies to William getting shot. I don't see what love and forgiveness have to do with anything. According to the preacher, those two things can get you through life's disappointments and tragedies. Horse hockey! I've seen what love and forgiveness can do. No, God admonishes us to love one another and to forgive seventy times seven, but when we try to follow, does he reward us? Does he even care? Hell, no.

The preacher winds down. Wanita makes the same dreadful sounds she made the night William died.

Brother Reynolds steps down from his pulpit. Arms outstretched, he speaks to the family in a long crooning hum. "Weep not, weep not, William is not dead." He rests his hands on Wanita's and Battles' shoulders. "William is not dead."

All the while, people are crying and shouting.

Brother Reynolds faces the congregation. "Weep not. William is resting, resting, *resting* in the arms of Jesus!"

The choir stands. Bass voices provide a mournful background, while sopranos and altos rise —

Were you there when they crucified my Lord?
Were you there when they crucified my Lord?
Oh, oh, oh, sometimes it causes me to tremble,

tremble, tremble.
Were you there when they crucified my Lord?

Wanita anguishes.

I glance at my parents, who look positively broken. Shaking with sobs, Angel presses her hands to her ears. Grandpapa sits straight and tall, but tears run down his cheeks, and he doesn't bother to wipe them away.

I tell myself, this isn't happening. But then we stand with the rest and file to the front of the church, to William's open coffin. I promise myself not to look. But I do. He wears a dark jacket, white shirt, and black tie. My strong, gentle friend — so still. And my ragged heart breaks.

Driving home from the funeral, everyone in the car is silent. Then Angel speaks, "Oh, my goodness. How those people carry on! I hope I never have to go to another colored funeral."

Tonight is the first time I've ever seen my parents really fight. I can hear their loud voices in the den. Mother starts out by asking Daddy if the outlaws have been charged with murder yet.

"How would I know? I'm not privy to special information."

"I figured you'd know, since you and the sheriff are such big pals."

Daddy says nothing.

"Aren't you sorry you took Battles and William out

174

to capture the outlaws?"

"Abby, I didn't insist they go! We were all trying to help out the sheriff, for God's sake!"

"You know how protective Wanita is of those boys. You shouldn't have involved any colored people, anyway. I don't blame Wanita for hating us."

"Who says she hates us? Maybe she's just in a state of grief. I didn't intend any harm. How could I know what would happen?"

"Jack, you *endangered her son*!"

"And who endangered your daughter? Wanita's the one who took Frankilee out to the shelterbelt. At least William had a reason to be there!"

"Wanita endangered Frankilee *after* you endangered William!"

"That's ridiculous!"

I hate what's happening, so I walk into the den. Daddy's sitting in his favorite chair, feet up on his ottoman, in front of the television set. Wearing one of Wanita's aprons, Mother's standing between him and the television with her hands on her hips. I speak up.

"Maybe Wanita blames us for a lot of things. What about the way Angel acted when William went out to the shelterbelt?" I ask. Looking at my dad, I can see he has no idea what I'm talking about.

"Oh, pshaw! Don't be silly," Mother answers. "Wanita couldn't have taken that little outburst seriously."

"Didn't you take Angel's outburst seriously?"

"Why no, of course not," she says.

"Then why did you slap her?" I ask.

Daddy looks from Mother to me and back at her again. "Tell me what happened," he says.

"We'll talk about it later." Then she says to me, "Frankilee, you made a mistake coming in here and interrupting us. As far as I'm concerned, you have interfered with things around here to the point of stupidity. You've become just about the worst busybody in town. It was your idea to go out to the shelterbelt, and I know it. I'm furious with you for lying to me, and I'm furious at Wanita for letting you do it."

"I agree," Daddy says. "You had no business out there at all."

"Why should William be allowed to go and not me?"

"Because he knew how to hunt!" Daddy yells.

I'm in a state of shock. They've switched from fighting with each other to being in cahoots against me. Their irrational behavior reinforces what I've known already — they share secrets, hoard information, make inane decisions, and plot against me. They're driven by some dark mysterious force of which I have no knowledge and over which I have no control. It's clear to me that Wanita is determined to protect her family from ours, and with good reason. My folks are crazy.

I storm upstairs. I bang around my room, and in a few minutes, Mother and Daddy are at my door. Jeez, pleeze, Louise. Daddy almost never comes upstairs, so he must be in a serious state of mind, or else Mother has coerced him in some witch-crafty way.

He does all the talking, which makes me even madder. "We're disappointed in you, Frankilee," he begins. "We all know you deliberately disobeyed your mother."

I'm too infuriated with these two idiots to speak.

"Ordinarily, we'd punish you. But you've seen tragedy beyond belief. Surely that's punishment enough."

In a few days the coroner's report becomes public. William was shot by a 30-30 rifle from about forty yards away. A single bullet entered his back, just beneath his right shoulder and traveled upward, exiting through his neck. The two accused criminals carried one shotgun. That's all. Members of the posse say William was always behind the outlaws, with the dogs. Meaning, of course, that William was shot by someone else.

For me, this is terrible news. Because now I have the photos I took at the shelterbelt, and I know who killed William. The person who knocked me down was James Colton.

The sheriff argues with the coroner over the report, but it does no good. Refusing to believe the Oklahoma boys are innocent, Sheriff Baines declares that they'll go to trial anyway and slaps a charge of attempted murder on them for shooting at him at the roadblock. His second charge against them is failure to obey an officer. He has no intention of extraditing them to Oklahoma for their crime of robbing a service station.

My dad comes home early from work one day and

reports all this. Immediately I call Shelly.

"I know," she says. "My dad has been appointed the boys' attorney. He says that the sheriff doesn't know his butt from a bass fiddle."

It's the first time we've laughed in a week.

A few days later, as Jerry Fred drives Shelly and me home from school, she tells us, "My dad says those Oklahoma boys aren't so bad. They're just two poor guys in trouble. And they have real good manners."

"I don't call shooting at people 'good manners,'" Jerry Fred says. Since his dad is the county attorney and will prosecute, his viewpoint is limited.

"Maybe they *didn't* shoot at the sheriff," Shelly says. "Maybe somebody's lying! We know they didn't shoot William Carver, and that was the main reason for keeping them here."

"Oh, go tell it to Perry Mason," Jerry Fred answers.

I break in. "You don't know a damned thing about what happened out there. Somebody shot William, and it wasn't those boys!"

"Of course not. They have good manners," Jerry Fred scoffs.

I'm beginning to despise my boyfriend, and I didn't like him much to begin with.

Chapter 17

I SIT IN my room and stew, while Elvis sings "Heart-break Hotel." He calms me down with his "And I'm so lonely baby, I could die."

Grandmommy used to say, "When you're sad, either buy a new hat or redecorate!" I decide to redecorate. I rearrange my furniture, then go down to the basement, and bring up a card table and chair. I take everything off my extra bed and spread a tablecloth on it. Now it's my college preparation area, and I arrange alphabetically the bulletins and catalogs I've been ignoring until now, along with admission forms to each school.

On the card table I organize files of my Elvis newsletter and my *Faith and Begorra!* school newspaper notes. On my desk I place my schoolwork, and on my nightstand I stack the books I plan to read soon. I hide the shelterbelt pictures behind books on a shelf, so Angel won't find them.

And I wonder what the two jailbirds down at the courthouse are doing.

The days get shorter, and the gray skies of winter set in. The world loses its color. At the end of October, we have our first snowfall. Swirls blow across the Texas plains and blanket Clover overnight, and in the following days the snow turns to ice, and then to wet brown slush. After school, I stand at my north bedroom windows, looking at the street towards town, watching cars drive by, their headlights beaming. Every day is bleakly the same. Wanita is truly not coming back to us. And I don't know what to do about James Colton.

I don't want to dress Jerry Fred up as some outlandish Halloween character and make him take me to the dance. I don't even want to talk to him on the telephone.

Mother's in a bad mood all the time. She complains that she can't keep up with the housework, the cooking, and the laundry, in addition to her own clubs and interests, Angel's lessons, and my ballgames. During one of her tirades, Daddy asks, "How do you suppose Wanita did it? You say it's impossible to accomplish everything. Not only did she do the chores around here, but she also kept her own house."

Mother looks at him, furious. "Don't you go driving me crazy, too!"

"Get someone to come help out!" he says. "For goodness sakes, hire somebody else! It's not as if Wanita is the only efficient housekeeper in the world. I'll bet lots of women would love to have her job."

Not true. "They're boycotting me," Mother says. "Wanita must have told them not to come to work here."

So I become Mother's helper. We agree we're both grieving and brooding and work will help us. She pays me well, and she teaches me to do the chores Wanita used to do. I hate them all.

Anytime Mother asks Angel to help, she's too busy, or she has a headache, or she's behind with her homework. If she does agree to help, she screws up the chore so royally we're sorry she got involved. Ask her to wash a load of clothes, and she'll bleach holes in them. So Mother usually lets Angel off the hook.

"Something's wrong here," I say to Mother one day. "According to the fairy tale, Cinderella was the one who had to stay home by the fireplace and work, and her stepsisters — *the true children of the mother in the story* — were the social girls who went out and had a good time."

Mother says nothing, so I continue. "Don't you understand? This must be a case of Cinderella Reversal. *I'm* supposed to be the carefree one, and *Angel* should stay home to do the housework."

"Don't be a smart aleck," Mother says.

I work like a damn dog, especially on Saturdays. Mother and I barely get through with a chore, and it's time to start the routine all over again. "Does housework never end?" I ask.

"Hell, no." She's started to cuss.

Early in November, my Aunt Georgia calls to remind Mother that a year ago, at Grandmommy's house, Mother agreed to have the family for the next Thanksgiving dinner. My mother starts groaning. Desperate, she drives down to the flats and parks her car in the middle of colored town. She walks from door to door, begging women to let her hire them just short term.

That night she tells us, "I used to think those people liked me, but they don't. They're punishing me."

"You're imagining things," says Daddy.

"Wanita hates us, and you know why!"

"Well, somebody should need the money enough to work for you."

"Those women are as poor as Job's turkey, but they still won't work for the Baxter family. Loyal to Wanita and Battles. They've all been so badly hurt they can't get over it. And I can't, either." Mother starts crying.

Later, we're sitting in the den, about to tune in a television show, and she says to Daddy, "Since my entire family is coming here for Thanksgiving, I need your help."

"Tell you what," he answers. "I'll stay home from now until Thanksgiving, and I'll do it all — housecleaning, baking, everything. I'll even cook the turkey and the dressing. And you can run the bank every day. Starting tomorrow. Is that a deal?"

"You're the most unsympathetic human being on the face of this earth," she says. "Not to mention, selfish."

"Listen," he continues, "if you intend to have your

damned family for Thanksgiving dinner, then get busy and figure out a way to do it without inflicting any of your schemes on *me*. As far as I'm concerned, you've inflicted one scheme too many on me already."

"And what do you mean?" Mother is frothing.

"I'm referring to 'The Angel Scheme.' You might ask her to help out around here occasionally."

"I do ask her," Mother rises from her chair in the den and walks through the kitchen, down the hall and into their bedroom. We hear her close the door. Next to Angel, she's the queen of drama.

Mother secretly wheedles and needles Daddy, so in the end, he agrees to help, and we all pitch in to assist Mother with Thanksgiving preparations. This is more holy-Moses-involved than I can say.

While Angel dawdles and conveniently disappears into the bathroom for hours, the rest of us clean the house, wash mirrors and downstairs windows, wax floors, wash and iron kitchen curtains, launder table linens, wash up china, shine silver, polish brass, re-arrange furniture, organize cabinets, closets, and drawers, pick up the yard, sweep the porch, terrace and driveway, and clean out the garage. Plus Mother buys a few decorative items to make the house look really swell.

She's happiest when she's making us work.

Then Mother sorts through recipes, writes out grocery lists, shops, organizes all the food in the pantry, and writes down everybody's work assignment. She gives us instructions for ham, bird, dressing, gravy, sweet potatoes, mashed potatoes, green beans, corn, jello salad, cranberry salad, relishes, rolls and butter. She gives Angel the very simplest of jobs that any half-wit could accomplish. Mother is solely in charge of desserts — fresh apple cake, pumpkin pie, cherry pie, Texas pecan pie. We'll have two of each kind of pie, because as far as Mother's family is concerned, pie is one of the major food groups.

Mother insists on serving guinea hens instead of a turkey. "My mother always served a turkey," she says, "and I want to do something different."

When Mother makes a statement like that, we realize how much she misses her own mother, and we work even harder to please her. And to tell the truth, we all have mixed feelings about this god-awful Thanksgiving dinner project.

Mother knows a farmer who raises guinea hens, so she and her friend Martini drive out to his property one morning and reserve eight guinea hens for the holiday.

"Have you ever cooked a guinea hen before?" asks my dad. "I think your plan is very risky."

"Nothing to it," Mother assures him. "Old Mr. Stephis tells me it's as easy as pie to bake a guinea hen."

"I'm not in favor of deviating from the norm," Daddy says.

"Do you want to run this project?" she asks him. "Because if you do, go ahead and take over, and I'll run the bank."

Mother is feeling very sure of herself.

Each of Mother's five sisters has a husband and, on the average, two and a half children. My aunts are smart and pretty, my uncles solid and reliable, and my cousins the kind of kids I can tolerate only once in a blue moon. Spending Thanksgiving together is just about all the togetherness any of us can stand.

I just hope to hell Angel keeps her paws off both Charlie and Grandpapa. I can just see it all now — the old geezer and the young whippersnapper competing for the attention of sleazy Angel Musseldorf. They might come to blows. Jeez. We might have to call the sheriff to break it up.

After the four of us work ourselves into a frazzle, a cold and blustery Thanksgiving Day arrives. My grandpapa, aunts, uncles, and cousins descend upon us, all commenting on the wind and the weather.

"That wind's so strong it just about blew me over!" each aunt exclaims, as the families crowd through the front door. "Oh, Abby, your house looks absolutely lovely! And my goodness, what is that wonderful aroma coming from the kitchen? Something smells downright larrupin! I'm so hungry I could eat a house! What can I do to help? Oh, you have worked so hard to have us all. Aren't you the sweetest thing? And isn't everything simply gorgeous! I'll swan! What a wonderful Thanksgiving! Oh, you darling child — how you have grown! Is everybody about to starve to death?" My mother and my aunts all sound just alike, say exactly the same thing, and talk at the same time.

During this hullabaloo, Angel quietly takes Charlie to her room. I watch them tiptoe up the stairs. Furious, I give them exactly two minutes together with the door closed, and then I bang on it and send a whole passel of cousins in.

When it's time to serve the meal, Mother tells everyone where to sit. My grandfather, aunts, and uncles sit at the extended table in the dining room. We cousins sit at various tables in the kitchen and the den. Some of us, Charlie, Angel and I included, sit on the floor at the coffee table. Since both the den and the dining room are next to the kitchen and the doorways are wide, it seems almost as if we're all in one large room.

After everyone is situated, Mother asks Grandpapa to say grace. Grandpapa prays and prays, and I can't imagine God having time to listen to the old man's requests, expressions of gratitude, and anecdotes, what with all of the millions of other things God no doubt has on his mind. Such as the Russians! Sputnik! The way Ed Sullivan treated Elvis!

Finally, the prayer ends with his usual altar call: "And now, Lord, if there's anyone here who is not a Christian let him make himself known and confess himself to Thee." Meaning Daddy, of course. The host.

Other than the time-wasting prayer, Grandpapa has been on his good behavior today. Unlike Charlie, he ignores Angel entirely.

Mother has figured that she'll need eight guineas to make a satisfying meal. To bake all these birds, she's used two of our neighbors' ovens, in addition to our own. So she, Daddy, Angel, and I have been up since dawn, running back and forth to our neighbors' kitchens through the god-awful wind. By the time we're ready to serve the guineas, we've been blown to pieces and we're practically constipated from exhaustion.

"Oh, for God's sake, Abby," my dad has said every time she's barked an order at us this morning.

Mother plans quite a lot of fanfare to accompany the presentation of the guinea hens. It would be appropriate for somebody to play a trumpet. Arranged artistically on platters, the birds arrive, two abreast. Mother, Angel, cousin Charlie, and I each carry a tray, and we march around the dining room table and then into the den. After our parade, Charlie, Angel, and I leave our fowl-filled trays in the kitchen. Mother sets her tray on the dining table, directly in front of my father, who stands, knife in his right hand, fork in his left, ready to carve with a flourish.

Daddy can't puncture the first fowl with his knife or with his fork, so he tries the next one. It's also too tough. Daddy uses his carving fork to hold the bird securely, and then he tries again. But the knife won't cut through the hen's hide. Daddy tries to saw it. Then he asks one of the uncles to hold the bird down while he wrestles with the fowl. But the table starts swaying while he tries to hack and chip.

He asks my uncles to steady the table. There they sit, each holding a table leg, while my father saws. The flesh of the hens is as hard as the ground.

"Must be really old hens," Grandpapa says. "Older than me," he chortles.

Daddy asks Mother to bring him two more hens. Red-faced, she retreats to the kitchen. The next two are just as tough, so Daddy takes the birds to the kitchen to carve. We all watch him there at the counter, working over each of our baked birds, trying to get a few pieces cut any way possible, so we all can get at least a bite. As we watch, he finally grabs a drumstick and asks Charlie to come and help. Together, they tug, as if the hen's legs were a gigantic pulley-bone, and they were each making a wish.

Mother's sorry she came up with the guinea idea. The adults all sit at the table in the dining room; the kids sit at their assigned places in the den, so Daddy has a large audience as he grapples with the birds. Finally, Mother laughs.

"Who wants a slice of ham?" she asks. And Daddy goes back into the dining room, still carrying his carving knife and fork. He pauses and looks at her for a moment, knife and fork poised. We all watch.

What goes on between two people who live together and love each other and have planned to serve the family a really swell dinner of guinea hens and then the plans all go to hell in a handbasket?

My daddy grins, and then he starts slicing the ham. Laughing and talking, we pass our plates to him. As Shakespeare would say, "Gadzooks!"

And speaking of Shakespeare, whom Coach Morris calls "The Bard" as if they were chums, we're studying *Macbeth* right now, and Lady Macbeth is one mean bitch. I wonder how she and Mrs. Musseldorf would fare if they spent a Thanksgiving Day together. When thoughts like this flit through my mind, I realize Angel probably can't help being a little shit, because she doesn't have a loud, obnoxious West Texas family like mine and hasn't known that she is dearly loved from the minute she was born.

My dad slices and serves, while I watch Angel rest her hand inside Charlie's thigh. It's clear he likes the special attention.

The rest of the meal is delicious, and we eat until we think we'll explode. When her sisters compliment Mother on her cooking, she says, "Pshaw! Cooking this meal was as simple as pie!" That's the perfect thing for a slave driver to say.

Later, when the families are preparing to leave, Aunt Georgia says, "Abby, it's too bad about the guineas. I'm surprised your kitchen help would let you buy those old birds. By the way, where is she today?" Aunt Georgia has the same qualities as Lady Macbeth.

"Wanita is at home with her family. Where else would she be?" Mother sounds frozen.

"I just assumed she'd be here today. She usually *is*," answers my aunt. "She's the one who lost her son, isn't she?"

"Yes," Mother says. It's plain as hell she's irritated.

Later, after everybody has left, Mother goes into the kitchen. She and her sisters have already cleaned up, so things are spic and span. I wonder what she's doing, so I follow her.

She's wrapping up the guinea hens — all eight of them. She puts them in brown paper sacks and neatly ties them with string. She looks up at me.

"I'm taking these birds to Wanita," she says. "I want her to have the damned things."

"Why?"

"Because I want to. Run down to the basement and get me a couple of cardboard boxes. Then you can go with me out to her house. See what *she* thinks of these tough guineas."

"But Mother, Wanita isn't responsible for them!"

"Don't sass me, young lady!" spits out Mother.

I bring a large box up from the basement and watch Mother pack the tough fowls in it.

"Get our coats," she commands. "Let's go, before it gets dark."

"No," I say. "I'm not going. You're acting mean."

By now Daddy has walked into the kitchen. "I'll go," he says. "Where are we going?"

"She's taking the guineas to Wanita," My eyes never leave Mother's.

"Why?"

"I just want to get my point across."

"What point?"

"That I miss her."

"It's cruel. I won't let you do it."

"Then help me bury the little devils," she says, as she sits down at the table. She puts her head in her hands and weeps.

"I'm so bitter, Jack," she says.

"I know," he answers.

"I'm bitter toward you."

"I know."

Daddy reaches down and pulls her up to him. He holds her, while I leave the kitchen and climb the stairs. When I come back down an hour later, they've turned out the lights and gone into their bedroom. The box of guineas is gone.

Chapter 18

OUR SMARTSY FARTSY courthouse stands smack dab
in the middle of the town square. A three-story square
gray granite building, it looms above everything else,
except the Hightower mansion on the hill. People from
all over Texas marvel at our super-duper art deco law
hangout.

Nearly every time we drive past it, my dad pro-
claims, "The Halls of Justice!" I assume he says that because he knows the judge.

In the summer, one-hundred-year-old elm trees hover,
shimmering and shading old men playing dominoes,
while fat dogs snooze at their feet. In the winter, the
scene is lifeless and gray, and the trees are giants against
the icy sky. On the north and south sides of the building,
wide white stone steps lead up into the foyer.

Inside, the walls are black marble, gray stucco, and
dark walnut paneling. The floors are a combination of
gray and green granite, and in the center of the ground
floor corridor is a huge bright green three-leafed clover, surrounded by a brass circle and letters which read

"Clover County Texas Courthouse."

The building smells of dust, books, tobacco, spittoons, and rumpled old lawyers. It consists of three stories and a basement, which houses the jail. In two cold, gray concrete cells down there, the boys from Oklahoma await their fate.

"Nobody to go their bail," the people say, when they discuss the case. "No doubt they've shamed their families so."

A few days after Thanksgiving I have an idea and say to my folks, "I've been hearing gossip about those two down at the jail. Sounds as if they have no homes, no families. They haven't had a single visitor since the night they were arrested."

"What about their lawyer?" Daddy asks.

"Besides him. You know what I mean. I'd like to know more about them."

"Don't forget — they're violent outlaws," Daddy says. "Dangerous men."

"Well, they're not dangerous now."

Mother chimes in, "Jack, you weren't too afraid of them the night you took William and Battles out to the shelterbelt." Sooner or later she winds up harping on that. I swear to God they'll drive me crazy. Sometimes Mother is so mean to Daddy I'm scared they'll end up getting a divorce.

I need a new project to cheer myself up because Angel has won Miss Homecoming Queen. Since she dates

James Colton, the most popular guy in school and the quarterback of the football team, it stands to reason the kids would elect her. I can hardly bear to watch that pasty-faced screaming ninny-harlot get crowned. And I could scream, thinking of James as royalty, after what he's done.

On the night of the Homecoming Dance, Angel looks gorgeous, dressed in a new red formal, escorted by hot-shot James, who wears a white dinner jacket and a red carnation. Those elegant bastards are crowned Home-coming King and Queen of Clover High School, while the band plays "My Wild Irish Rose," and everyone prac-tically bows in adoration. Wearing last year's formal, I stand in the shadows with Jerry Fred. I squinch my eyes nearly shut and pretend he's Elvis Presley in disguise.

I can't stand being so mealy-mouthed and inactive, so when it's Ladies' Choice, I make a beeline for James. "May I please have this dance?" I ask.

Smiling, he takes me in his arms. Almost immediately I say, "I haven't had a chance to talk with you since that night in the shelterbelt."

"What do you mean?"

"I wanted to ask you what you were running away from? Why you knocked me down."

He doesn't answer.

"James, were you responsible for William Carver's death? I have to know!"

"I don't know what you're talking about." With that, he walks away, leaving me alone in the middle of the dance floor. I realize I must refine my interrogation techniques.

After the dance, Angel comes home almost an hour past curfew. Her dress is wrinkled, her make-up smeared, and my folks give her holy hell about it. They ground her for two weeks. Good.

After Mother and Daddy ream her out, she barges into my room. "What did you say to my boyfriend? He was no fun at all after he danced with you."

"Then why did you stay out half the night with him?"

"Who says I was with James?"

"Who, then? Not Jerry Fred."

"That creep? I wouldn't have Jerry Fred Porter if you served him on a platter!"

The next night, Jerry Fred takes me to a Dean Martin-Jerry Lewis movie, but the show's so damn dumb we leave. After our routine whirl around the square, Jerry Fred drives out of town, past the golf course, where most kids go for serious parking. I can't believe he's so stupid. I don't want to park with him any time or any place. Jerry Fred knows how I feel, but his mind is made of mush.

"I want to remind you of the couple that parked one time and nearly got killed," I say. "Apparently they were really going after it, and then they heard something scratching on the driver's side of the front window. They both looked, and there at the window was a hideous man, tapping with a hook, instead of a hand.

"The young lovers drove away, both about to die of heart attacks. When they got to town and into a lighted place, they looked over at the window. And there, attached to the window was the bloody hook! Oh, pain, agony, and vomit. Ever since hearing this story, Jerry Fred, I've refused to park with anybody. Tonight is no exception."

"That's just an old wives' tale," he argues.

"I believe it."

Furious, he drives back into town and takes me to the Dairy Queen for cherry Cokes. "Someday you're gonna wish you'd been nicer to me. Just hope I'm still around to hear you apologize."

"Jerry Fred, I'll never park with you, so get used to the idea."

"That smarts, Frankilee. That really smarts."

We're headed home when we see the sheriff driving like a bat out of hell toward Hightower Hill. I make Jerry Fred follow him. The sheriff zips into the driveway, and his car quickly disappears behind Miss Mabel's house. Parking in the drive, we notice several neighbors running toward the garage apartment where Coach lives. The air smells smoky, and when we reach the back of the mansion we see why. There in front of Coach's home is a burning wooden cross. It's about three feet tall, and every inch is ablaze. I wish to God I had my camera.

"I wanted you to see this before I put out the fire," Coach tells Sheriff Baines.

"I see it. Now get some water," says the sheriff.

A neighbor has hooked up a hose, and he sprays water on the fire, which immediately fizzles. Coach and the sheriff go to the back door of the mansion to tell Miss Mabel what's happened.

"I thought I heard voices out here," she says. "What's wrong?" The men step inside. I never see Miss Mabel, but I hear her yelling.

Soon both men come back out, and the sheriff says, "I want everyone to go home now, but if you see anything suspicious, call me. And I want one of the neighbor ladies to stay with Miss Mabel." When I raise my hand, he says, "Not you, Frankilee. I want a grown woman."

I'm late for my curfew, but when I tell my folks about the fire, they're as sweet as pie about it.

Everyone in town knows about the burning cross. Daddy says the worst thing about the whole deal is that now people will start suspecting each other of bad things. He's right. If I had to bet on who did it, I'd say James Colton. I remember his father speaking against integration at the town meeting. And there's no doubt in my mind that James shot William.

People say Coach Morris is obsessed, and they wish he'd let up on integration. They say he's a troublemaker, and they don't want any trouble.

"Can you imagine Clover filled with those nasty liberal Yankee reporters?" they ask each other. "What if we got a lot of bad publicity?"

Football season has ended now for both the Lepre-chauns and the Eagles, with the Leps barely winning one game and the Eagles taking the colored teams' State Championship. I don't blame Coach Morris for practically going berserk on the subject of integration, because he'll probably never even get close to athletes like William and his friends any time during his coaching career.

Daddy says it's a doggone dirty shame the two teams couldn't be combined, and he rants and raves about it until Mother says, "Jack, you're making everybody in town mad!"

"Well, I don't care if I do!" he answers. Holy Moses! The man's just nuts about sports. He's even crazy about our crappy girls' basketball team and always comes to our games.

Coach Morris says we'll improve. He has several books on women's basketball, and he draws up diagrams of complicated plays and mimeographs them in messy purple hand-staining ink. He runs us through practices and drills until our tongues hang out. For the actual games, I'm on the second string, playing center defense. I only get to play when one of the first string players is tired.

"Frankilee, I wish you'd started playing basketball earlier," Coach says to me one day. "You have great potential. If you weren't graduating, you'd be one of my best players next year." This isn't true, but that's the kind of coach he is. Never mean to his players, but always encouraging.

By saying I have potential, he gives me hope. At night, when I pile Lucy and Desi on my bed and then crawl under the covers, I think about my potential and relax, listening to rock' n' roll on the radio. Every night, listening to songs like "Only You" by the Platters, or "Teddy Bear" by Elvis, I yearn for something out there — beyond the gray sky and the city limits of Clover — something bright, accepting, and wonderful. Somewhere there's a place — and a person — for a too-tall, flat-chested, stringy-haired sarcastic girl like me. If I could find a man as encouraging as Coach, as lovable as Cornel Wilde, and as sexy as Elvis, I'd have a *hunk* of a man. And if I had a husband like that, and a job I loved, and adorable little cats and children playing at my feet, wouldn't my life be just perfect?

After school lets out for the Christmas holidays, Mother and I clean house, bake cookies, make candy, and decorate the tree. We wrap jars of apricot preserves in cellophane and deliver them to the neighbors. Angel always has an excuse and never helps. But when she sees the garlands and mistletoe we've hung, she says, "What's that for, Frankilee? Is that the only way you can get Jerry Fred to kiss you?"

"Oh, go to hell, you hump-road hussy," I say, and when I reach for her hair she shrinks back, so I know I haven't lost my scary touch.

I still want to meet the two jailbirds and to ask them if they know *who* shot William. Sheriff Baines has acted as if it doesn't matter who shot William, since it's been proved those guys didn't do it. Well, I think I know who did it, but I'm also sure no one would believe me. So what good would it do if I told somebody?

I decide to go to the jail and ask the sheriff if I can interview the outlaws for our school paper, my alleged purpose being to deter crime among potential juvenile delinquents in Clover. The sheriff is just about dumb enough to fall for it.

I get the Christmas spirit and buy men's mittens and scarves from the five-and-dime on the town square. I wrap these gifts and take them to the jail, but Sheriff Baines makes me unwrap them to prove I'm not smuggling in a dangerous weapon. Then he lets me use his Scotch tape to rewrap the gifts.

"No telling where all I can get this article published," I tell him. "Your name will be mentioned, of course, as the lawman in charge of the whole thing."

It's no trouble at all to get the sheriff to let me in.

Robert and Terry Slocumb are cousins but look like brothers. Both have sandy hair and brown eyes. Up close, they look even younger than they did the night at the shelterbelt. They're both seventeen. Each quietly stands alone inside his cell, with hands in pockets, swaying from heel to toe in white socks and rundown shoes. String thin, they both wear baggy jeans and large men's blue-gray jail shirts. Acting as if they're glad to meet me, they both stick their hands out between the jail bars to shake my hand.

"Before we get started with the interview," I ask, "is there anything I can bring the next time I come? What about something to read?" I'm looking in their cells, and all I see is religious stuff, nothing entertaining. No Christmas gifts, but what could they expect?

"Could you bring us some magazines?" Robert asks.

"Or comic books?" Terry adds.

I ask them about the night of their capture. What was it like to be chased down by dogs? Were they afraid? At the time they were hiding, did they know that nearly a hundred men with guns were out searching for them?

Then I wedge in: "Do you have any idea who might have shot William Carver?"

"Young lady!" Sheriff Baines calls from the far end of the hall. "Don't be getting above your business!"

I try again. "About the night you were arrested, when William Carver died — "

"You ain't their lawyer! Can't talk about it!" the sheriff yells.

I excuse myself and walk to the end of the hall. I speak in a low voice. "Sheriff Baines, you're not letting me do research for my article. Please allow me to ask questions."

"You're acting like a fool reporter," he answers. "I'm not letting you ask about William Carver's death."

"Sheriff, for my research, I have to ask all sorts of questions."

201

"You mention William Carver again, and you're out of here."

"What about Freedom of Speech? You know the Bill of Rights?"

"You mention the shooting again, and I'll put you in jail."

As I go back to the cells, the Slocumb boys watch me. "I don't know exactly what we can talk about," I tell them. With my back to the sheriff, I get the photograph of James out of my pocket. Slowly I show it to each of them. "Have you ever seen this person?" I whisper.

They shake their heads.

"Can you tell me anything about that night?" I ask.

"How's this? The white guys sent a big old nigger into the shelterbelt to get us!" Terry says.

"Man, yes! Talk about a monster!" Robert adds. They both begin ranting about Battles' strength and size.

I can't believe it. Already mad at the sheriff, now I'm so mad at the Slocumbs I could tear them apart. This is what Daddy means when he says some people, no matter how pitiful, have to pretend they're better than others.

When Robert and Terry stop carrying on, I ask, "Are you glad to be alive?"

"Oh, sure," they say. "We're real happy about it."

"Well, if it'd been left up to those white men with guns you'd be dead now, because one of them would have shot you. The father of the boy that was killed saved you."

They say nothing.

"The tragedy is, the white men shot that boy instead of you!"

I have a feeling they know they're not getting those comic books.

"Tell you what," I say. "You two jailbirds can get your own goddamn magazines. And Merry Christmas."

I put on my coat, leave the jail, and climb into Daddy's car before I realize how badly I'm shaking. Rat shit! Jesus told us to visit people in prison. No doubt he meant for us to be decent about it. If there's such a thing as hell, I know for sure I'm going there.

The packages under our tree look meager, but I'm so worried about the state of my soul, I don't have time to even think about unwrapping them. Plus, I'm picking a bone with God over letting William die, so I can't get into a holiday spirit. On Christmas morning, I'm surprised as hell and also thrilled to a pink string to receive five pieces of matching tan Samsonite luggage, unwrapped, stacked under the tree. Angel receives the same thing, only in a baby blue that matches her eyes.

"We decided to go all out, girls," Mother says, "because we know how much you'll need luggage in college next year."

On Christmas afternoon my grandfather comes by. For the first time in my life, he doesn't carry gifts into the house. Instead, he hands Angel and me each an envelope with money inside.

"I don't know how to shop for young ladies," he says in his cracking voice. "You'll have to buy your own gifts. I hope you don't mind."

We all sit in the brightly lighted, warm living room, the adults drinking coffee and Angel and me guzzling no-liquor eggnog. We eat thick slices of fruitcake made from Grandmommy's recipe, topped with rich whipped cream. The house smells of pine needles, cedar, and cinnamon.

"Norther's coming," says Grandpapa, looking out the window. "After another cup of coffee, I'd better git."

"Why don't you spend the night?" Mother suggests.

"No, miles to go before I sleep," Grandpapa looks at me and winks. "You do know Robert Frost, don't you?" Suddenly I love the old man the way I used to, before he went gaga over Angel.

Christmas music wafts from the phonograph player in the den. Daddy's turned the volume up, so we listen to Bing Crosby singing "White Christmas." On the next record, Elvis croons, "I'll have a blue, blue, blue Christmas without you." I look at my lonely grandfather, whom I've told atrocious lies about. I watch my parents, whom I disobey frequently, and I look over at Angel, whom I've tried to permanently embald for life. Then I remember the two ignorant jailbirds I've insulted, and tacky Jerry Fred, who I treat like shit on a regular basis — and I suppose I could just keep going on and name everybody in the world I've treated badly. And then I think about

Grandmommy, William, and Wanita, and how terribly much I miss them.

It really is a blue, blue, blue, blue Christmas.

Chapter 19

THE WRETCHED WINTER continues, and the overcast West Texas skies add to my gloom. Everything I see is gray. Just for kicks and grins, I take to wearing my red sweater nearly every day, until finally Mother conspires against me and hides it.

At school, everyone is in a rotten mood. "No sun!" Mrs. Rickers exclaims in biology class. "We're just like the Eskimos in Alaska! If we don't get some sunshine soon, we'll all become a bunch of alcoholics!"

Every time I open my mouth, I make somebody angry. Angel says I'm hateful, Mother says I'm irritating, Daddy says I have a smart mouth, Coach Morris says I'm sarcastic, Jerry Fred says I'm bossy, and my best friend Shelly says I'm an obnoxious know-it-all.

"Sharp tongue!" says Grandpapa. "Frankilee's afflicted."

"Well, she can be unpleasant," Mother agrees. "But sometimes Frankilee is extremely witty."

"When Frankilee says something hateful, I'd send her to her room," Grandpapa advises. "And I wouldn't put up with her cussing for one minute!"

"That doesn't do any good. When she's home, she spends most of her time in her room anyway. Maybe to punish Frankilee for being unpleasant I should make her spend time with Angel," Mother laughs.

On Valentine's Day, Jerry Fred Porter brings me a box of chocolates and asks me to go steady. The box is huge, with three tiers of candy. As a twosome, Jerry Fred and I are a pair of towering beanpoles, and we go practically everywhere together. But I still can't stand him.

"Let's not go steady," I say. "I appreciate the offer, and I really do like you, but not enough to go steady. Let's just be friends."

"I want more than friendship. If you were my girl-friend, you'd be nicer to me."

"But we really aren't that serious about each other. Can't you be realistic?"

"I'm serious about you. I'm in love with you. Don't you love me even a little?"

"No, I don't, Jerry Fred. Not even a smidgen."

"So," he says and then pauses. "If you won't go steady with me, I won't ask you out anymore."

"Suit yourself."

Jerry Fred leaves his box of chocolates and goes home.

Breaking up with Jerry Fred isn't an act of kindness, but what happens to Coach Morris is much worse. For

Valentine's Day, someone sends him a red heart-shaped box, which is labeled "Poisoned Candy." On the morning after Valentine's Day, the coach holds the candy box up for our class to see. Then he asks, "Do any of you know about this?" He opens the box, which contains chocolates and a note, which he takes out. Unfolding it, he reads aloud: "Stop pushing for integration."

He looks at each of us as if we're suspects. "Someone in this school knows who sent me this package — and this warning. Whoever it is needs to realize I'm not afraid. I won't be threatened or intimidated. The culprit is wasting his time."

Coach Morris may not be frightened, but the rest of us are. Since we girls are all half in love with him, we're furious he's being mistreated, which may be the reason for what I do next. This is when the shit hits the fan.

It's the Tuesday after Valentine's Day, and Monkey Woman Mabel is in a snit. For the first time in all my years of taking lessons from her, she doesn't bore me to death with music theory. Nor does she nag about my laziness. Instead, she wants to talk about her boarder, Coach Morris.

"He's as bad as a carpetbagger," she fumes. "I don't know what I was thinking, renting my garage apartment to him!"

"He's a very good teacher," I turn to her. She's dressed in her long brown sweater, a gray skirt, and black lace-up shoes. Her eyes have devilishly red pupils, and her lop-sided gold-rimmed glasses hang practically off her nose. As always, her dyed black hair looks like it should be stuck to the head of a Japanese doll.

"He's a troublemaker," she answers. "He's causing the ruination of the town!"

"Why? Because he wants to integrate the schools?"

"Because he's a fool!" She breathes down on me. "White children going to school with the niggers! Everyone's in an uproar about it!"

"Miss Mabel — " I clear my throat to make a speech.

"I've a good mind to kick him out of my house. Let him get a cross burned on someone else's property!" Miss Mabel reminds me of a gargoyle.

I realize this is my supreme opportunity to quote Battles' famous cliché. I stand up and look down at her dramatically. Just call me Ethel Barrymore.

"What are you staring at?" she asks.

"Miss Mabel, is there a hole in your head where the brains leaked out?"

Suddenly, everything about her changes. Something shrinks back inside her. Her expression hardens, and I realize I'll pay for this dearly. In the silence that follows, even Pope Pius watches with hostility. The room is cold.

"Stack your music," she says. "We will forgo your lesson."

I do as I'm told.

"Tell your mother I wish to speak with her," Miss Mabel says.

"Yes ma'am," I answer and walk to the door. My

heart pounds wildly. Before I leave, I turn around and say, "See you later, alligator." But her back is to me, and she doesn't reply.

As I walk home in the freezing grayness, I realize I've crossed a line, and things won't be the same — not with Miss Mabel, and maybe not with my parents either. What seemed like such a good idea at the time wasn't a good idea at all. I wonder if I do have a serious personality disorder. And I wonder if I can stand to be grounded for about a year.

The next afternoon Mother waits for me in Daddy's den. Angel is warbling her heart out in the living room.

"I thought you had bridge club today," I say, surprised. I've found Lucy hiding from Elvis in the backyard bushes. I carry her close to me.

"I found a bridge substitute," Mother answers. "I wanted to talk to you about your music lessons. Sit down."

It turns out, of course, that Miss Mabel has called Mother and reported my rudeness. She has decided to discontinue my lessons. She simply can't tolerate ugly behavior from a teenager. Angel, of course, will always be welcome, and Miss Mabel wants *her* to continue.

"Suffering shit! Don't you want to hear my side of the story?" I ask.

"Don't say *shit*," Mother says, as she lights a cigarette. "I know what you said to her. And I can imagine her comments about the Negroes were terrible."

Angel walks into the den. "Are you in trouble, Frankilee?"

"Why do you ask that?"

"Because you always *are* in trouble."

"Angel, this conversation is between Frankilee and me," Mother says.

"Did I hear you say Miss Mabel's kicking Frankilee out?"

"Get back to your practicing, Angel," Mother says.

"Well, Miss Mabel would never kick *me* out! I'm the best student she's ever had!" She leaves the room and soon starts playing the piano with a flourish.

"Oh, honey, why did you do it?"

Moving around the bouncing Elvis and still carrying Lucy, I leave the kitchen. I have a headache and feel like I've been kicked in the stomach. Suddenly I'm worn out, exhausted, disgusted, and as mad as hell. I can hardly climb the stairs, and I move slowly. Upstairs, inside my room, Desi sleeps on my bed, still unmade from this morning. After putting Lucy next to Desi, I take two aspirins, and then I climb in under the covers and quietly cry myself to sleep. When I awake, it's suppertime, but I have no appetite.

A few days later, Jerry Fred comes by my locker after English class and says, "My mother has been giving me hell for breaking up with you."

"Tell her there was nothing to break."

"I need to talk to you," he says. "Let me drive you

home after school."

At three-thirty, he waits for me outside his car, and he opens my door for me. "I don't want to ride around a lot," I tell him. "Just take me home, say whatever you have to say, and make it snappy." I don't care that I'm hurting his feelings.

Then driving down the street to our house, I see her — Lucy — just a tiny speck in the road. What is happening can't be real — a living creature can't lie so still. As we come closer, and Lucy doesn't move, I scream at Jerry Fred to stop. He slowly pulls into the driveway. I run into the street.

Lucy is stretched out on the pavement, lying on her side. Not moving, not breathing.

"Go to the bank and get my dad."

"Where's your mother?"

"She's not home! Go get my dad!"

I stand in the middle of the road while he backs out of our driveway and heads to town. Then I kneel and gather Lucy in my arms. She's as straight and stiff as a cat-statue. She weighs nothing. I sit on the curb, holding her on my lap.

I'm watching the entire scene from someplace else — from a cloud or a treetop. I'm watching a girl in slow motion, picking up her cat. She sits and she waits for someone to drive by, stop, and tell her, "This animal isn't dead. She's only sleeping."

I wait until my daddy comes with Jerry Fred. Still carrying Lucy, I walk with them to the back yard. I watch as Daddy gets a shovel from the tool shed and digs a deep hole next to the terrace, while Jerry Fred finds a box in the basement. Then I ask Daddy to bring a bathroom towel for me to wrap Lucy in. He brings two, and we make her a cozy bed in the box, put her inside, and fasten the lid. We put the box in the hole, and Jerry Fred shovels dirt on top of it.

Daddy holds me next to his woolen suit coat. The top of my head is even with his ears. I smell a hint of Old Spice and cigars, and I hear the crinkling stiffness of his shirt. He kisses my forehead and rocks me in his arms. "Honey, baby, please don't cry," he says.

But I'm not crying. I'm a zombie.

When Angel gets home from her voice lesson, she comes to my room. Walking in without knocking, she says, "I hear your old cat died. Too bad, but if she was so dumb she got into the street, she deserved it."

"I wouldn't say that about your dog." Angel is making me too tired to fight.

"Well, my dog isn't that stupid, so you won't have to."

The next morning I'm so exhausted I can't get out of bed. "Tell Mother I can't go to school," I say to Angel when she comes into my bedroom to snitch a sweater. "I don't feel like getting up." And I sleep.

The next day I go to school, and during fifth hour I find Coach Morris. He's sitting at his desk in his office, grading homework from our literature class.

"I'm sorry to disturb you," I say, "but I have

something for you." I hand him my basketball uniform. "I'm quitting."

"Why are you quitting now?" he asks. "The season's almost over. Why not stick it out a couple more weeks?"

"I want to quit."

"I know how you feel. Sometimes I feel the same way."

"What do you mean?"

"Having a cross burned in my front yard caused me to think about a lot of things."

"Do you think you'll quit? Will you leave Clover?"

"No, giving up is not an option."

"Maybe not for you, but it is for me," I say. And then I leave Coach Morris sitting at his desk, grading our papers.

Chapter 20

I FEEL SHITTY, and I'm blaming it on Angel. Mother says, "Don't say *shitty*," but that's how I feel.

Mother says I'm still grieving for Grandmommy and William. She tells me most days she feels the same way. Shelly says I'm in shock from finding Lucy dead in the street, Daddy thinks I miss Wanita and also I'm humiliated about being kicked out by Mabel Hightower, and Mrs. Rickers is certain the cloudy days are doing me in. But I say the blame lies with Angel. Before she came to live with us, I was a happy girl, and now I'm downright miserable.

One of the basic rules my mother preaches is, "Don't ever take to your bed!" The women in her family have a tendency to do this in times of trouble. Mother believes it's a weakness and an escape from reality. She cites the females in her family who have taken to their beds: Aunt Tommie, when she got jilted by her first fiancé; Aunt Teddy, when her car caught fire and the family's Christmas gifts were burned up; Aunt Jim, when her kitchen help ran away with her silver; Aunt Georgia, when her eldest daughter brought a derelict home from college and announced their engagement. Mother ridicules those sisters, because she believes in facing your problems.

So when I want to take to *my* bed, she isn't sympathetic. "Get up, now, Frankilee," she says every morning as she flips on the light and pulls the covers down. "Start a new day!"

I reach down, retrieve the covers, and drift back to sleep. Regardless of how much Mother preaches or threatens, I can't make myself move.

"I just don't feel like going to school today," I say, as I roll over. "I think my throat's sore."

"Well, then, I'll take you to the doctor."

"I'll go to the doctor tomorrow if I don't feel better."

Then every evening she comes to my bedside and asks, "How's your throat?"

"Fine," I answer.

"Good. I'm expecting you to get up tomorrow. Everybody's worried about you. Your friends miss you."

On about the fourth day, I tell her, "I really don't give two pig farts. Maybe I'll get up tomorrow, and maybe I won't."

Now Mother's angry. She sends Daddy, then Angel, then Shelly to talk to me, but I don't want to talk. I just want them to leave me the hell alone.

One afternoon I awake, and I'd swear I'm dreaming.

"Wanita, is that you?" I ask. She sits in my study chair, with her feet on the bottom of my bed, as she looks through my schoolbooks. I watch her for a while, and then she looks in my direction. She leans toward me and says, "I come to tell you I sorry about Lucy. Such a sweet little cat. You got a right to be sad."

Wanita pulls a chair over next to my bed, while I sniffle. Then I say, "How have you been able to stand it? Losing William, I mean. I can't even stand to lose a cat, much less a son."

"I *can't* stand it. But I know that loving and losing sometimes mean the same thing."

I refuse to let Wanita make me cry again.

"I'll tell you one thing. I'm mad at God. Why does he let such horrible things happen to people? In a way, I can understand why Grandmommy died. But why William? It makes no sense at all."

"Course it don't make no sense. My William dying *don't* make no sense."

"I'm furious, and it's hard for me to believe in God now. I haven't said a prayer since William's funeral."

"Now listen here. Don't you go laying this onto Jesus. Him and God both up there watching us, but they don't protect us from all the bad stuff. We supposed to do that for each other. You think God Almighty pulled the trigger on the gun that killed my boy? Uhhh uhhh! Some white man out there done it by accident, and he's too scared to tell the sheriff, maybe afraid of what somebody colored might do to him. Or maybe it was a man too drunk to remember what he done. Or maybe some white man who always wanted to shoot a colored boy finally got his chance. Lord God didn't do it."

"Still, God could have kept it from happening," I say.

"Maybe Lord God don't work that way. You think he planned for my people to be slaves all them years? You think he jump around making some people suffer and some people have the life of Riley?"

"I don't know what to think."

"No, we is what we is. He just help us to hang on." She sits still for a minute. "And I'm hanging on. For my Rootie, if for no other reason. Frankilee, there ain't nothing easy about living or loving."

I sit up in bed and across the room I see myself in the mirror. "I look horrible," I say.

"Honey, you in pain. But being white-girl pain, you got a chance." She looks at me. "Now, colored-girl pain — that don't ever let up. Uhh uhh!"

"Wanita, everything has been going wrong."

"Listen here, you and your mama done bit off more than you could chew when you brung that Angel into this house. But your mama don't quit. She going to do all that she can to help that girl."

"Sometimes I think Mother is nuts."

"Your mama could use a kind word from you right now. She ain't had no relief. Think she have an easy time after her own mama pass on? Uhh uhh."

We sit silently for a moment, and then she says, "Tell you what the Lord God do for me. Every morning I say, 'Just get me through this day, Lord, that's all I ask. Just

218

help me make it through this one day.' So far, Jesus stand by me and give me the strength."

"Wanita, I'm so glad you're here. Maybe tomorrow I'll feel like getting up and going to school."

"I wants you to get out of that bed right now. Besides Rootie, you my favorite living child. Why, look at you. Pretty and smart. A real beauty."

"I'm tall, skinny, and ugly."

"You ugly now because you been crying. Listen, girl, you one of them ducklings that get to be a swan. You think you could belong to your papa and mama and not be beautiful? Listen, honey, golden retrievers don't birth silly little lapdogs. Ain't nothing prettier than a golden retriever."

Wanita makes me smile.

She pulls me by the hand. "Get yourself together now! Let's go into the bathroom and wash your face. I wants you to drive me home."

"Will you come back to us, Wanita? I don't have anybody to talk to."

"I don't think so."

"Why not?"

"I've took care of you since you was a baby. But now I ain't got no truck with your dad . . . or Miss Angel, either."

"Daddy feels terrible about William."

"How you know that? He tell you that?"

"I know by the way he acts."

"Well, he didn't tell me! Just sent us a damn check

to cover the funeral expenses."

"He cares about your family, Wanita."

"He didn't care about us when he took Battles and William to the shelterbelt."

"They wanted to go!"

"Ha! Rich white banker say 'jump!' and all the darkies jump. Afraid not to! Well, not no more. Not Wanita."

We're both silent for a moment, and then I ask, "What about Mother?"

"I miss your mother, but not enough to put up with your dad."

"You can't forgive him."

"Come on, get dressed," she says. "I told you — I wants you to drive me home."

I stand up and walk to my closet. Pulling a pair of jeans off a shelf, I ask, "How did you get to our house, Wanita?"

"Why, your mama brung me. How do you think? Your mama at her wits' end about you."

We walk into the bathroom, and she runs water in the sink and hands me a washcloth. "The problems you got won't last. Ain't you going to college next year? You be rid of Miss Angel then."

"I blame Angel and her goddamned dog for my cat getting run over. Elvis probably chased Lucy into the street."

After handing me a towel, Wanita puts her hands on my shoulders and looks at me square. "You ain't the

220

only one have a hard time handling Miss Angel. That girl got squirrel-cage ways."

She reaches over to brush my hair out of my eyes, and then she flattens her palm against my forehead. "Mercy sakes, honey," she says. "You hot as a boiled owl! Is you sick?"

Chapter 21

MONONUCLEOSIS IS DR. Thatcher's diagnosis. "It's called the 'kissing disease,'" he says, "and it's fairly common among college students. To the best of my knowledge, yours is the first case in Clover County."

Mother tears up, and Daddy turns pale as the doctor reads aloud from his medical journal. Then he says, "Sometimes when a person gets physically or emotionally run-down, the body loses its ability to fight off viruses. The immune system gets out of whack. That's what's happened to your daughter. I'm recommending a round of antibiotics and complete bedrest. To keep an eye on Frankilee's blood count, I want to put her in the hospital."

We somberly go home to pack my things. If I were heading for the Clover County jail, I wouldn't be more frightened. The way things are going, I won't be surprised if I die in the hospital before daylight. I call Shelly to tell her my bad news.

"Promise you'll have a conniption fit if Mother lets Angel sing at my funeral."

I become the town celebrity. Nobody in high school has ever heard of mononucleosis before, and the next day during visiting hours, my friends bring presents and flowers. They report that in all the science classes Mrs. Rickers gave a lesson about the disease by drawing circles on the blackboard with red and white chalk to illustrate the workings of my blood. According to them, she practically went into a rapture.

After school on the following afternoon, Mrs. Rickers shows up at my hospital room with a diagram to explain the characteristics of my illness. Old, gray, dull Mrs. Rickers is so thrilled she almost jumps up and down. She tells Mother and Daddy, "Your daughter has an unusual blood disorder. It isn't leukemia, but it's almost as exciting!"

Gadzooks! On this same evening Coach Morris calls Mother and says he'll talk with my other teachers and get my homework assignments. So he begins a ritual of bringing my books and papers to the hospital every afternoon during his fifth hour break. Pulling up a chair and sitting close to my bed, he explains every assignment carefully. He offers to help me, especially with Algebra II, if I can't solve the problems without major cheating by looking at the answers in the back of the book. Now I elevate Coach to an even higher plane, although he's not quite up there with Elvis.

The kids say Angel wanders around school, wringing her hands, crying, even refusing to eat her lunch in the cafeteria.

"Oh, how can I eat?" she asks, "When my sister may be dying?"

Her behavior is ridiculous. My friends are on to her now, saying she's milking my illness dry. But she won't come to visit me. Instead, she sends me a get-well card with kittens on it, along with a note telling me she can't risk getting sick herself, since I have a highly communicable disease. The dumb twit misspells *communicable*.

She and James Colton are the only kids in the senior class who don't come to visit me in the hospital.

My most regular guest is Jerry Fred, who keeps begging me to kiss him. Every evening, Jerry Fred either sits on the side of the bed or pulls up a chair as close to my face as possible. He inhales my air and gives me claustrophobia.

"All I want is a French kiss or two," he says one night during visitors' hours.

"That's disgusting," I tell him.

"Just a teeny weeny French kiss? I brought you roses." It's true. I had hardly checked into the hospital before Jerry Fred stomped into my room, carrying a dozen red roses. At that weak moment I reinstated him as my boyfriend.

"Do you want my disease?"

"Yes! Then everyone will know we're intimate."

"But we're not intimate."

"I want people to think we are."

"No! If you want to be sick, go get your own disease!" Honestly, sometimes Jerry Fred gives me the fruit-fly heebie jeebies.

One day, after explaining my assignments, Coach Morris leans back in his hospital chair and says, "I should tell you that the school board probably won't extend my contract. I've made a lot of enemies." His brown hair flops over his forehead after he runs his hand through it.

"If it's because you pushed integration, they're dead wrong."

"They don't see it that way."

"You did what you thought was right."

"How does anybody know what's right?"

I pause and then say, "Speaking of what's right, I have to ask you something. What would you do if you knew a horrible secret about somebody? Something you didn't want to know. Would it be right or wrong to tell it?"

"It would depend on what the secret was. Whether it was dangerous to other people, I suppose."

"What if you knew who killed William Carver?" I can't look at him.

He speaks slowly. "If I could prove it, I'd tell the authorities. If it were only a hunch, I'd keep it to myself. You could do a lot of damage with an accusation like that." He puts his hand over mine. His dark brown eyes have black circles underneath, and they fill my chest with a jagged pain.

"How could you possibly know that, Frankilee?" he asks.

"I saw someone in the shelterbelt that night, right before I found William. He was running away, and he knocked me down. I hadn't intended to tell anyone this."

"But it was dark out there, wasn't it?"

"I got his picture."

Coach takes his hand away from mine, and then clasps his hands together and bends over, as if he's received a blow. "Whew!" He looks at me. "Do I know this guy?"

"You know him well."

"Do you want to tell me who it is?"

"No."

"Does he know you know?"

"I've told him."

"And his reaction?"

"Denial."

"Of course."

"It's driving me crazy, Coach."

"Of course it is."

"You're the only person I've told."

"Not even your parents?"

I shake my head.

"You should tell them."

"They've got enough problems. Mother's furious at Daddy for taking William out there in the first place, and Daddy acts mad or sad most of the time."

"They've said all along it was an accident," Coach says.

"It probably was. I don't know."

"This is a very serious situation, Frankilee. Possibly dangerous. You must tell your folks. Your dad will know what to do."

"I'll think about it."

He slowly stands up, and then he pats my shoulder. He promises to come back tomorrow.

Later, Daddy comes, just a few moments before visiting hours end. Agitated, he sits on the side of my bed and looks out the window at the black sky. He's still wearing his navy blue business suit, but he's taken off his tie. He's so tall his legs stretch down straight, and his feet touch the floor. He hunches his shoulders as he looks out into the night.

"You know," he says, "I've spent twenty years in this town, and I've made a good living here. But sometimes I don't like the citizens of Clover."

"What's happened?"

"The sheriff has closed his investigation into William's death. He and the coroner have finally finished their report. William's death was officially ruled 'accidental.'"

"Does that mean he isn't holding anyone responsible?" I ask.

"It's lousy, isn't it?" My dad looks sick.

"Did Sheriff Baines even *try* to find out who shot

William?"

"Apparently not."

"Didn't try to find witnesses?"

"Didn't even try to find out who was carrying 30-30 rifles. Although that might be hard to do, I'll admit," Daddy says. "But he has those two kids in jail, and that's all he cares about."

"Do you think the sheriff knows who shot William?"

"I doubt it. But the point is, he doesn't care. Just think what that says to the Negro community. 'You can come help us out when we need you, but if you get hurt or killed, we don't give a damn.'"

"How will the colored people react to this?"

"They're probably expecting it. They won't be surprised at one more disappointment."

"Is there anything we can do to help them?"

"I don't know. I've done everything wrong. The Negro people don't like — or trust — me because they think I involved William in the manhunt. And I did. The white folks don't like me because they think I'm fond of the Negroes. And I am."

"I had no idea people felt that way."

"As a result, the bank will suffer. Already does."

"But yours is the only bank in town!"

"Doesn't matter. People will drive fifty miles to bank elsewhere if they get mad enough. And some folks have."

"Oh, Daddy, I can't believe people would be that unreasonable."

"Well, they can. Honey, don't be surprised if our board of directors asks me to step down. And if they do, it's all right. I hate for you and your mother to have to suffer, though. And I sure hope they don't fire anybody else at the bank. The whole damn thing's a mess."

After a pause, I say, "I don't want to add to your troubles, Daddy, but I've had a long talk with Wanita. She's so hurt she can't think straight. And you're right. She does blame you. Go to Wanita and Battles, Daddy. Tell them how sorry you are about William."

"What's the point? They already know."

"Wanita doesn't know."

His voice quavers. "I don't think I can."

"She's hurting, and she needs you. Even if you both break down, you should go."

"No, Frankilee. It won't do any good."

Chapter 22

AT THE END of two weeks, I leave the hospital.

"I want Frankilee to curtail all activities except going to class. No parties, no senior class trips, nothing. She's been a very sick girl, and the only way for her to recover is by getting plenty of rest." Dr. Thatcher acts as if I'm not even in the room. Dammit to hell!

My mother makes me follow the doctor's instructions, and I swear to God I'll die of boredom. There are only thirty-five graduating seniors this year, and our class needs me to help them raise hell. I tell Shelly I'm in a major depression, and she says, "It's just as well you're missing some of this senior stuff. If you could see the way Angel and James Colton carry on, you'd urp."

"What do you mean?"

"I mean they hang all over each other and smooch until you want to vomit!"

Angel is due for another hair pulling. The little bitch will probably get pregnewton before the end of the school year. Just what we need.

Jerry Fred calls me every evening. One night he says,

"I want to have mononucleosis, because I figure if you have to stay home I might as well, too. After all, as lovers we should stick together."

"Jerry Fred, we are *not* lovers. We will never be lovers, except in your warped imagination. Ask one of the other girls to be your date to the prom, and take somebody else to all the other parties. I can't go. Don't even *want* to."

Stacks of college catalogues fill the corners of my bedroom. I've filled out applications to several and am waiting to hear if I've been accepted. My first choice is State. Thanks to Coach Morris, I know a lot about that school. He says they have a terrific journalism department, which is where I'm headed.

Angel wants to attend a smaller private school, because of its theater and music departments. "I plan to major in music and then head to New York City," she tells anybody who'll listen.

One evening she announces. "Just as soon as we finish my skin treatments, I'm going to try my luck in beauty contests."

"Angel," Daddy says, "that sounds expensive. I'm not made of money."

"You should try to get scholarships for school. Maybe we can somehow manage the rest." Mother is always a little off target.

I read, take the ACT and the SAT, and I rest, attending

only those functions my mother and Dr. Thatcher will allow. Angel prepares for scholarship auditions. She practices singing and dancing early in the morning and then again at night. Playing the piano madly, or singing like a wild German opera star, or hoofing up and down our polished hardwood floors, she causes more dither and makes more noise than a train full of squawking peacocks.

Angel puts records on full volume, as she dances on *pointe* in her hard-toed ballet shoes. Elvis races after her, his feet sliding as he crashes into walls and furniture. I hate that maladjusted little bastard. But with a mistress like her, he has no chance for a normal life. I pick him up and scold him, then hold him in my arms and feel his small head next to mine, his spotted face and soft ears smelling peppery. He clings to me. His left paw is on my right shoulder, his right paw in my left hand. Then Elvis and I dance.

One April afternoon, Angel tells us Miss Mabel wants her to practice for auditions on her famous grand piano.

"She told me to come any evening after her students have left," Angel says. "So I plan to go over there regularly."

"That's amazing," Daddy says.

"It certainly is," Mother agrees. "I wonder if Miss Mabel has any idea what a hypocrite she is."

"What do you mean?" Angel asks.

"I'm referring to her hateful treatment of Frankilee,"

Mother says.

"Oh, that!" answers Angel. "She never mentions Frankilee. She loves *me*. And she wants to help with my artistic endeavors."

"Your artistic endeavors," says Daddy. He's as mad as an old ant lion.

"Oh, let her go," Mother says. "Let her get all the help she can from the nasty old crone."

"I have misgivings," Daddy says, looking at Mother.

"If Angel auditions on a concert grand piano and she's used to practicing on one, she'll have an advantage," Mother says.

"I suppose."

So a new routine for Angel: voice in the early morning, dance after school until supper, and piano at Miss Mabel's mansion until bedtime. Angel insists on walking from our house to Miss Mabel's, and after her session, she walks home by herself. Bored to death, sometimes I sit on the front porch after dark and soak in the heavy spring air. The streetlights shine on the neat sidewalks, the black velvet West Texas skies are packed with a brilliant moon and stars, and April is deliciously warm. Children play in their yards after dark. I can hear them, laughing and calling.

One night Mother and Daddy attend a banker's dinner in Amarillo. I watch my favorite shows on television while Angel practices at Miss Mabel's home. Wearing my shortie pajamas and a robe, I sit in the den on the couch,

Elvis on one side and Desi on the other, both snoozing.

All day the air has been unusually warm, muggy, and still. "Bad weather's coming," Mrs. Rickers announced to her classes at school. The sky has been an ominous green.

At about nine o'clock, Mother calls. "We've just heard a weather report. There's a big storm coming through. You girls get to the basement."

"Angel isn't home yet."

"Call Miss Mabel and tell her to send Angel home now. I want you girls safe."

I hang up and dial Miss Mabel, dreading to talk to the old bitch. But no one answers. I try again and decide the phone must be out of order. I grab the car keys and head up Hightower Hill, as the first drops of rain begin to fall.

Driving through the entrance to the estate, I'm hoping Angel's left Miss Mabel's and is hurrying home. The house stands in total darkness — not even a porch light. Suddenly the world is as bright as daylight, and then a crack of thunder shakes Hightower Hill. I hear the crash of tree limbs and nearly jump out of my pajamas.

I'm not anxious to get hit by lightning and have somebody find me sprawled out in the driveway, fried, tomorrow morning, so I stay in the car and think what to do next. Surely Angel is on her way home. But how could I have missed her?

The storm rages, with more flashes of lightning, followed by deafening thunder. A huge section of one of

Miss Mabel's trees flies through the air. Torrential rain covers the windshield, and the wind shakes the car. Suddenly, the tornado siren blares. Attached to a light pole near the Hightower estate, it wails on and on. I inch the car down Miss Mabel's wide circular drive and then drive home.

When I arrive, I grab a warm sweater from Daddy's den, some towels from the utility room, and then dig in a drawer for a flashlight, in case the electricity goes off. Desi, Elvis, and I head for the basement. Carrying a book in one hand, and holding the cat, scrunched up to my chest with the other, I descend the steep stairs.

Soon I hear Angel coming through the back door above me. She appears at the top of the basement stairs, wet from the rain.

"Are we supposed to have a tornado?" she asks, her wet blond hair haloed by the light behind her.

"Where have you been? Didn't you hear the siren?"

She looks down the stairs at me stupidly.

"I went to get you at Miss Mabel's house!" I yell up at her.

"Oh."

"Were you with James Colton?"

Angel laughs, as she comes down the stairs. The wind and rain are as loud as an orchestra.

"Listen, Angel, this ain't my first time at the rodeo. Did you lie to Mother and Daddy about practicing at Miss Mabel's so you can carry on with James? Were you screwing?"

"You really went up there?"

"Stop playing dumb. How long has this been going on?"

She hesitates. "Not long. Only a couple of times."

A loud crash of thunder.

"You'll ruin your life!" I yell. "And Mother's and Daddy's!"

"I'm not going to ruin anyone's life. Least of all, mine."

"What if you get pregnant? You stupid bitch! Don't you know what can happen?"

The storm pitches as more thunder crashes.

"Don't worry." She hesitates again. "We're very careful." She comes over to me. "Hand me one of those towels."

"What do you mean — you're very careful?"

"I mean, before we *do it*, we always wrap his weasel in plastic."

"You do *what* to *what?*"

"You heard me."

"Do you mean his *penis?*" I ask.

"I mean his *weasel!* And don't act so holy. We don't do anything you and Jerry Fred haven't done."

"We've never done *anything*, you slut!"

The wind howls so fiercely above us I can hear boards in the house creaking.

"If you dare tell Mom and Pops where I've been tonight," Angel says, "I have plenty to tell them about you and Jerry Fred."

"Are you crazy?"

"Don't say that again, you tall, ugly chunk!" She spits at me.

The lights begin to dim.

"I'll *make* you stop!"

"You *can't* make me stop!" She spits again.

The fluorescent basement light comes back up full strength and turns Angel's curly mane a soppy delicious yellow. I watch my right arm stretch out, a thin rubber band, pulled to its limit by some cosmic force. My fingers grab. My rubber arm pulls back into its socket. And Angel's hair is attached to my hand. I've been waiting for this.

She yowls, and the lights go out.

"I won't let go until you promise to stop meeting James and pretending to be practicing at Miss Mabel's." I'm calm, considering the circumstances.

Then the lights come back up and I drag her around the basement a few times until she has tears and snot mixed together on her face.

"Frankilee," she cries, "so what if I make out with James? I can't practice the piano *all* the time!"

"There's something you should know about James," I say. "You are a totally worthless shit, but he's even more totally worthless than you." I yank her head and hold her fast.

Finally, she says, "I promise."

"You'd better be telling the truth," I say. "Or I'll rip you bald-headed."

"I know how much you hate me," Angel cries. Her face and scalp are as red as a West Texas sunset.

But the black storm rages on, while we crouch in the basement and curse each other. Finally, it subsides shortly before midnight, just before Mother and Daddy return.

"No tornado, just a bad storm," Daddy announces as they greet us.

Mother's so relieved we're alive and the house is standing she brings a dessert out of the freezer to celebrate. She asks Angel if she had any trouble getting home from Miss Mabel's. Looking at me, Angel says, "No trouble at all." By now her face and head look almost normal, with only a trace of red.

I don't know whether to tell anyone about Angel's lies. Who would believe me? Besides, she's so capable of deception I'm convinced of her power to ruin me. Angel's worse than any god-awful character I'd ever read about or seen in a movie. Worse than Roger Chillingsworth in *The Scarlet Letter*. Worse than Lady Macbeth. Worse than the elephant trainer in *The Greatest Show on Earth*.

So now I carry Angel's ugly little secret, along with James' secret, which is a million times worse. I wish to holy hell there *had* been a tornado, and they'd both been blown away.

Chapter 23

DOWNTOWN AT THE courthouse, everybody's getting ready for the Slocumb boys' trial. Shelly, Jerry Fred, and I want to skip school to watch their dads, Mr. Cox and Mr. Porter, work in the courtroom.

"I wholeheartedly agree that you kids should go to the trial," Daddy says, when I ask him if I can cut classes. "You'll learn more by observing the court in one day than you would in a month of school." One thing I love about Daddy is his realistic view of education.

The dark, paneled courtroom is packed, and we squirm in our seats. First, the jury, which was selected yesterday, files in. I know nearly everybody in that box, and I'm amazed to see James Colton's dad among them.

Everyone in Clover County has waited for this trial all winter, and it begins with Judge Dawson explaining the rules of the court. A lot of what he says is mumbo jumbo. Finally, the judge asks the Counsels for both the State and Defense if they're ready. When they indicate they are, he hands the reins to Jerry Fred's dad, Mr. Prosecutor, who presents the State's accusations.

Only two witnesses will testify for the State — Deputy Bart Jebson and Sheriff Billy Joe Baines. As far as Shelly and I are concerned, both act super retarded. They've claimed that the Slocumb cousins crashed through the roadblock and shot at them. Bart Jebson is questioned by the prosecutor, and he makes a poor show of it.

Cross-examined by Mr. Cox, the defense attorney, Bart Jebson says, "I'm telling you, I was rattled. I might have been a little mistook about what happened."

"Were you carrying a weapon that night?" Mr. Cox asks.

"I can't hardly remember the details," Bart answers. He's shaking like a small frail stick.

"Think about it. If you weren't carrying a firearm, why would the defendants shoot at you?"

"What do you mean?" Bart is as dumb as a rock.

"Mr. Jebson, you have claimed that you were shot at. I'm asking you how it happened."

"I might have took my pistol out of the holster when them two knocked down the roadblock. I might have shot it."

"And did the accused — these men before you — did either one of them take your pistol from you?"

"Not that I recall."

"Did either of them shoot your pistol?"

"Not exactly."

"They carried one shotgun. Is that true?"

"Yep."

"Did they shoot it?"

"Maybe not."

"Then tell us exactly what *did* happen."

"I might of accidentally shot my own pistol," Bart Jebson answers.

Voices in the courtroom buzz loudly. No one expected this.

Now the prosecution takes another turn.

"At the preliminary hearing, you made the statement that you were shocked that they ran through the barrier, and at that moment you were shot at. Is that true?"

"I didn't get shocked. I got shot at. There's a difference!" Bart says. He doesn't like Prosecutor Porter.

"Tell us who shot at you."

"Sheriff Baines told me to stand at the roadblock. We stopped a few cars and asked questions and let them on through. But then these two guys come and didn't even slow down. They knocked down the barrier and would have knocked me down too, if I hadn't jumped out of the way. I took my pistol out of my holster and got ready to shoot out their tires. But I was shaking, and I might of accidentally shot the wrong way, in the direction of the sheriff. I never done no work like this before, and I guess I was nervous."

The prosecutor asks, "Mr. Jebson, do you remember telling us at the hearing that the defendants shot at you?"

"Not really, sir."

"Your witness," Mr. Porter nods to Mr. Cox. He sits down and shuffles papers.

I look at the defendants. Wearing white shirts and slacks, they lean on the table next to their attorney and watch Bart Jebson expectantly. Shelly has told me that neither of them has any family attending the trial. I wonder how it would feel to be in trouble, facing a possible prison sentence, without any family or friends to say, "Good-bye. We love you. Don't forget to write."

Mr. Cox takes his turn again. "Mr. Jebson, why do you carry a firearm?"

"I want to."

"Are you required to carry a firearm?"

"Do you mean do I *have* to?"

"Yes, does your job require you to carry a firearm?"

"Sure."

"Have you ever needed to use it?"

"No. I don't need it, because I carry it. That's the way it works!"

"Let me ask you this, Mr. Jebson. Do you remember either of these two defendants — the men on trial here are the defendants — did either of them ever point a firearm at you? Remember you're under oath."

"Under oath?"

"You've promised to tell the truth. Did either of these men point a gun at you?"

"I can't remember, exactly."

"Are you saying they did not shoot at you?"

"I can't hardly remember, but I think maybe they didn't."

"To your knowledge, did they shoot at Sheriff

Baines?"

"Probably not."

"They didn't point their firearm at either you or the sheriff, and they didn't shoot at you. Is that true?"

"I reckon," says Bart.

"Just answer yes or no, please."

"What was the question again?" Bart asks.

"You *must* answer the question," says Judge Dawson.

"Did these boys shoot at you?"

"I can't hardly remember."

Mr. Cox looks at the jury and then looks back at Bart and then sits down.

Next, it's Sheriff Baines' turn to testify. His testimony rocks along well for the prosecution, until out of the blue he says, "I don't like this business of Oklahoma juvenile delinquents running across the state line into Texas. We got to put a stop to it." Emphasizing his statement, he turns and points to the jury. "You all make an example of them. Send them up the river without a paddle!"

"Objection!" shouts public defender Cox.

Judge Dawson says, "Sustained." Then he tells the sheriff to keep his comments appropriate and to the point, and Sheriff Baines's face turns even redder than usual.

During his summation to the jury, Mr. Cox pounds his fist into his hand as he makes his points. "Of course, the defendants ran the roadblock! They're seventeen-year-old kids who panicked. Who wouldn't be afraid?

"It's clear from Deputy Jebson's testimony that these boys probably did not shoot their shotgun at either of them. Now the sheriff probably thought they were shooting when Deputy Jebson accidentally misfired. That's why he charged them with shooting at an officer. But we have no real proof they did it.

"What else do we know about these kids — the age of many of our sons and daughters? We know they didn't shoot anybody in the posse, and from what we can tell, they didn't even try. We know that when they were caught out in the shelterbelt they gave up without a struggle and never fired a shot.

"And last, we know they have both been model prisoners during their stay in jail."

The jury files out.

We wander out into the cold gray hallway to wait. While the jury deliberates, I ask Daddy, "Why weren't *you* asked to testify as a witness? As a member of the posse, I mean. I think they've left you out of the whole deal."

"This is a trial, Frankilee," he says. "It's not a social event."

The jury deliberates for forty minutes. When they come back into the courtroom, we're all so excited we whisper and fidget expectantly, like bright, sharp-headed wild birds. Judge Dawson raps his gavel a couple of times to calm everybody down, "Order in the court!"

Then the foreman of the jury stands. It's James Colton's father. I remember seeing him waving his rifle the night William was killed. Today, wearing a white shirt, coat and tie, he stands with dignity and delivers the verdict: "Not Guilty."

Judge Dawson orders the Slocumb boys held for their extradition hearing the next day. So their next stop is Oklahoma, where they'll go on trial for robbing the service station, after spending months in the Clover County jail.

"Well, was I right, Frankilee?" Daddy asks as we drive home. "Did you learn more today than you would have in school?"

"I learned so much it's pitiful."

Daddy clears his throat. "All my life I've tried to be on the side of the Negroes. Tried to help them whenever I could. And I'm the one responsible for hurting them the most. For the stupidity we saw in the courtroom today, William Carver died."

"Daddy, do you know who did it?"

"Nobody knows who shot William. You saw how it was out there. Could have been any one of dozens of men. But I'm sure it was an accident."

"So no one's responsible for William's death."

"Oh, that isn't true. We were all responsible. Me more than anybody else. When I saw how dangerous it was — how some of those guys were bragging and drinking — I should have sent William home. I put a kid in a dangerous situation, and he died." His voice is deep, husky, and his face is pale.

I don't know what to say. How much worse would it be if I told him what I know?

"I've decided to take your advice," he finally says, his voice still strange. "I'll talk with Wanita. Let her know how sorry I am."

Chapter 24

SAD AND DISTANT, Wanita finally returns to us. Early one morning, she comes in through the kitchen door and begins cleaning up after our breakfast, as if she's never been gone. I'm so glad to see her I hug her neck, but she says, "Go on, now. Get ready for school."

Later, I hear my dad ask, "Wanita, how's Battles?"

"Not so good. He's took to drinking pretty regular now."

"When I went out to your place to talk with you the other day, I didn't see the dogs."

"Sold them. Wanted to sell Alice, but Rootie talked Battles out of it."

"I suppose he's staying busy with farm work?"

"Yes, but he ain't hisself."

"Maybe when he puts in his garden he'll feel better."

She says nothing.

"What can I do to help?"

She looks at him and shakes her head.

"Maybe I'll ask him to take me fishing."

Wanita comes back in time to save my sanity. Every minute I'm suspicious of Angel and irked with Mother. Because she gives Miss Angel-face too much damned attention, I finally confront Mother about her birdbrain love for the girl.

"Don't be ridiculous!" she says. "I do *not* love Angel more than I love you. If you *must* know, I'm not crazy about the way she acts around boys. We've talked about this before. She's love-starved. And the only way I know to control her shenanigans is to monitor her day and night."

"What boys are you talking about?" I assume she refers to James Colton.

"One old boy in particular, and that's your grandpapa," Mother answers.

Oh, yes, Angel's slutty behavior with Grandpapa. But I could make a list: Grandpapa, Charlie, William, the soldier on the bus, Coach Morris, James Colton. Practically every guy she's met, except Jerry Fred Porter. Which shows how bad Jerry Fred really is. Not even a desperate nymphomaniac wants my boyfriend.

I worry and stew, while Angel continues her frantic pace — going to school, taking lessons, pulling the disappearing act, and practicing every livelong waking minute. She plans to present her senior recital toward the end of the month, which involves rehearsals in the high school auditorium. Also, she and Mother go to doctors in Amarillo every Saturday for a final series of skin treatments. The one weekend Angel isn't doing the skin crap, Mother takes her to her dream school for auditions. To add to the pace, Angel fills out applications for beauty contests and a music camp after graduation. When they're home, Angel and Mother have their heads together, totally excluding Daddy and me.

One day Daddy asks, "And how much is that camp going to cost me? I sure hope our board of directors is happy with how I run the bank."

"Well," Mother says, "you're the main shareholder, aren't you?"

"We own less than fifty percent of the bank, Abby. We care what the other shareholders think."

"My stars! We're doing all right financially! I heard you telling my father about how well you're doing."

"That was only bragging, Abby. With nothing to back it up."

"What are you saying?"

"I'm asking you to hold down the girls' expenses."

"I'll be careful with your precious money," she says. My mother, the know-nothing, has become the queen of snide.

I've rested until I'm sick of resting, but the rat-fink Dr. Thatcher says, "Rest some more!" As a disease, mononucleosis leaves a lot to be desired. I'd rather have tuberculosis. I could languish with a hacking cough, and people could feel sorry for me with good reason. Important people have died from TB. With mono, nobody hears you coughing and looks at you with pity and then says, "My God, you poor thing!" You can look pathetic and lounge around, all right, but after the novelty of your disease wears off, nobody gives a rat's ass.

I can't talk on the telephone absolutely *all* the time, so to keep from going stir crazy I bring the card table to the den and start some projects. First, I write another "Ode to Elvis," which isn't an easy chore.

> *Oh, Elvis, my Elvis, when your concert tour is o'er,*
> *Dear Elvis, sweet Elvis, please appear upon the*
> *   moor —*
> *The great plains of West Texas, along Highway 66,*
> *And carry me off to Memphis, 'cause mono's got me*
> *in a fix . . .*

But I get bored to a green bean, so I start typing my autobiography. I'm revealing everything, and listing the personality flaws of everyone in our family, starting with Angel and her hot pants ways.

During the first week in May, our high school annuals arrive in huge brown boxes addressed to the school. Everyone's so excited about our senior edition of *The Blarney Stone* we're about to wet our britches. Coach Morris brings in the annuals during English class, so all the seniors open our books at the same time. Squeals, cries, and gnashing of teeth. Even though I'm on the annual staff, I don't know who has won all the contests.

Angel's been elected "Most Likely to Succeed" and also "Most Beautiful." Her pretty smiling face in both photographs makes me gag. What's even more putrid, Jerry Fred Porter and I have won "Most Intellectual Senior Boy and Girl." Our pale faces stare up from the pages. With the Clover High School library as the background, we look startled, like scared rats. Only our mothers would love that picture.

The night after the annuals arrive, Jerry Fred calls and asks me to the prom.

"Ask another girl," I tell him. "I'm not well enough to jitter-bug all night."

"Please go with me," he begs. "You're the only girl for me. We don't have to dance much, just some of the slow ones." Then he says, "Here, listen to this," and he places the telephone receiver down beside his record player: "For your love . . . I would do anything . . . I would do anything . . . for your love."

"That's our song," he tells me.

"No, Jerry Fred. We don't have a song."

"Well, then, it's *my* song."

Poor guy. I agree to go to the prom with him.

The next day at school, Principal Johnson calls Jerry Fred and me out of English class. "Please follow me to my office," he says. Looking at each other, we wonder what we've done wrong.

After Mr. Johnson gets us seated in front of his desk, he announces, "You both have identical grade averages.

I'm giving you a choice. You can either take a comprehensive test to determine which one of you will be valedictorian, in which case the one with the lower score would become our salutatorian. Or you can share the title and all the honors and prizes that go with it."

I look at Jerry Fred. This is a test of his love and loyalty.

"Who would make up the test?" asks Jerry Fred.

"Your teachers, of course," answers Mr. Johnson.

"That in itself could be a problem," I say.

"It surely could," Jerry Fred agrees. "If the test is slanted toward math and science, I'd probably win, but if it's slanted toward language, literature, and history, Frankilee would win."

"And if the test is evenly balanced?" asks Mr. Johnson.

"Then we'll have a tie again," says Jerry Fred, "and we'll put Frankilee through a lot of pressure for nothing. I vote we split the honor."

Holy roly miracle. I look at Jerry Fred with new eyes. He's really a decent guy, and in love with me. But I'm Jerry Fred's unrequited love. It's a colossal flaw in the universe.

Mr. Johnson, Jerry Fred, and I talk about the graduation ceremony. We'll each make a speech, and to determine who'll talk first we draw straws from the janitor's broom, which rests against the wall next to the principal's door. Long straw for first, short straw for last. I draw the short straw, so I'll give the last speech at grad-

uation. I'll leave this brick shit school in a blaze of glory
— if only I can think of something to say.

Mother tells Daddy that Angel and I need new prom
dresses as well as graduation outfits. So on Saturday I
come out of mono seclusion and ride to Amarillo with
Mother and Angel for a shopping spree after her skin
appointment.

"I want a strapless dress," I announce, as we drive
down Route 66. I'm riding in the back seat of Daddy's
Chrysler, and Mother and Angel sit up front. Whenever
we travel together, I insist that Angel ride on the front
passenger's side because *Reader's Digest* calls it the "sui-
cide seat." More people are killed there than any other
place in the car.

"This year I want to buy a strapless dress," I repeat.

"Not a good idea. You don't have anything to hold it
up," Mother says.

"That's what you said last year. This year I want a
strapless dress." Is she deaf?

"You have the same problems with your figure this
year. You'd look ridiculous in a strapless dress."

"Boobs don't hold up the dress. Those little plastic
stays do it."

"I know what holds the dress up technically. I'm
talking about the looks of the thing. You don't want
great wads of fabric on your chest with nothing to fill
them out."

"Hollow wads!" laughs Angel. Who gave her the

right to interrupt?

"Hush, Angel, I'm having a serious discussion with Frankilee." Mother says, as she turns off the highway and heads toward the medical complex.

"Why don't we talk about this while Angel is in the doctor's office?" I suggest.

"No, I need to talk to the doctor too. Let's resolve this issue now."

Angel chants, "Nah, nah, nah, nah, nah. Frankilee has flat boobies!"

"I want a son of a bitching strapless dress!"

"Well, you're not getting one," says my mother, as she pulls into the parking lot and cuts off the ignition. She turns around, eyes flashing. "Listen," she hisses. "I'm getting sick of you! Sick of your hatefulness and sick of your bad language!"

"Is Angel getting a strapless dress?" I ask.

"What a cruel thing to say!" Angel wails. "You know I can't because of my scars!"

"But not because of the size of your breasts! And I'm sick of hearing about those son of a bitching scars! You may be sick of me," I glare at Mother. "I am doubly sick of both of you!"

"I'm grounding you because of your language."

"Well, ground me! Son of a bitch! Son of a bitch! Son of a bitch!"

"Come on, Angel, let's go inside," Mother says. "We'll leave Frankilee out here screeching like a banshee. Frankilee, don't come into the reception room unless you can behave."

Fortunately, I've brought a book, *The Great Gatsby*. I read it during Angel's time with the doctor; I continue reading it while Mother and Angel go into the downtown cafeteria for lunch; and I finish it while they're shopping for Angel's formal and her graduation dress. What happens to Jay Gatsby in that book shouldn't happen to a dog.

Periodically, Mother asks me, "Won't you come along and shop with us now?"

"Well, son of a bitch, no," I answer each time. "I don't think I can behave."

When she parks the car in front of the last dress store on her list, Mother turns to me and says, "Better settle down and go in with us, Frankilee. This is your last chance."

"Only if you promise to buy me a strapless," I answer.

Mother's madder than an electrocuted cat. "You're acting like a three-year-old. You just wait 'til I get you home."

"I'm in a hell of a lot of trouble already!" It gives me infinite pleasure to goad Mother and embarrass her in front of Angel. I figure whatever punishment she can dish out will be worth it.

Sitting in the back seat and smiling, I give each of them the finger. Angel gets Little Orphan Annie eyes, and her mouth opens up into an O. Mother presses her lips into a tight straight line. She gets out of the car and slams the door.

I guess I showed them.

When we get home, Mother and Angel carry their packages into the house. I have nothing to carry, and I don't feel quite so god-awful smug. After supper, Mother tells Daddy and me to go sit in the living room for a style show. I don't want to do it, but I can't fight with Mother as long as Daddy's breathing down my neck, so I sit beside him on the sofa. Mother tells me to hold Elvis on my lap, so he won't jump up and damage the goods. She has bought three beautiful outfits for Angel: a gold tulle prom formal, a white eyelet graduation dress, and a red and white striped cotton summer frock. Also, three sets of underwear and three pairs of shoes. One white straw handbag, a summer robe and nightgown, and a whole new line of makeup. Angel swirls and dances and curtsies. No one says a word about No-New-Clothes Frankilee.

Grandmommy used to warn me: "Don't cut off your nose to spite your face." Watching the beautiful blond Angel, I realize I've done exactly what Grandmommy preached against. How could I have been so son-of-a-bitching stupid?

On the following Monday morning Daddy knocks on my bedroom door. He's pissed. "This place is a mess, Frankilee," he says, looking around as he walks in. Then he looks at me. "I want you to come by the bank this afternoon. Straight from school. Can you do that?"

I worry all day, imagining that he has some really drastic punishment in mind. When I arrive at his office, he stands, ushers me to a chair, and closes his door. To quote Holden Caulfield, that goof-off in *The Catcher in the Rye*, he's a phony with friendliness, and he treats me as if I were a valued customer, applying for a loan. Cheerful. Formal. Not my dad.

"I understand you had a dispute with your mother about your prom dress," he says. When I start to speak, he holds up his hand. "I don't want to hear about your grievances against her and Angel. Believe me, I understand why you might be unhappy with the arrangement, but your mother didn't cook it up by herself. As I recall, you were responsible for Angel coming to live with us. But that's not the issue."

"Why did you ask me to come here?"

"I'd rather not get involved, but your mother wants me to help you get some new clothes. Here's what I want *you* to do. Tomorrow, go to Sally Mae's Clothes Fountain and ask Sally to send a formal home with you. I don't know why you all shop in Amarillo when we have a perfectly good ladies' store here in Clover." Daddy is clearly irritated with the women in his life. "Oh, and also get a dress for graduation and then one for all occasions. I want you to buy three dresses, just as Angel did. But bring home several, so Wanita and I can help you decide which to keep."

"Can I have a strapless prom dress?" I ask, hoping

Mother didn't give him too many details about our argument.

"I don't care," he says.

"How much money can I spend?"

"Spend whatever you have to. Try not to be extravagant."

The next day Shelly and I go to Sally Mae's and we bring eleven dresses home on approval. Angel is at her piano lesson, and Mother's playing bridge. Daddy comes home from the bank early, and I model all of the outfits for him and Wanita. Shelly stays around to help me change. "This is strange!" she says.

Daddy holds a notepad in his hand and makes notations with his blue fountain pen. As I model, he writes down comments in four categories: style, fit, appropriateness, and color. Then he adds a fifth column — price — which he says will serve as a tiebreaker. At the end of the modeling session, Daddy, Wanita, Shelly, and I discuss each outfit, and we make our selections.

Shelly and I load up the rejected dresses and take them back to Sally Mae's, barely making it before she locks the door. I ask Sally Mae to send my dad the bill.

This is how I get my strapless dress. It's pale pink tulle, with lace gathers and ruffles, and it brushes the floor. Yards and yards of soft flounces. The bodice is full and makes me look like I have great breasts.

In addition to that, I buy a white lace graduation dress and a yellow summer sundress with spaghetti straps. All of these clothes are pretty; all are perfect.

When Mother comes home, I ask her to look at them in my room.

"I don't think so, Frankilee. I'll see them when you wear them," she says. She doesn't mention strapless dresses, nor do I.

Knowing that it was her idea to buy me the new clothes, I'm not angry with my mother any longer. Although it would have been more fun to select my clothes with her, in a pinch, a girl could have no better friends than Daddy, Shelly, and Wanita.

On the night of the prom, Jerry Fred wears a white sport coat and a pink carnation, just like the song, and he brings me a yellow cymbidium orchid. When he sees my built-in breasts, his eyes nearly pop out of his head. I can tell he wonders where the fabric stops and the real me begins.

"You look beautiful," he breathes, as he walks me to the car.

"And you look handsome." It's true. We both look about as beautiful and handsome as we'll ever look in our entire lives. It's depressing as hell.

Arriving at the prom, we walk into the school gymnasium, which has been decorated by the juniors. The theme is "20,000 Leagues Under the Sea." Those kids have spent months making shiny paper fish and stringing them on invisible wires from the rafters in the ceiling. Thousands of iridescent fish float above our heads. In one corner of the gym the decorating committee has built a coral reef, upon which sprawl six mannequins, borrowed from Sally Mae's dress shop. They're outfitted as mermaids. They're supposed to be sexy and alluring, but they just look like six pale old mannequins with out-of-date hairdos. The kids have stuffed them into green homemade scaled-tailed fish suits.

In another corner there's a cardboard submarine, really refrigerator boxes from Sears, taped together and painted silver. Fake green and purple moss hangs around the door. Inside, benches are lined up next to windows cut in the sides of the vessel. Outside the submarine the photographer has set up his equipment, and that's where he takes the prom pictures.

The theme continues to the refreshment table, which holds a punch bowl in the shape of a shell, and plastic seahorses encased in ice-cubes, swimming in the punch. Some of the mothers have loaded up trays of cookies and cupcakes.

If you're a senior, you're supposed to pretend to be grateful for all this tacky shit. You must rave about the cookies and punch. You go on and on, telling the decorating committee what a good job they've done carrying out their theme. The teachers have instructed us about our duties as guests of honor. Walking from group to group, Jerry Fred and I thank everyone for the hard work. We take care of this social obligation as quickly as possible, because we're afraid the whole mess might fall apart any minute.

We dance a few slow ones and then walk up to a

group of chaperones. Coach Morris stands in the center, and he smiles as we approach. He takes a step toward me and then looks at Jerry Fred.

"May I have a dance with Frankilee?" he asks. And then he leads me away, as the jukebox plays "Young Love."

"In case I'm not able to talk with you again," he says, "I'd like you to know how much I've enjoyed having you in class . . . and on the basketball team."

"What do you mean, if we're not able to talk?"

"I found out this morning that my contract won't be renewed. I'll leave the day after graduation."

"Oh, no! They can't do that!"

"I'm afraid they can."

"This makes me sick. What reason did they give?" I'm about to cry.

"I'm a troublemaker, Frankilee."

"But you're a *good* troublemaker! They should let you stay!"

"I was hoping they would. For several reasons."

I pull back and look into his eyes. "What will you do? Where will you go?"

"I'm not sure. Right now, I'll go to my folks' house on the Gulf, and then I'll make up my mind. Probably head to Korea."

"This makes me sad," I say.

"Not as sad as it makes me."

We dance a few more steps and then he asks, "Did you talk with your folks about the shooting?"

"No. The picture I took proves nothing. I realize it could've been taken anywhere. Coach, I hate to stir up more trouble, just when things are settling down."

"I still think you should tell them."

We continue to dance, slowly. His body is strong, tight, and he holds me close to his chest. I wonder if he feels my soft fabric boobs through his jacket. He sways to the music. We are temple-to-temple, cheek-to-cheek.

I love that man right down to the ground.

Because of our conversation about the shooting, I do something radical. When Jerry Fred and I walk over to the submarine to have our picture made, Angel and James are there. We watch them pose for the photographer.

"Angel, I want a photo of you and Jerry Fred," I say. "Just for kicks and grins, you two have your picture made." I find a bench inside the submarine. "I need to rest for a while. Join me, James." I pat the bench beside me. There's a long line for the photographer, so I can work on James for a while. Through a cutout window, we watch the photographer and all the couples.

James sits. "For Christ's sake, what do you want, Frankilee? This isn't about William again, is it?"

"James, it's driving me crazy."

"Then forget about it."

"Are you kidding? Listen, if you don't tell someone you shot William, I will!"

"You wouldn't do that. You have no proof."

"Yes, I would. We'd both sleep better nights."

"I sleep okay."

"I don't."

We sit there, watching all the happy, dressed-up kids smiling into the camera. Finally, James says, "Look, there were a lot of us out there that night, and I fired my rifle just like everybody else. I heard the yell, knew I'd hit someone, but I didn't know who."

"Well, you know now. Do your folks know you shot William?"

"My dad does."

"Did he want to serve on that jury?"

"Yes, he was glad when he was called. He thought the charges against the Slocumbs were ridiculous. He said too many teenagers' lives had already been ruined."

"What about *my* life? Does your dad know that I know?"

"Not yet, but I'll tell him."

"Oh, you do that!"

"You're making a big deal out of this, Frankilee. Mind your own business. It's over."

"It is my business because I know the truth! And it's not over!"

James moves close to me and growls, "Don't you understand how it looks, Frankilee? The white mediocre quarterback shoots the perfect Negro quarterback in the back. I'm more scared of the Negroes than I am of the law! Now leave me alone! It was an accident, goddammit!"

He stands up and walks toward Angel, while she and

Jerry Fred smile before the camera. Leaving the submarine, he doesn't turn around, and suddenly I have the feeling that neither he nor his dad will ever let me tell the truth. Maybe they would do anything they had to to stop me.

Angel's senior recital, organized to demonstrate her vast talents, is held on the Sunday afternoon after the prom. I'm surprised so many people attend. She begins with a dramatic reading, "The Swallows of Capistrano." This piece celebrates the instinctive return of some goofy birds to Capistrano in California. I think the whole piece is too emotional for words and pretty much a pile of shit. Who cares if a bunch of birds fly back to the same place year after year? But, even though Angel is over-coached and over-rehearsed, she looks gorgeous in the formal Mother bought her on our dismal day in Amarillo.

Next, Angel plays the piano, and she is damned good. All those months of listening to her practice, I tuned her out, but I know she's practically a musical genius. She winds up this part of the program with Chopin's "Polonaise in A Minor," which is the most beautiful piece of music in the whole world. No one can believe she's become so accomplished at the piano in only two years. It's a downright miracle. Listening to her play, I'm sure I've been cruel to her because I'm jealous. I'm a sorry bitch.

We have a short intermission, giving Angel time to catch her breath and change her clothes, and then the vocal portion of the program begins. Wearing her white graduation dress, Angel belts out song after song, accompanied on the piano by the church choir director, tackling patriotic scores, church hymns, and Broadway tunes. My favorite is "People Will Say We're in Love."

Angel ends her program by dancing across the stage, tapping like mad. Imitating James Cagney, she performs "I'm a Yankee Doodle Dandy." The Cloverites go crazy. For an encore, she sings, "America." The audience gives her a standing ovation, and she flings kisses to everyone.

At the beginning of the week, I had an idea — something to get me back in Mother's good graces, after I treated her so shittily. "I'd like to hand Angel a bouquet of flowers at the end of the recital," I said. "It would be a nice touch."

"Frankilee, coming from you, it would be a completely meaningless gesture," Mother answered.

"I agree. But I want to do it anyway."

Probably she was feeling weak — or hopeful — because she gave in.

So on the day of the recital, Mother hands me a dozen yellow roses to carry onto the stage. I'm wearing my boring navy blue sailor dress. Very much aware of the contrast between us, I feel like a slug crossing the stage with roses for Angel. A goddamned slug wading through mud in slow motion.

But I'm glad Mother let me do it, because it gives me the opportunity to see the audience from a different perspective. Smack dab in front of the stage are

Mother and Daddy, who've supported Angel these past two years — Mother, more than anyone could imagine. Next to them is Miss Mabel, beaming. No doubt Angel is the best student she's ever had. There's Grandpapa, smiling like a sly old fox. Who knows what that old coot is up to? James Colton and his entire family. Shelly and Mrs. Cox. Mrs. Porter and Jerry Fred. Mother's best friend, Martini. The Reverend and Mrs. Farnsworth. Mrs. Rickers. Wanita and Rootie. And many others.

Looking out over the happy people — all convinced they've witnessed the debut of a Broadway star, I'm able to see a person in the back, half hidden, several rows behind everyone else. Dressed in a dark cotton housedress, Mrs. Bridget Musseldorf applauds wildly.

Chapter 25

ON THE FOLLOWING Friday night, the high school graduation of 1958 is held in the same auditorium. This event starts out like every other commencement in the state of Texas, with the place filled with families and friends. As we march to the front, Shelly Cox plays "Pomp and Circumstance" on the piano, and then Angel sings "America the Beautiful" before the speeches and giving out of diplomas.

Jerry Fred's nervous, and I'm glad he'll deliver his address first. I'm nervous too, but I feel a strange exhilaration. We've read each other's speeches and rehearsed them together until we're both sick of them. Jerry Fred's message is perennial: hearts and flowers, our wonderful parents, rah-rah-rah, and now let us go forth to do our best for God and country, rah-rah-rah, shish boom bah! He delivers his talk all right. When he sits down, his face is pale and dripping. The audience gives a polite applause. But it ain't exciting, honey.

Now it's my turn. I start out the same way: rah-rah-rah, aren't we wonderful? Thank God for our town, curlicues!

I look out at the audience. The houselights are up, and I can see perfectly well. They're people I've known all of my life, and I'm as disgusted as hell with them. They look like a bunch of hungry birds, expecting too much from us. They want me to spout the same old valedictory shit. They think they can count on me, the banker's smart, ugly daughter. I step away from the microphone and clear my throat. I remember Coach Morris, sitting alone in his office, after a wooden cross was set afire in his front yard, saying, "Quitting is not the solution."

Looking into the smug faces of our neighbors and friends, at my grandfather and my parents, I think — what the hell.

"I've decided I don't like my original speech," I say loudly, and then I pause. "So this one's from the heart!" I look around to make sure the microphone is carrying my voice. "Everyone in this auditorium knows what hypocrisy is. We know about narrow-mindedness, pig-headedness, and cruelty. We've all seen those things here in our hometown. It seems that if you're rich enough and powerful enough, or if you happen to live in a fancy mansion, you can afford to make stupid mistakes. People may laugh at you behind your back, but they'll put up with you. And even if you're not rich, if you were born here and everybody knows your family, you might just be able to get away with murder."

I sigh and feel my shoulders drop. "But if you're poor

or different or alone, you're asking for trouble when you come to live in Clover, Texas. Especially if you live in the flats. Or if you're a teacher with great new ideas.

"What I hope for my alma mater and my home town is this — I hope the federal government steps in to integrate the schools very soon. I wish our local school board had done it while my class was still here. I wish I could have gone to school with the kids in the flats. Most of all, I wish my classmates had known William Carver.

"Integration had better happen soon. Because until then, this town is going to go on destroying the schools, the teachers, and the students — white and colored."

I have no more to say, so I sit down. The applause is feeble, and I feel woozy. Maybe I'm about to have an out-of-body-experience, or a mono relapse.

After the recessional, people avoid me. I think *pariah* is the word for what I am. Mother and Daddy take Grandpapa back to the house without saying a word. Later, after we turn in our caps and gowns, Jerry Fred walks me to his car. He, too, is silent.

"Well?" I ask after he climbs in on his side and closes the door.

"Well, what?"

"What did you think? About my speech?" I strain to see his face in the dark.

"I think my mother is right about you," he answers.

"Oh, really? And what does she say?" I can barely make out his features as other cars pass through the parking lot.

"She says you're too much to handle."

"And after all this time you agree with her."

He starts the engine. "I thought I was in love with you, Frankilee. But I don't know."

I sit there, watching him. "You don't have to love me. I don't want you to. But the last thing I need is for you to shut me out. Aren't we friends?"

"One of these days, somebody's going to break your spirit," he says. "And I hope I'm around to watch it happen."

"You cruel bastard." I'm too royally pissed off to cry.

We drive to the Dairy Queen for Cokes. Then I tell him I want to go home.

Jerry Fred says, "I'm sorry, Frankilee, but I can't understand why you have to make a major issue out of everything. Why couldn't you give the speech you practiced? What am I supposed to say when people ask me if my girlfriend's gone off her rocker?"

"You can start by telling them I'm not your girlfriend."

He drives down Route 66 to a country road outside of town. Just north of the cemetery, overlooking Clover, you can see the town's lights sparkle against a black backdrop of earth and sky. With no horizon line, the vast area twinkles, as if Fourth of July sparklers were scattered in the distance.

This is not the place for serious parking. This has always been the place for serious dreaming. We kids are never able to distinguish stars in the sky from the house lights in town, and we find the phenomenon eerily wonderful. Ever since electric lights were brought to Clover, it's been a favorite pastime of high school students, particularly those with wanderlust, to drive out to this area and exclaim, "Look at the lights! Look along Highway 66! Clover looks just like a big city! Not like a hick town at all!"

Jerry Fred stops the car. "Let's not be so serious," he says. "I'm sorry for what I said. You gave the speech you wanted to give. What's done is done."

We look out into the darkness, but instead of the usual bright lights, a portion of the town is enveloped in a dark cloud.

"Is that a storm?" I ask.

"More like smoke," he answers. "You don't think the school's on fire, do you?"

As fast as we can, we drive back into town on Cemetery Road, past the school, which isn't engulfed in flames at all. Hearing the fire siren, Jerry Fred turns right at the next intersection, and then he drives up the hill. Miss Mabel Hightower's mansion is wrapped in smoke. The sky gleams purple, and orange flames lick out from the downstairs library windows. The rest of the house is silhouetted against a murky fiery glow. The Clover, Texas, fire truck is parked inside the gates, and volunteer firemen rush around toward the garage. People gather on the fringes, huddling together, wringing their hands.

I jump out of the car before Jerry Fred parks it.

"Where's Miss Mabel?" I yell, when I see her neighbors clinging to each other.

"We think she's out of the house," a man says. "The firemen are looking for her."

"We don't know where she is!" says another neighbor.

"We think that them boys got out of the garage all right, though," yells another man. "Them's the ones that started the fire!"

"What boys?" Jerry Fred asks.

"Them high school boys!" screams the man, over the noise.

"Get out of the way!" yells a fireman, as he pushes me aside.

I turn from the beating heat of the fire. Walking across the driveway behind the house, I see people watching and waiting beneath a tree on the lawn. I recognize Coach Morris and a few of the senior boys, James Colton among them.

"What happened?" I ask.

"Frankilee, I've made a serious mistake," Coach says.

"What are you guys doing here?" I ask the boys.

"Playing poker. We were minding our own business when she came running in, screaming, with that fire. Scared us to death."

I turn around for Jerry Fred, but he isn't here.

I find him in front of the house, where it's dark but

not so smoky. I hear him before I actually see him. He's yelling, defending himself from the fury of a small pale-headed figure dressed in a white robe that trails on the ground. She carries a large flaming cross, and she tries to hit him with it, as he ducks and moves away from her. I run up to them, and when she turns, I recognize Miss Mabel. Without her thick brown wig, her white hair stands straight up, making her look like a character from *The Night of the Living Dead*. She pokes the tip of the cross at Jerry Fred and spouts out gibberish. Her face contorts as if she were a wax figure, slowly melting.

"Talk to her, Jerry Fred! I'll get help!" I yell, as I start running toward the back of the mansion. "We've found Miss Mabel!" I scream. Several people follow me, and we try to catch her arms and hold her. Coach is successful in getting her to drop the cross, and the boys begin stamping the fire out on the ground. But she eludes Jerry Fred and me, running to the back of her house toward the flaming garage apartment. We follow close behind. But no one wants to tackle her; no one wants to hurt Miss Mabel.

She moves more quickly than we can comprehend, and she heads straight for the fire.

When they realize she's running into the house, Coach and the boys move quickly. They follow her to the door, as the firemen yell, "Get back, you can't go in there!"

Then a couple of firemen run into the burning apartment.

Jerry Fred and I stand in the driveway and watch, while firemen spray water into the apartment, and neighbors try to help by bringing buckets. They also work with garden hoses.

Soon a fireman comes out, carrying Miss Mabel, as if she were a tiny rag doll. Her hair is singed and small flames creep up the bottom of her robe. Coach grabs one of the garden hoses and puts out the flames. Miss Mabel and the fireman are black, burned. Looking at her lumpy face, we can tell she's gone beyond crazy.

Her face looks awful, but her lips move rapidly. I swear I hear her say, "Niggers . . . white trash . . . Mousetrap."

Suddenly Mr. John Williamson of the funeral home is there, having driven his hearse, which the hospital uses as an ambulance. As the fireman places Miss Mabel onto the gurney, her robe falls open, and we can see her spindly white legs and her chalky, soft stomach.

From nowhere my mother has appeared, and she climbs into the back of the ambulance with Miss Mabel. She speaks in soothing tones, bending over her and saying, "It's all right. Everything's going to be all right." Then they drive away.

By now Coach's apartment is destroyed. Meanwhile, inside the mansion, moving from the library into the rest of the main floor, the fire continues to spread. We stand under the trees and watch the firemen fight the blaze. Finally, we sit on the ground and watch.

Sometime after midnight, the firemen get control of

the fire. Mother comes back with the news that Miss Mabel probably won't live until morning.

"How did the fire start?" Mother asks.

Daddy takes off his glasses and wipes them with his handkerchief. "A group of boys and Coach Morris were playing poker. The fire started in his apartment."

"Miss Mabel started it," I say. "Jerry Fred and I saw her, running with a burning cross."

"She was out of her mind," Jerry Fred says.

Suddenly I remember Pope Pius. "What happened to Miss Mabel's cat?" I ask a fireman walking by.

He looks at me in surprise. "I have no idea."

"All right, everybody," I say. "We've got to find the Pope. Come on! I hope he's still alive!"

Firefighters and a few onlookers, along with Sheriff Baines, still hang around. We rush up to the now-smoldering house. Jerry Fred and I explain the lost-cat situation to the sheriff. Then under my direction, our family, the remaining firefighters, and even the sheriff fan out and search for the Pope.

The electricity is out, so we carry flashlights, provided by the firemen and the neighbors. The mansion is a mess. Burned, smoke damaged, and waterlogged, it's amazingly intact, but it can never be the same. Here and there, various valuable items and art pieces lie broken on the floor. The famous Hightower piano is ruined.

Nobody knows the house plan but me, so I get to boss everybody else around. Which only goes to show that sometimes it pays to be a snoop. I give them assignments, and then say, "Jerry Fred, come upstairs with me." We stop by a linen closet and take a pillow-case.

I know where to look for that decrepit Persian cat. I lead Jerry Fred into Miss Mabel's room and open her closet door. "You stand at the door and catch him if he tries to run away. I think he'll be in here." Sure enough, we find him in a sad huddle. He's smushed himself into a ball behind the trunk that holds Miss Mabel's weird treasures. He's gray from smoke, and he trembles, as Jerry Fred pulls the trunk away from the wall and I pick him up, but he's all right. We drop the Pope into the pil-lowcase.

It's no trouble to persuade my parents to let me keep him.

When we get home, Angel is in a tizzy, furious be-cause James Colton hasn't shown up for their late date after the poker game. When we tell her about the fire and Miss Mabel, she says, "Well, what do I care? I was about finished taking lessons from her anyway."

Chapter 26

"I'M WONDERING WHY you did it," Daddy says. He's sitting in the passenger seat as I drive. The Saturday morning after graduation everyone in the family needs the car, so I've been elected to drive Daddy to the bank.

I've dreaded this moment, knowing he'll quiz me about changing my commencement speech. "Are you mad at me?"

"Of course not. I just want to know what you were thinking," he replies.

"I don't know, Daddy. It seemed like the thing to do." I slow down at the corner and turn. Then I stop the car at the side entrance of the bank. He pulls his keys from his trousers pocket and selects the right one. Then he puts his hand on the door handle.

"Be prepared for the consequences of your actions," he says.

"What do you mean?" I ask.

"I've told you that since I spoke up at the town meeting last year, a few families have closed their accounts with our bank." He turns his head to the right and looks out his window. "I don't regret speaking out in favor of integration. I'd do it again. In fact, at the time I felt I *had* to speak up. But, as a result, the money will be tight for you and Angel in college. Even with your scholarships."

"I'm sorry, Daddy. I've made things even harder."

"Don't be sorry," he says and looks at me. "You spoke up in public for what you believe. I did the same thing. Sometimes you have to do that. But be prepared to accept the consequences for every action you take — good or bad, noble or rotten."

"I understand. Coach Morris is noble, and look what happened to him."

"Yes, he's a good example of a good person being punished for doing what he thinks is right."

My throat hurts. "What do you think will happen to Coach?"

"He'll find a better job. Be better off," Daddy answers.

"Not if he has to go to Korea."

"No, probably not."

"Daddy, I just wanted to change people's minds about the colored kids going to school with the white kids."

He looks tired. "I know. But we don't always get what we want." He opens the door and gets out of the car. He leans down, looks in at me and says, "That doesn't mean we shouldn't try."

He closes the door. I turn and watch him while he

slaps the rear end of the car, my signal to pull away from the curb. Such a relaxed and natural action, you'd think he were slapping the rump of one of Grandpapa's riding ponies. Then he unlocks the side door of the bank and lets himself in.

One more rule to learn, I tell myself, heading home: Don't go around acting holier than thou and trying to prove other people wrong. When, I wonder, will I have learned all of life's shitty little lessons?

Two weeks after graduation, the brainless Angel will go away to music camp. She's received her letter of acceptance, and you'd think she'd been given an Academy Award. She nearly drives me crazy with her preparations and packing. I keep finding my things in her suitcases and retrieving them. Saying nothing, I hide those articles from her. Then, saying nothing, she snitches some other belongings of mine. I find those things and hide them also. In this way, we wage a silent battle.

"I'll swear to God," I say to Wanita one day, "Angel is doing her best to steal all my stuff!"

"That little sucker full of stunts, uh huh."

All the while, I wonder how Daddy can afford this. Still, nobody seems to worry about that except me. Maybe Daddy really doesn't have financial burdens at all, but wants to keep the rest of us from spending. If that's his strategy, it isn't working, as far as Mother and Angel are concerned.

Since Angel never does a lick of work around the

house but causes constant confusion, I'm so happy when she leaves I could dance up and down the walls of my bedroom, like Fred Astaire in *Royal Wedding*. I do a little jig as she climbs into the backseat of the car. Hot damn, peace and quiet at last!

Mother and Daddy drive Angel to the camp, which is held on the university campus in south Texas — an eight-hour drive away. I can imagine them being cooped up with the giggling, goofy, warbling Angel. Mother deserves it, but Daddy doesn't.

While my parents are gone, Wanita stays with me, and I go to the swimming pool every day. Because I've recovered from mono so well, Todd Mason has hired me full time. And when Mother and Daddy return, we're back to being a three person family. Praise the Lord and pass the ammunition.

Except for the sad death of Miss Mabel Hightower and her burned-out house, along with the banishment of Coach Morris, the town returns to normal. Mother's so relaxed she quits smoking. She and Daddy begin planning a vacation in Colorado in late July. They'll stay at a friend's summer cabin. I hope while they're on the trip, they'll start liking each other better.

The summer starts out swell, and the swellness lasts until mid-July. At that time Mother announces we should all drive to music camp to watch Angel perform in the Summer Follies. She brings up the subject one day at lunch, and Wanita and I look at each other. She's refilling glasses of iced tea, and she jerks her eyes away from mine.

"I can't possibly go," Daddy says, irritated. "The girl's been gone for only six weeks. Why don't we just let her perform this time without us?"

"You've never liked recitals. Admit it, Jack," answers Mother.

"Abby, I want to head for Colorado next week. It'll be good for us to get away."

Mother agrees but says she feels compelled to attend the follies also. "We should go to be supportive," she says.

"I'll go with you," I say. "It'll be fun."

"Uhhhh-uhhhhh!" Wanita sings an emphatic "no" as she slams the tea pitcher down.

Mother ignores her. "What about your job?" she asks me.

"I'll have to get a substitute lifeguard, but that's not a problem."

"That's it! Frankilee, you and I can drive to see the show!" Then she and Daddy agree to leave for Colorado the day after we return.

"I'll call and get two tickets and I'll also reserve a motel room." Quitting smoking has caused Mother to act nervous and flighty.

"Let's not tell Angel we're coming, Mother. It might be fun to surprise her."

Right away, Mother starts planning. I watch Wanita, who's turned her back and rakes leftovers into the garbage disposal. Then I glance at Daddy, who's taken off his glasses and gently rubs his eyes with stiff fingers.

"Fine," he says. "You two go. I, for one, am not overjoyed by the invitation to travel for eight hours in a hot car to watch Angel hoof her head off with a bunch of other college girls. But I'll be ready to leave for the Rocky Mountains when you get back."

Early the following Friday morning Mother and I head south for our grand weekend with Angel. As we leave, Mother tells Daddy not to expect us until Sunday night, which will give us Saturday to loaf around the motel swimming pool, shop, and generally relax. Mother has called the box office and reserved tickets for the Friday night performance. She's hoping to get last-minute tickets for the Saturday evening performance as well.

Mother says her nerves are shot from not having a cigarette in over a week, so I drive. We arrive at the motel by mid-afternoon. I swim while she naps. Then we grab a bite and head for the show. Again, I drive and Mother navigates. We find the parking lot easily and enter the Fine Arts Building ahead of the crowd. Because we bought our tickets so late, our seats are in the first row of the balcony. Mother's disappointed, but I'm quite happy with our cool bird's-eye view. Soon other people — friends and families of the performers — swarm in, laughing and hooting, finding their seats.

Before the show begins, I excuse myself to go to the ladies' room and find it down a hall near the back of the stage. I enter and choose the middle stall. I hear a couple of women enter and can't help but listen to their conversation.

"So glad ya'll could come," a girl says. She sounds like Angel.

"We are, too," an older woman answers.

"Are you proud of me?"

"Course we are. We pulled it off!"

"They never suspected a thing."

"Because you're such a great little actress." Other women enter the restroom and their voices mingle. I strain to hear.

"You'll have a brilliant career."

"Thanks to you!"

"No, thanks to you, my little Katharine Hepburn."

"It'll be worth all I've had to put up with from that horrid Frankilee." It *is* Angel!

I yank up my underpants and leave the stall as fast as I can. Looking around the restroom, I see no one familiar, so I open the door and look down the hall. Strangers, every one.

I meander through the lobby, back toward the auditorium, past the refreshment stand. Noticing that other people are buying soft drinks to take inside, I stop and buy a couple of Cokes. Then I cross to the other end of the lobby and climb the stairs. Wondering if I'm headed in the right direction and if I've chosen the right flight of stairs, I slow down. But I can't get my bearings. At the landing, I turn and gaze back at the lobby. This is when I see a familiar-looking man. He stands in the midst of the crowd, not the least bit remarkable. Small and scrawny. Just like *Mr. Musseldorf.*

I return to Mother before the house lights dim and the curtain opens. She's excited and doesn't notice my state of shock.

During the first half of the show Angel appears in two numbers. She performs just like all the other girls — no better, no worse, but she's definitely prettier than most. As she smiles at the audience and twirls around the stage, I remember all my past grievances against her. Why the hell did I come here, anyway?

Maybe my fears are a result of food poisoning or the flu. Maybe I'm paranoid because I've been cooped up all day with a reformed smoker. But I swear to God I'm almost overcome by Musseldorf phobia.

During the intermission, while Mother is reading her program again, I look down from our perch and spot them right away — Mr. and Mrs. Musseldorf.

The rest of the performance blurs. What will happen when Mother notices Angel's other family? What if she goes berserk in the university auditorium? Will she scream and cry or freeze up like an ice goddess? What if she has a heart attack and falls down dead on the spot?

On the other hand, what if Mother never notices the twosome having such a high-heeled good time below? Then I'll have to live with the knowledge that Angel is obviously in close communication with them, and what does that mean? If I tell Mother I've seen them, she might not believe me.

I wonder if there's any logical, acceptable, or honest reason we're all here, watching the shitty Angel Musseldorf dance.

At the finale, Mother's on her feet, applauding. I look at her, with light from the stage splashed across her face. She's truly happy.

When the show ends, the houselights go up, and the audience moves into the aisles. Mother says, "Let's go backstage." She pauses, as she looks down toward the crowd on the first floor. "My gosh, there are so many people here, it'll take us forever to find Angel!"

We stand in the balcony as it slowly empties out, while girls and guys of various sizes and descriptions — some costumed, some in street clothes — come out and greet their families. Mother's back is to the stage, but I watch as the Musseldorfs approach and Angel emerges from behind the curtain. Laughing, shrieking, hugging, Angel and her mother act like two survivors from the *Titanic*, glad to be together. Angel embraces and kisses Mr. Musseldorf, her not-so-long-lost dad. Then Angel and her mother, giggling and chattering, link their arms and bounce up the aisle together, followed by Mr. Musseldorf, as smoothly choreographed as if they were members of a wedding party.

Angel wears the red and white striped dress Mother bought her last spring, when we three went to Amarillo. The day I sat in the back seat and gave them both the finger and called them sons of bitches.

By the time Mother and I leave the balcony, nearly

everyone downstairs is gone, and we hear only muffled sounds from behind the curtain. Then the janitors begin sweeping.

Chapter 27

"IT WAS A mistake not to tell Angel we were coming," Mother says, when she shakes me awake in our motel room at 8:00 A.M. "I've tried calling her dorm room and no one answers. Maybe we should run by there again. Where could that girl be?"

Where indeed? I know she's with the Musseldorfs, and I should tell my mother, but I can't force myself to share this awful secret. Not until it makes some sense.

"If we can't find Angel right away, let's get back home as soon as we can," she says, while I brush my teeth. "I can use an extra day to finish packing for our trip, and we can tell Angel on the phone how much we enjoyed the show."

We go to Angel's dorm room, as we did the night before, and she's still not there. The dorm counselor says, "Angel's spending the weekend with her parents, who came to see her show."

Mother looks at her as if she's a moron. "You must be mistaken," she says.

"Mother?" I ask tentatively when we're in the car,

"what if she's with the Musseldorfs?"

"Don't be ridiculous, Frankilee." She looks at me as if I were a moron, too.

Driving home might be a good time to remind God that the circumstances are dire. Still, I refuse to ask for help, so I compose a one-liner: "Oh, Lord, I am confused!"

Daddy is anxious to leave for their trip, so early the next morning he and Mother head for the Rocky Mountains, leaving Elvis, Desi, the Pope, and me in the care of Wanita. Mother has told me that Daddy will be looking at some banks in the area, in case his board of directors doesn't settle down.

That afternoon, the phone rings. It's Angel. I tell her Mother and Daddy have left for Colorado.

"How was your show?" I ask.

"Oh, it was great! I never had so much fun!"

"We were sorry we couldn't come. Did James Colton or anyone from Clover make it?"

"No! Nobody at all."

"That's a shame, Angel. Mother was sick she had to miss it!"

"I called because I'm invited to spend next weekend with a friend from Houston. I met her parents this weekend. Do you think Mom will let me go?"

I know she's lying, planning to be with the Musseldorfs.

"I'm sure it'll be all right, Angel. Just be sure to let us know where to find you if we need you."

"Great. I'll send you my friend's address and phone number."

"You do that," I answer.

I spend the rest of the afternoon thinking about the Musseldorfs. For the past two years, whenever I've been exasperated with Angel to the point of murder, everybody — including Wanita — has reminded me that I myself brought all of this about. It's true: I befriended Angel, saw her scars, believed her story, feared Mrs. Musseldorf, involved my mother, and helped Angel run away from home. Since I got us into this mess, I'm the one to get us out of it.

Wanita cooks bacon and eggs for supper, but I'm not hungry. After I feed the pets, I sit down to watch television with her. We're watching *The Ed Sullivan Show*, but I can't concentrate.

"You fidgeting too much. What the matter with you?"

"Oh, Wanita, I've found out something about Angel."

"Oh, goody. Tell me quick!"

I tell her about seeing the Musseldorfs and Angel together at the show.

"What you think?" she asks.

"I think the whole damn thing about Angel being beaten and burned by her Mother may have been a lie!"

"What you know about them people?"

"We don't know *anything* about them."

"Not even where they from?"

"Nothing. I need more information. And I know where to find it."

I go upstairs and call Jerry Fred. Then I come back down and tell Wanita, "I'm going out for a while. Don't wait up for me."

"That'll be the day!" she says.

I'm carrying a flashlight and my camera as I climb into Jerry Fred's jalopy. I wear black pedal pushers and a dark shirt, and I carry the black shirt from the Elvis costume for Jerry Fred. So far, so good, but convincing him to sneak into the Musseldorfs' house may be harder.

"That's called breaking and entering, Frankilee, and it's against the law. My dad would kill me!"

"No, your dad would represent us, you ninny. He'd get us off. But we're not going to get caught. Just drive down First Street, and I'll show you."

At the end of the street, the Musseldorfs' house is isolated and dark, with no houses nearby. A streetlight shines on the yard, which is a tangle of weeds.

"If that light were out, Jerry Fred," I say, "there'd be no way in hell anybody could see us."

Jerry Fred takes a small stone, spits on it, aims, throws, and shatters the bulb.

We sit in the dark on the broken steps leading up to the rotting porch and survey the neighborhood. No activity anywhere. If we're going to do it, this is the perfect time.

"You're asking me to commit a serious crime," he says.

"Angel's parents have used mine shamelessly. I aim to put a stop to it, if it harelips the President."

He puts his arm around me. "I don't want you to go to jail all by yourself."

"Just help me get inside and keep a lookout."

Jerry Fred and I walk around the house, trying to open windows. He figures he'll have to break one. "Vandalism," he tells me. "The cops can add another charge."

But to our surprise and relief we find a window we can raise. He helps me climb over the sill, handing me the flashlight and my camera once I'm inside.

I probably could turn on the lights, and no one would know, but I don't. Fortunately, I know the sparsely furnished house fairly well, and I start looking — for what, I'm not sure. I look through several desk drawers in the living room and find nothing. Nor is there anything in a pile of bills on the dining room table. I'm burning up and getting discouraged when I go into the bedroom. There, in a small desk I find a fat file, stuffed with papers. Among them is the birth certificate of Angelica Gaines, baby girl, born to Herbert and Winifred Musseldorf Gaines, March 10, 1940. Angel's birthday. In the same file, among other legal documents, are death certificates for Herbert Gaines and Winifred Gaines, both apparently killed in a car accident. A yellowed newspaper mentions a young daughter who survived the crash. So the story I heard Angel tell the horny soldier on the bus long ago was true, and I was too stupid to realize it.

The house is unbearably hot. I go to the front door, unlock and open it, and whisper to Jerry Fred. "Come in here. I need you to see this." We leave the door ajar, so we won't pass out from heat exhaustion.

Jerry Fred looks for adoption papers while I spread the certificates out on the floor. Then I pull down the shades, close the door, turn on the lights, and quickly take several pictures of each document. There are no adoption papers. Nor is there a marriage license.

In one of the bedroom closets we find shoeboxes filled with pictures. All strangers, except for an old family picture with several children in it. On the back of the photo someone has listed their names. Alfred and Bridget are among them. We search the faces until we can identify them.

"This means that Mr. and Mrs. Musseldorf aren't husband and wife," Jerry Fred says.

In Angel's room we find a scrapbook filled with pictures of Angel. First as a toddler, posing with a young Bridget Musseldorf. In some of these pictures Angel is with Alfred. Then pages of her as a girl of about eight or nine, with a smart looking young couple. In one of these photos, Angel wears a long dress and sits at a piano. So she hasn't miraculously learned piano in two years.

"No wonder she went through those John Thompson books so fast!" I say.

Other pictures of her in dance costumes. At the top

of one page someone has printed in block letters, "The Axtons."

Then additional pages of pictures of Angel. Three grinning children and Angel, flanked by a mother and a father. At the top of a page, "The Worthingtons," in the same block print.

Then Angel as a teenager, probably taken shortly before she moved to Clover. In one, Angel and a woman are seated at a baby grand. Angel wears a formal and a corsage. Other pictures of her in dance costumes. The label reads "The Jacksons."

Finally, Angel in her Homecoming formal, her senior prom formal, and her graduation dress. Labeled "The Baxters."

"So this is their game," I say. "The Musseldorfs move into a community, set up a business, join a church, and find a family to provide a home, as well as music and dance lessons for Angel."

"Why would a family take her in?" he asks.

"Mrs. Musseldorf pretends to batter Angel. Makes her into a pitiful victim."

"There's more," he says, showing me a handful of medical papers. "Angel has been to several doctors besides the ones in Amarillo. All having to do with her scars."

Again, I remember her conversation with the soldier. "She was burned in the same car accident that killed her parents," I say. "Mrs. Musseldorf never tortured her at all."

"What good'll this scam do the Musseldorfs? I mean, in the long run?"

"Well, someone else pays for Angel's music lessons. Someone else buys her clothes and pays all her bills."

"I'll bet there's more to it than that," he says.

He discovers a lock-box in a bottom drawer of the bureau. We find a hammer in the garage and break the lock. Inside, a stack of letters is held together with a rubber band, the envelopes addressed in the same block print, many of them mailed from El Paso. They're from Alfred. The most recent letter is on top.

Dear Sis,

What have you got on Baxter? A mistress? Illegitimate kids? Hanky panky at the bank? Theft? Shady loans? What about the mother? Drinking? Lovers? Or the girl? Bad reputation? Cheating at school? Drinking, etc.? What about her and that nigger kid? Find something or we'll have to pull the kidnap scheme. Damned lot of trouble.

Things in E. P. are fine. Dealing with illegals hard way to make a living. See you next weekend. Have something for me.

Alfred

Here's the incriminating evidence Jerry Fred's looking for. And finally, it's clear that Bridget and Alfred Musseldorf are brother and sister.

Although it's as hot as Hades in this house, my bones

turn cold. "They're going to blackmail my daddy," I say.

I take pictures of everything, because Jerry Fred won't let me take any evidence home. "We're going to be in enough trouble already," he says.

We put everything back, lock up the house, and drive away. Looking at my watch, I see it's nearly midnight. "Wanita's going to have seventeen cats," I say.

And I'm right. "Where you been?" she yells when I walk through the back door. "I about to send old Sheriff Baines after you!"

"Wanita, you need to know this," I say. And then I tell her everything about Angel.

"Well, well, well," she says after I finish.

Then I tell her, "Whether she likes it or not, Angel is moving away. Will you help me pack her things?"

"When we start?"

"Let's box up her stuff. Hopefully, Mrs. Musseldorf will still be gone tomorrow night, and we can dump everything on the porch."

Chapter 28

WHEN I GET home from the pool the next afternoon, we start packing. It's amazing how much Angel's accumulated during the past two years. And it's doubly amazing how much of it belongs to me. I take inventory and list everything under either "Really Angel's" or "Stolen by Angel." I put the items in the last list back in my room where they belong.

I'm glad Wanita and I are doing this job; otherwise, no telling what Miss Twitchy Butt would carry off. Retrieving my junk renews my hatred for her, big-time.

"What you think your mama gonna say when she come home and find Angel's stuff gone?" Wanita asks me, looking around the near-empty bedroom. Stacks of books and phonograph records are in the middle of the floor, along with a couple of cardboard boxes. Nothing else is left, except the old mahogany four-poster, along with its matching bureau, dressing table, and nightstand. We've stripped the bed, and the gray and white striped mattress and pillow look desolate.

"What can she say? We're helping her out."

"Uh-uh. You and me enjoying this too much. I probably be fired. And you be in a heap of trouble."

"We'll plead insanity," I tell her.

A few minutes later, I hear Wanita say, "Oh my. Oh, Lord have mercy."

I'm on the floor, sorting through records. I get up and walk over to the dressing table, where she sits, holding a small blue box. I know what's in it, but I take the box and open it anyway. My grandmother's sapphire and diamond earrings. The ones Grandpapa tried to give to Angel and Mother refused to let her take.

"How did she get these earrings?"

"What you think?" asks Wanita.

"Did Grandpapa sneak around and give them to her?"

"Could be."

"Please don't tell Mother, Wanita."

"Oh, no, honey. She don't need to know."

"You know how Angel acts around Grandpapa. Do you think they've been meeting secretly?"

"Maybe, maybe not."

"It makes me sick! How could he do this?"

"Don't know, honey. May just be one last flirty fling before he head to the graveyard. Or he may have met her only one time, to give her them earrings."

I put the lid back on the box. "I'll take these back to Grandpapa's house and put them with Grandmommy's things." I start to cry.

"Them earrings is between him and her. They ain't

yours. Ain't got nothing to do with you."

"What are you saying? That I should let her keep them? She might have stolen them!"

"Just because she be a thief, don't mean you be one too," Wanita answers.

"It isn't just the earrings, Wanita. It's what she did to get them."

"You don't know nothing about it, honey. Nothing for sure. Put it out of your mind. Let it go."

Crying, I walk into the bathroom and dab my eyes with a cold, wet washcloth. My smeared mascara makes me look like a raccoon. When I'm all cried out, I take the blue box, with Grandmommy's earrings inside, and pack it with the rest of Angel's things. Then I come back and squat on the floor, next to a pile of records.

Wanita says, "I thinks finding them earrings is a sign from the Lord God Almighty."

"A sign? I thought you didn't believe God interferes in our lives."

"The Lord didn't *cause* none of this. But you and me's smart enough to figure out signs along the way. Them earrings a sure sign we needs to get rid of Miss Angel Pussy." Wanita can always make me laugh.

At about eleven o'clock we load the car to the gills and make our delivery. It takes two trips, bouncing across town, laughing and feeling good. No lights shine at the Musseldorfs' house.

The rotten Angel never sent us the name and address

of her imaginary friend.

We leave Angel's stuff on Bridget Musseldorf's screened-in back porch. As I carry things from the car, I wonder what the old bat will do when she realizes Angel's stint with the Baxters is over.

"You suppose Mrs. Musseldorf will come to us — screaming and carrying on?" Wanita asks.

"This has probably happened before."

"You think that old hog-woman gonna stay in Clover?"

"I have no idea. She'll have to figure out how to pay for Angel's tuition and college bills. But Angel may have enough scholarship money to take care of it. She might not suffer at all."

"Oh, they gonna suffer one way or another, child."

I work all week at the swimming pool and don't hear a word about Angel. I'm so nervous I can hardly eat or sleep. On Friday I go to the drugstore and pick up the pictures I took at the Musseldorfs' house. After looking at them, I call Jerry Fred.

"We've got to go back," I say.

"What are you saying?"

"The letter from Alfred is illegible in the photograph. We have to get the real thing."

This time it's super simple to climb through the window, open the bureau drawer, and snap open the lockbox. I grab all of the letters. Two shakes of a lamb's tail.

Now we have proof of the Musseldorf schemes, in

Alfred's own handwriting.

"Don't ask me to do this again," Jerry Fred says, as we drive home.

"What do you mean?"

"I mean I'm through with this game. It'll get us in trouble."

"For God's sake, Jerry Fred! You of all people should understand how important this is!"

"Then go to the sheriff, but leave me out of it." He pulls into our driveway.

"What's come over you?" I ask.

"I'm serious," he says. I get out of his jalopy and slam the door.

Holy Moly. I've committed a few crimes, I've gotten rid of Angel's stuff unbeknownst to my parents, I've involved Wanita, and now I've lost my accomplice. I'm as nervous as a whore in church, wondering what will happen next.

Chapter 29

ON SATURDAY, I stop by the post office to pick up the mail, and I find a tan envelope addressed to Mr. and Mrs. Jack Baxter. Printed in familiar block letters, there's no return address, but the postmark says El Paso. I stare at the envelope, carry it to the car, and then I open it. The letter is from Alfred Musseldorf. I'd recognize that block printing anywhere.

On Big Chief notebook paper, torn ragged at the top, Alfred has written, "We're holding Angel for $50,000 ransom. Do not call the police or she will get hurt. You'll hear more later."

I take the note home and show it to Wanita, who picks up the phone to call my parents and the police.

"You know what an idiot Sheriff Baines is," I say, taking the phone. "He'll foul up the whole deal. And I'm not going to let you spoil my parents' trip. They're practically having a second honeymoon, for goodness sake. And they need it."

Now Wanita is angry with me. "That ain't it at all, Frankilee. You afraid they be mad at you for throwing out Angel. You got to tell someone about this letter! I ain't responsible if you don't."

I call Jerry Fred.

"You should tell the cops," he says. "Kidnapping is a terrible crime."

"But it isn't a *real* kidnapping, Jerry Fred. Remember Alfred's letter to Bridget? This is their last resort."

"What if it *is* real? You're already in so much trouble — and so am I!"

"Don't chicken out on me," I say.

He hangs up. The guy who yearned for my kisses, would do anything in the world for me, and even wanted to share my mono. What a drip.

That night Mother calls from Colorado Springs. When I hear her voice, my hands immediately get clammy.

"We're going to shorten our trip," she says. "Your dad thinks he'd better get back to the bank."

"Have you found any prospective banks in Colorado?" Killing time, while I think what to say next.

"Not really. Your dad thinks he'd better repair some fences back home."

"Oh, stay a while," I beg. "It's hot and dry here. Downright miserable."

"We'll be home in a few days," she answers. Jeez, pleeze, Louise. Maybe they'll have car trouble. I need some time! I remember Mother saying that I am the most interfering person she knows. Man, is she going to hate me now.

Later, just as I'm getting ready for bed, the phone rings. I don't recognize the man's voice, but I assume it's Alfred Musseldorf. He asks to speak to one of my parents and seems confused when I tell him they've gone away. He hangs up but then calls back a few minutes later.

"You'll have to talk to me," I say. This is the ransom call. I've got to show some grit.

"Tell your parents I have Angel Musseldorf. I want fifty thousand dollars for her."

"We don't want Angel back."

"Miss!" he yells. "Where are your parents?"

"You must be certifiably crazy to believe my folks have that kind of money. And you're stupid to think they won't call the police. More like the FBI. You're lucky you're dealing with me, not my dad. Now listen here. *You can keep Angel.*"

He slams down the receiver and doesn't call back.

I wake up in the night, sweating. What if I've made a mistake? What if the man wasn't Alfred Musseldorf? After all, I really don't remember what Alfred's voice sounds like. What if Angel is really in the hands of a cold-blooded killer who's torturing her at this very moment? What if he murders her? I was so sure I was right, but now I'm wavering.

Where is that Angel? With the Musseldorfs in El Paso, I presume. I've already checked with her school, and she hasn't returned to dance camp since the week-end of the recital. The program director says Angel told her roommate she'd be gone for a few days.

Since I can't sleep, I begin writing a confession for Angel to sign. If she isn't dead, she's part of a scheme to trick my folks. And if she turns up here again, I'll be ready for her.

To Whom It May Concern:

I, Angel Musseldorf, admit to being part of a plot to fool the Baxter family. I lied, making them believe my mother beat and burned me. Bridget Musseldorf, my aunt, and Alfred Musseldorf, my uncle, were behind this scheme. The Baxters fell for my lies and in the past two years they have taken care of me by providing food, clothes, shelter, as well as music, dance, voice lessons, and medical services to help erase my scars. Since they now know the truth, I understand why they are making me leave their home.

Typing it up, I put "Admission of Involvement" at the top of the page and mark a place for her to sign at the bottom. Although the confession doesn't sound like a legal document, it should do the trick.

I turn out my light and finally get back to sleep.

The next morning, I call Jerry Fred. "I've written a confession for Angel to sign when she returns," I say. "It needs to sound more lawyerly, and I want you to help me fix it up. I'll read it to you."

"Forget it, Frankilee," he says. "I meant it when I said I'm through with this mess."

"Then I guess this means you're through with me, too," I say.

"Yes, I guess it does." He pauses for a minute, and then he hangs up.

My chest feels a dull ache, a hole in there somewhere. Not because I loved Jerry Fred, but because I thought he loved me. I was so sure of his help, and now I'm not sure of anything.

Mother and Daddy are due Wednesday night. It looks as if we'll still have the Musseldorf plague when they return. Disappointing, and maybe even dangerous. Plus, I don't trust my fruitcake mother to support me about kicking Angel out, even after she knows the truth.

In my bathing suit and cover-up, I walk through the back door after work on Wednesday afternoon. The telephone rings, and Wanita answers it. I hear her say, "Yes, Angel, somebody be right there to pick you up. Wait at the bus station."

Wanita looks at me. "Looks like ol' Angel done escaped from her kidnappers."

I'm so relieved I could cry. "Just as I thought. Angel wasn't really kidnapped, was she? It's all a part of their game." I pick up my car keys again. "Wish me luck."

"Honey, we both go."

"I want to do this myself."

"Uhhh uhhh! Your mama not going to be happy

about this. No telling what that girl might do! By now she know you didn't want her back."

"Don't worry, I'll be fine. This will be simple. I'll take Angel back to Mrs. Musseldorf's house. And I'll tell her she's in a powerful lot of trouble."

"Don't threaten her."

"I won't threaten. I'll just say we never want to see her again."

I drive out Route 66 to Brown's service station, which also serves as the bus stop. Angel is furious. The little creep has blown her good life with the Baxters, and she knows it.

I doubt that Angel rode the bus all the way from El Paso — or wherever she's been — and I look around for the Musseldorfs' car but see nobody familiar. Probably Mrs. Musseldorf let her off and then high-tailed it to her own house. By now she's found Angel's things on the back porch. She may be coming for me, so I've got to make this fast. I start to worry even more.

Angel's wearing her red and white striped dress, and her hair is done up in a ponytail. We load her blue luggage into the car. She yells, "What took you so long? I thought I might have to spend the night at this nasty bus station!" She stamps her foot with rage.

"So sorry," I say, starting the car. "After your ordeal with your kidnappers, I'll bet you're exhausted. You look pretty damned good to have gone through such hell."

"Shut up, Frankilee!"

"Did you come all the way from your kidnapper's lair in El Paso? How'd you get away?"

She pauses and then says, "I crawled out a window, you stupid bitch."

"With all that luggage? How stupid a bitch do you think I am?"

"Listen, I didn't appreciate the fact that you wouldn't give those people any money! Wouldn't even call Mom and Pops! I might have died in that horrid town with those terrible people!"

"Who were they?"

"How should I know?"

"Actually, I was hoping they'd do you in. Tell the truth now, how'd you get away?"

"Go to hell, Frankilee."

I drive toward town.

"I can't wait to have a long hot bath," she says.

"Then I hope they paid their water bill."

"Why? What?"

I've decided not to confront Angel on Mrs. Musseldorf's property, or even within yelling distance of her house. Instead, I drive to the town's square and park in front of the bank. I turn off the engine and roll down my window. Lots of people drive by, most of them on their way to Wednesday evening church services. If I'm attacked, there'll be witnesses.

Angel screams at me. "Why are you stopping? Can't you see I'm worn out from spending all day on that bus?"

"Mother and I attended one of your performances at music camp," I say. "The one on Friday night. It was supposed to be a surprise. Turned out we were the ones surprised. We sat in the balcony and saw the whole thing."

Angel says absolutely nothing but looks straight ahead down the street.

"It doesn't matter if you say anything or not, because I already know. You're an actress in an elaborate scheme to find someone else to pay your bills and educate you. And I'll have to hand it to you. You had us fooled."

"Why do you think that?"

"I also know that Bridget Musseldorf is not your mother, but your aunt, and Alfred Musseldorf is really your uncle. And I know that you squeeze everything you can from people like us."

"I don't know what you're talking about!" she snaps.

"It's pretty sorry to take advantage of people by pretending your demented mother beat you and burned you."

She turns to me. "Do Mom and Pops know what you're doing?"

"Of course! Listen, we can send the three of you to jail. You've committed a serious crime. Extortion, isn't it? Look over at the courthouse, Angel. Want to spend months down in the basement, waiting for a trial? Ask the Slocumb boys about the Clover County jail."

Suddenly she looks at me and smirks.

"I mean it, Angel. If you don't cooperate, I'll have you arrested. I'll walk right over there to the sheriff, and he'll come get you. Good luck getting your hot bath then."

"What do you want from me?" She doesn't sound worried.

I open my purse, take out the sheet of typing paper, and dangle it before her. "If you're smart, you'll sign this."

"What's is it?"

"It's a confession of your deceptions. Your lies about being battered. Your scheme to mislead us."

"Give it to me."

I hand her the "Admission of Involvement." Without even looking at it, Angel tears it in two. "Here," she says, throwing the pieces of paper at me. "Now take me home, shitface."

"Aren't you the least bit sorry, Angel? Don't you feel at all bad for treating my parents this way? And the ransom scheme!"

Angel laughs. "Boy, have you got a lot to learn."

I look across the street at the courthouse. It would be easy to get the sheriff. But do I really want to involve stupid Sheriff Baines if I don't absolutely have to? My plan isn't working out. I start the car and drive to Musseldorfs.

"I said to take me home," Angel says.

"Exactly. *Mi casa* is not *su casa* anymore."

I haven't driven down this street in the daylight for a

long time. The Musseldorf house looks worse than ever. Mrs. Musseldorf's car is in the driveway, which is very bad news. But more proof that the old witch just let Angel off at the bus station and then drove home.

I pull up in front of the house. "I've packed every solitary thing you own and left it on the back porch. The only thing you can't keep is Elvis, because I don't trust you with a living creature. If Elvis were a *spider*, I wouldn't let you have him."

Angel snorts.

"Get out of this car and take your suitcases with you. Good-bye and good riddance." My chest tightens up.

Angel doesn't move. "Oh, Frankilee, you are so funny. You're a freak."

"Get out!"

"You're a jealous hag. You couldn't have James Colton and had to settle for Jerry Fred. And William — "

"Out!"

"Listen, Frankilee, if you don't take me home, I'll ruin you. I'll tell everyone you were in love with William Carver. How you went to all his ballgames. How you wanted the schools integrated so you could be with him. Then see how easy it is to pledge a sorority. See how well Pops' bank does, if people think you sleep with niggers."

"You're crazy! William was just a friend!"

"You'll be an old maid. Nobody'll have you."

"Don't be ridiculous!"

"And everyone will believe me, after your stupid

graduation speech."

"Angel, I have proof of your lies. I have the ransom note."

"You can't prove anything."

"I found Grandmommy's earrings in your things. I'll have you arrested for stealing."

"Grandpapa gave them to me!"

"What do you suppose Mother will do when she finds out about the earrings? Do you honestly think she'll love you then? And Daddy will think you're a tramp! Now get out!"

"You can't make me get out of this car."

"Angel, if you don't get out, *I* will. I'll walk home, call the sheriff, and tell him you've stolen our car. I'll have you arrested within half an hour."

"Always going to have me arrested. How creative!" Her face is red with fury. Her gorgeous hair begs me to pull it, but I resist the temptation. She doesn't move, so I get out and pull her suitcases out. I line them up on the uneven sidewalk.

"At least you don't have a tacky box of Kotex right here in front of God and everybody," I say.

And then my biggest fear. The front door opens, and Mrs. Musseldorf flies out. "What's happening here?" she yells, running down the porch steps.

She isn't a killer, I remind myself, only pretends to be.

"Why are Angel's things on the back porch?" She's racing down the walk.

"We're on to you. Your scam is over. Angel's coming back here to live." I wish Mother and Daddy were here. Wanita, Jerry Fred, the sheriff, a neighbor, *anybody*.

Mrs. Musseldorf grabs my arm and spins me around, as she slams my back up against the car. "You stupid little bitch, I'll ruin your family if you don't do what I say." Her face is an inch away from mine. Yellow teeth and white whiskers. "Now put those bags back in your car." Still holding me, she looks into the front window. "Angel, stay right where you are. I'll bring your things back to the Baxters' house." She lets me go.

"I'll leave you two," I say, intending to walk home. "You can explain to the sheriff why our car is on your property."

Mrs. Musseldorf grabs my neck and knocks me against the car door. I'm on the edge of the curb.

She screams, "I'll tell everyone you were pregnant with William Carver's baby when he died. That you had an abortion and pretended the mono thing! Everyone in town will believe it."

"You're nuts. Who would listen to that cockamamie story?"

"The Mary and Martha class."

"They'd never believe it!"

"Of course they would, you fool. People always want to believe the worst!" Now she's choking me so that I can't get my breath. I grab at her wrists and struggle to push her away. She lets up a little, and I try to slip out of her grasp. But she tightens her hold on my neck and slings me around. Free from her, I back up. Then she pops me in the face with her right fist. I'm stumbling backward when she advances and smashes me with her left, and I feel my nose explode. Twisting away from her, I lose my footing and trip over Angel's suitcases. Then I fall over, headfirst, onto the broken sidewalk. A jagged piece of concrete tears through my face and forehead, and I smash down on my nose. I lie there in blackness for the longest time.

"She's dead! You killed her!" Angel screams through the god-awful ringing in my ears.

Slowly I pull myself up. The suitcases lie in a heap, and I try to negotiate around them. I stagger to my car, my face wet with blood, sure my skull is split in two.

"Get out, Angel," I say. "Or take me to the doctor."

"Stay in the car," Mrs. Musseldorf yells. Looking at me she says, "I didn't do it! I didn't do anything to you!"

"You deserved it!" Angel shrieks, through the ringing in my ears.

I climb into the car. I have nothing to stop the blood that's streaming from my forehead and into my eyes, so I use my terry cloth cover-up. My nose hurts and my mouth and gums bleed so much I'm afraid my teeth will fall out. I turn the ignition key.

"You and your terrible temper," Angel yells at Bridget, jumping out of the car.

"Shut up, stupid! You sorry little bitch. Did you at least get the earrings?" Bridget Musseldorf screams.

I pull away from the curb. Holding my shirt against my forehead and cheek, I drive slowly. Barely able to see, I weave from one side of the street to the other, sometimes hitting the curbs. Inch by inch by inch. Everybody in town must be at church services, and there's no one to notice I'm desperate. Remembering that Dr. Thatcher makes his rounds at this time every day, I drive to the hospital. It takes forever to get there.

I park, cronkey-jawed, in the driveway and stumble through the hospital door. Inside, a nurse, dressed in white from her winged cap to her hospital shoes, stands at the reception desk, filling out a form. I lean toward her, and when she looks up, she jumps. My blood drips everywhere. I can see it puddling around my sandals. And the ringing is so loud I can't hear anything else. When I tell her who I am, my voice sounds far away, and my throat chokes with blood and sobs. The nurse buzzes for Dr. Thatcher, then has me lie down on a gurney nearby. The old man sprints down the hall toward me and tells her to call Sheriff Baines immediately.

"Tell him to bring Wanita," he says.

They wheel me into the operating room. Then Dr. Thatcher gives me an injection to kill the pain. "I don't want to put you out completely, my dear," he says. "So you must tell me when you hurt. I'll do something about it." He begins cleaning my face.

Wanita arrives with the sheriff, running. She holds my hand while the doctor sets my nose. "You can expect very black eyes from this break," he tells me.

314

"Can you sew my face back on?" I ask.

"I'll fix you up as good as new," he promises. "I'll take tiny stitches, Frankilee. I don't want you to have any scars." When he says that, I start crying all over again. So he stops, and while Wanita croons to me, he gives me another injection. Everything becomes quite hazy.

Seated, Wanita holds my hand, while the doctor works. She hums, and he talks as I drift in and out of consciousness. "She's lucky her jaw isn't broken," I hear him say.

Sheriff Baines hangs around until I'm stitched back together. Afterwards, I tell him as much as I'm able about the Musseldorf scam. Wanita fills in whatever I've left out. But we both neglect to mention the part about Jerry Fred and me being such good amateur detectives.

We go home, and Wanita puts me to bed downstairs in Mother and Daddy's room. She follows the doctor's orders, props me up, and makes ice packs for my face. She wants to wait for my folks to arrive before she gives me more painkillers, and when they finally come, we tell them the whole story. I have the ransom note, my photos of the scrapbook pictures, and the letters from Alfred to Bridget. In my drugged up state, I can't tell whether they approve of Jerry Fred's and my actions, but they're outraged by the Musseldorfs.

"Thank heavens Angel's gone," Mother says. She's climbed in the bed and is holding me.

"Let's not be too cocky," Daddy warns us. "We may

not have heard the last of it."

That night, the sheriff serves Mrs. Musseldorf with a warrant for her arrest: assault and battery and attempted extortion. He also takes in Angel, as an accomplice to the crimes. The next morning he comes by the house to tell us there's a warrant out for Alfred Musseldorf also, for extortion. Looking at the letter from Alfred to Bridget that Jerry Fred and I stole, he says, "If we can't get him for extortion, we'll get him for smuggling in illegal aliens. Lawmen all over Texas are after him now."

The sheriff asks me why I have this particular letter. Where did I get it? Fortunately, I'm drugged up enough to go to sleep immediately, without saying a word.

Where is Alfred Musseldorf? Everybody wonders, but nobody knows. As long as he's gallivanting around the countryside, I don't feel safe. Even in my fog, I realize there's no telling what damage he might do. Maybe none. But maybe a whole lot.

Chapter 30

NOBODY EXPECTS SHRIMPY little Mr. Musseldorf to come back to Clover under these circumstances. But he does. Bridget and Angel have been in jail for a couple of days when he appears at Daddy's bank. Disheveled and smelling of liquor, he approaches a teller and demands to see my dad. My friend Shelly is working there for the summer, and she recognizes him.

When Alfred Musseldorf is ushered into Daddy's office, Shelly immediately runs across the street for the sheriff.

"Want you to know I don't appreciate what you've done to my family," Musseldorf says, refusing to sit down in Daddy's office.

"Are you aware there's a warrant out for your arrest?" Daddy asks.

"Don't care about that," Musseldorf answers, his eyes glazed red. "Just want you to know I'm gonna kill you for what you've done. Kill you and your girl."

He pulls a gun from inside his jacket and aims it at my father's heart. He pulls the trigger. My daddy is hit, and he starts to fall. Then he decides the one last thing he can do to protect me is to kill Alfred Musseldorf.

Daddy lunges at the smaller man and knocks him down, fully intending to grab the gun and shoot him. But Alfred beats him to it. The gun goes off again, and Musseldorf lies dead. Daddy falls back on the floor, sure he'll die, also. And Sheriff Baines arrives with handcuffs, too late.

Mother, Wanita, and I hear all about this incident from Rinky Fines on the radio, only moments after it happens. All three of us become hysterical, wringing our hands and crying. Suddenly the doorbell rings. It's Deputy Bart Jebson, come to take us to the hospital. He's a stuttering, nervous wreck when he discovers he has three screaming women to transport — one black, one white, and one all bandaged up. But he gets us there.

When we arrive, Dr. Thatcher is heading into the operating room with Daddy. The doctor speaks to us quickly. My dad's shoulder has been hit, and ligaments were torn. It may bother him for the rest of his life. But he'll survive, thanks to a poorly made firearm and the shaky aim of Alfred Musseldorf.

As we wait during the surgery, the president of the board of directors at the bank appears. Reporters from Amarillo, Pampa, Wichita Falls and Lubbock drift in, and he talks to them. He calls Daddy "the bank's ulti-mate hero."

When Daddy comes home a few days later, Mother fixes up their bedroom for his makeshift hospital room.

She, Wanita, and all the aunts smother him with attention, and when he's well enough he entertains callers in his den. He's practically a celebrity now. Members of the bank board bring food and send flowers. They all come to visit Dad frequently. And Grandpapa, looking sheepish, drops by to check on him every day. Grandpapa never says a word about Angel, but he gives me a hug or pats my head every time he has a chance. The old coot.

When it's time to have my own stitches removed, I insist on going to the doctor's office alone, despite Mother's and Wanita's wanting to come along.

"I can stand only so much mothering," I say. "Come on, Wanita, I'll take you home before my appointment with Dr. Thatcher."

We drive to her farmhouse, talking about the events of the past few days. "Lord Jesus smiling on us now," she says, as I give her a hug and let her out. Then I turn the car around and wave to Battles and Rootie, who are working with a new bird dog.

On my way back into town, I'm surprised to see James Colton, his mother, and his dad driving toward me on the dirt road. I can't imagine where they're going, but when we pass each other they all wave. Since I look like a mummy in my bandages these days, it's amazing how many friends I have. Everybody except Jerry Fred, who really meant it when he said he was through.

In his office, Dr. Thatcher has me lie down on his examining table, and his nurse stands beside him with gleaming instruments. He assures me that my god-awful nose will heal straight, and then he takes my stitches out. Bending over me, he's nervous and makes chitchat, not wanting to talk about my face.

"Have you heard the latest scuttlebutt, Frankilee?" he asks. "I heard at the drugstore this morning that they finally know who shot William Carver. It was James Colton."

I'm shocked to pieces. "How do they know? I mean, who told on James?"

"Oh, he told on himself. Went into the sheriff's office yesterday afternoon and said he did it. Finally had to tell somebody. Couldn't stand it anymore."

"What will happen to him?"

"He could be charged with manslaughter, but I doubt it. He's going to talk with William's parents. Wants to confess and apologize. I expect that'll be the end of it. Wish he'd told the truth straight off, would have made folks feel better, maybe." So that's where the Coltons were headed today when I saw them on the road to Wanita's. I think I may cry.

He's finished with the stitches. I want to see my face, so I stand up and walk across his office to a mirror. A red scar stretches across my forehead, down my right temple. Under my left eye is a network of jagged marks. And on my right cheek, three seams travel from my cheekbone to my jaw. Still swollen, and every color of black and blue, I look like the bride of Frankenstein.

"I did my best, my dear," the doctor says. "In time, these scars will fade. They will be barely noticeable, but I'm afraid you'll always have them." He clears his throat. "Think of them as your badge of courage. You're the bravest girl I know."

The nurse has left the room. I look at Dr. Thatcher, and he has tears in his eyes. He reaches into his pocket for a fresh handkerchief, and then he blows his nose.

"The bruises, of course, will disappear in a few weeks," he says. "When they do, you'll look better."

With his arm around me, he walks me past the waiting room, through the front door, to the porch outside his office.

"It's all right," I tell him. "Please don't be upset." And I move toward my car.

I find Sheriff Baines there, waiting.

"I have something for you, Miss Frankilee," he says, not looking at my face. "Angel Musseldorf asked me to bring this. Had me go to her house to get it." Eyes to the ground, he hands me a shoebox with a rubber band around it. He adds, "Angel asked me to tell you something. *Tell her I want her to have these.* That's exactly what she said. Had me repeat it, to get it right." Isn't that just like Angel? Giving orders to her jailer.

I thank him and take the box, and with his head still hanging, he turns and leaves.

And isn't it just like Angel to try to hurt me even more? From the outside of the box I can tell she's sent her size five red satin shoes, the ones dyed to match her beautiful homecoming dress, which she wore when she was crowned Queen. Another insult, one last brag, since my shoe size is nine, before she goes to the pokey for good. One last time to remind me of her petite figure and spectacular beauty. One more reason for me to hate her. But it's too late. I'm tired of hating Angel.

I look so awful I don't want anybody else to see me just yet. I can't imagine what Mother and Daddy will say when I walk through the door. Needing some time to brace myself for Mother's wails and tears, I decide to drive to Hightower Hill.

When I enter through the open gates to the estate, the afternoon is waning. I steer the car up the wide drive-way to the back of the house to look at Coach's burned out garage apartment. I'm amazed to find that the area has been cleared off, with no trace of a building. No sign that my teacher ever lived there.

For some reason I think of Angel's shoebox. Cutting the engine, I reach for it. Opening the box, I find the high, pointed red heels, wedged together tightly in tissue paper. Taking out one of the shoes, I see what Angel has intended. Lodged between the heel of one shoe and the toe of the other, there's a small blue box. I know what's inside. Opening it, I find Grandmommy's sapphire and diamond earrings.

Tell her I want her to have these, Angel had told the sheriff.

How many shocks and jolts can a girl stand? First my bloody face, then the news about James Colton, and now this from Angel.

I thought I knew Angel . . . and James . . . and even

322

Jerry Fred. But I really didn't know any of them very well at all. And I certainly never expected an act of decency or remorse from Angel Musseldorf.

"Angel, you're beyond redemption," I once told her. Now I'm not so sure.

I drive around to the front of the damaged mansion, and I park. Getting out of the car, I walk around the house and look to the west. As the sun sets, the town, stretched out below the hill, is bathed in violet shadows. Above Clover the wide orange western sky holds purple streaks, and golden lines sliver through long, flat indigo clouds.

Suddenly, despite Daddy's injury and my scars, I'm happier than I've been for quite a spell.

Life is full of unanswered questions, painful losses, and huge surprises, and if you think about them too much, you'll go crazy. Grandmommy once told me that, and now I know it's true.

Admiring the fiery sunset, I feel a door opening inside my chest. Call it the getting over mononucleosis door, or the Angel exiting door, or the grieving for William door.

As for Elvis ever coming to Clover, Lord knows, I've been hankering for the impossible for far too long.

LYNDA STEPHENSON grew up in a small town in Texas and now lives with her husband and her cat, Elvis, in Edmond, Oklahoma. *Dancing with Elvis* began as a short story, but Lynda decided to "stick with Frankilee and see her through her troubles." The result is this book, her first published novel.